ALSO BY MUR LAFFERTY

Playing for Keeps

Nanovor: Hacked

The Shambling Guide to New York City

Ghost Train to New Orleans

Six Wakes

MUR LAFFERTY

Based on the screenplay by
Jonathan Kasdan & Lawrence Kasdan

arrow books

1 3 5 7 9 10 8 6 4 2

Arrow Books
20 Vauxhall Bridge Road
London SW1V 2SA

Arrow Books is part of the Penguin Random House group of companies
whose addresses can be found at global.penguinrandomhouse.com.

Penguin
Random House
UK

Mur Lafferty has asserted her right to be identified as the author of this
work in accordance with the Copyright, Designs and Patents Act 1988.

First published in Great Britain by Century in 2018
First published by Arrow Books 2019

www.penguin.co.uk

A CIP catalogue record for this book is available from the British Library.

ISBN 9781787466562

Printed and bound in Great Britain by Clays Ltd, Elcograf S.p.A.

For Fiona

TIMELINE

TIMELINE

A long time ago in a galaxy far, far away. . . .

It is a lawless time. CRIME SYNDICATES compete for resources—food, medicine, and HYPERFUEL.

On the shipbuilding planet of CORELLIA, the foul LADY PROXIMA forces runaways into a life of crime in exchange for shelter and protection.

On these mean streets, a young man fights for survival, but yearns to fly among the stars . . .

PROLOGUE

Han summoned speed, but his boots could only run so fast.

He had meant to be on time, but there had been a Sabacc game going on and most everyone respected the need for a good game of Sabacc. Anyone worth playing Sabacc with, anyway.

And he *was* on time, if you considered half an hour late to be on time, and who counted half hours anyway, when you're meeting a shady back-alley dealer in a shady back alley in the poorly lit hours of the morning?

Unfortunately for Han, Kilmo, the shady back-alley dealer, was waiting for him. He, apparently, counted those half hours.

Han came skidding to a halt in front of him, his engineer boots sliding in some industrial goo. He grinned a hello, hoping his charm would win him some points here. "Hey, Kilmo, you're looking good," he said, barely recognizing the tall, lanky human lurking in the shadows. A couple of larger shadows moved behind him. "And Kilmo's friends. Hey."

Friends. Lady Proxima had said nothing about Kilmo bringing friends.

"You're late," Kilmo rumbled. He sounded even taller than he was. Han wouldn't have said someone could sound tall, but that was Kilmo for you. He moved into the light, his pockmarked face half hidden by greasy blond hair.

"Only a little bit," Han agreed amiably. "But I'm here now, and I've got what you need." He winked, hoping they could see he was no threat.

One of the tall shapes behind Kilmo stepped forward. It looked like a Sabetue, gaunt, skeletal, and skin the rare, pure white indicating they were genderless. Han had never seen a white Sabetue before, but no matter their color, he thought it would be a good idea to keep his eyes on the claws. You really didn't want to deal with the claws on either their hands or feet. At all. Ever.

"Less talk," they said. "More showing."

Han fished around in his right-hand pocket, pulled out five small metal vials, and showed them to Kilmo. "The finest hyperfuel credits can buy." Kilmo reached out his hand eagerly, but Han jerked his away. "If you brought the credits, that is."

The Sabetue seemed to be the brains of the outfit, because while Kilmo's eyes gleamed with greed, their ugly face frowned, adding at least two more degrees of ugliness to it. "We agreed to seven vials of refined co-axium."

Han's eyes went wide. "Seven?" He looked at his hands and made a show of counting the vials. ". . . three, four, five. I could've sworn she gave me seven."

The Sabetue stepped forward, flexing their claws, and Han took a quick step back. "Hang on, hang on, let me see if I misplaced them," he said, holding up one hand to stop the advance as his other hand grasped the coaxium.

He rooted around in one trouser pocket, and then the other one, awkwardly reaching across his body while his right hand tightly grasped the treasure the gangsters wanted. His fingers brushed another vial, and he fished it out, sighing in relief. "I misplaced it!" he said triumphantly. "Here you go."

"That's still only six," Kilmo said, finally catching on. "Where's the last one?"

"Well, I'm sure Lady Proxima will accept a reduced payment for a reduced number of vials," Han said. "You were going to pay forty-one thousand for seven? How about twenty thousand for six?"

The gang advanced as one, and Han backed up, scrabbling for another answer. "Eighteen? Sixteen! Give me a number! I can be reason—uh-oh." He had backed into something. It wasn't a wall, but it was about as solid, and a lot angrier.

If he'd thought Kilmo and his friends were large, they were nothing compared with this person. Another human, a man, but bigger than any he had ever seen. The person was enshrouded in shadow, but Han could feel the muscles move under his skin, like busy rocks putting their affairs in order before an avalanche. Hands fell on his shoulder, and he staggered under the weight.

"Another friend?" he asked, smiling weakly and looking up. That's when Kilmo hit him.

The first punch landed squarely on his left eye, rocketing his head backward and making him see stars in the overcast sky. The second attack was the lucky one, though. It was a one–two that glanced off his nose and hit him in the gut. It was lucky not because the punches didn't hurt—his eyes watered from the pain and he doubled over, desperately trying to get his breath back—but because they drove him backward into the man who held him.

Since Kilmo had been so helpful as to give him some extra force, Han drove back with his elbows as he hit the man behind him. He would have liked to slam his head back and break the guy's nose as well, but the guy was too tall. Besides, Han was doubled over from the force of the blow to his stomach, but he could still hit the guy behind him so he, too, could feel the pleasure of a gut punch.

As Han had hoped, the man staggered backward, doubling over and losing his grip on Han. The coaxium vials fumbled through Han's fingers and rolled to the ground as he forced himself to run, still doubled over. At least hunched over in pain was a good position to avoid the Sabetue's attempt to grab him as he scrambled away.

He gave one last mournful look at the coaxium, now being gathered by Kilmo's greedy hands. "Blast," he said under his breath—except it was more like a croak, since his breath hadn't returned. He hadn't wanted to leave without the payment. Not having the credits would be a problem when he returned to Lady Proxima, but if Han had learned anything in his years on Corellia, it was to get away with your life first, and then later you could deal with all the other problems that getting away had caused.

His middle stopped spasming and he took in a great whoop of air. Han straightened up, stretched his legs, and ran.

CHAPTER ONE

The predawn light began to tentatively touch the pills of Coronet City, making the dark-gray connected islands somewhat lighter gray, before the sun would rise and turn them to their glory of, well, a little bit lighter gray than that. The city was always gray in some shade or other.

Through the dark gray, Han sought an answer to the question that seemed to come up a lot: How *was* he going to get out of this with his life? Kilmo had not been content with letting him go; after he and his gang had gathered up the metal vials, they'd started after him.

All in all, this mad dash for his life was not unlike all the other mad dashes for his life. Adrenaline surged as he ran down the alley, dodging trash, boxes, leaking canisters of he-didn't-want-to-know. Feet, human and non-human, pounded the street behind him.

Ahead lay Narro Sinear Boulevard, one of the bridges that connected the island pills of Coronet. He aimed to cross it and hit the alley on the other side, lose the pursuers in the maze of power generators and desalinization units. It was a solid plan, one that had saved him countless times in the past. He definitely didn't want to move from the shadows into the street that had just started to wake, with L-1g droids powering on and getting to work, but something caught his eye.

Kilmo had been driving an M-68 landspeeder—shiny brand-new, and just sitting there. *I guess you don't worry about leaving your speeder in a bad part of town when you're what makes the town bad,* Han thought. Still, Kilmo should have known better than to leave a street-racing-quality speeder—an open-air model at that!—just sitting there with only its security system to protect it.

This speeder was treasure. Treasure that would lead to freedom and a ticket away from this grimy and down-trodden life.

He threw himself out into the street, dodging around the tall droids, some of them protesting that he was impeding their work. He hoped they would shield him from his pursuers—but there weren't a lot of droids or people out at this time of day. When he reached the speeder, he ducked down and rolled under it, panting and watching.

Feet wandered past his hiding place, most of them human engineering boots and droid feet. No surprise; the best barely-living-wage jobs were in the factories. The Corellians were famous for starship designs and con-

struction. Most jobs on the world had to do with building starships, testing the mechanical and electrical parts,
and designing them—and those jobs tended to work you
to death. They were marginally better than the other
jobs on the planet: no fish guts.

The local jobs that paid less consisted of fishmonger,
sailor, and thief. Han, like most orphans, outcasts, and
runaways in Coronet City, held the last job.

Most respectable jobs had dried up since the Empire
had claimed the planet as its own and put its citizens to
work building Imperial ships. Gangs and crime had
risen in the subsequent years as more and more desperate people looked to find a way to feed themselves. And
there were the rat gangs, taking orphaned and poor
kids to their bosom, offering food and credits for lifted
goods. Joining the White Worms had seemed like a great
idea at the time, a family to replace the one he'd had. Or
at least a place he could sleep off the streets.

Unfortunately this "family" also came with danger
on the street, beatings within the grimy lair, and a constant reminder that you were worth much less than the
clothes they put on you and the portions they grudgingly gave you. And if the authorities caught you outside doing the Worms' dirty jobs, you were on your own.
No one would come and help.

Han had fallen into this life as a boy, and there was
still no end in sight.

Imperial feet wandered by the speeder, white boots
stepping with smart certainty. He hoped they would
keep his pursuers at bay, but no such luck. Kilmo and his
gang soon came into view. Their pace slowed somewhat,
likely due to the Imperials, but they still came. Human

feet, Sabetue claws, three legs belonging to one being, and then a tail sliding in the street. He hadn't even seen whom the latter feet had belonged to, but he guessed they had been ready as backup for Kilmo. They hurried toward him, coming closer and closer, and Han held his breath, knowing that if they caught him, he couldn't get away again. They'd probably kill him right there in the street, claiming to have found a thief.

They weren't entirely wrong about that, but technically they were the thieves this time.

The feet paused. They were so close Han could see that the Sabetue needed a pedicure badly; they had a split claw that oozed, as if it had recently been tearing at something. It looked painful, but Han couldn't make himself drum up too much sympathy as he wondered who had been at the other end of those claws.

He swallowed nervously and kept perfectly still. If Kilmo decided to search for Han in his speeder, Han would have an entirely new set of problems very quickly.

Then the feet moved on, disappearing down the alley.

That should be all of them. Han popped up and looked around: Imperials were gone. The thugs were gone. Then he looked at the console of the speeder. He grinned and hopped inside.

A gritty metal taste filled Han's mouth as he held his light between his teeth to see in the early dawn. He took his tools in his hands and smiled to himself. It was child's play, really. Especially because he had been doing this kind of thing since he'd been a kid.

"Come on," he muttered. He bypassed the alarm before it could even wake up to alert anyone, and then broke through the security system. He shook his head, the light bobbing back and forth across the console. Whatever Kilmo paid for his security system, it was too much. He was about to learn an expensive lesson.

Once security was disabled, Han reached under the steering wheel. His hands knew what they were doing; they moved almost without him thinking about it. Switch this, push that aside, strip a mechanism down to the wires. With surgical precision, he united two wires and gave them a twist.

"Come on," he urged, the wires sizzling but nothing happening. He popped his head up and looked around, seeing Kilmo's back only a few meters away.

"Come *on,*" he said a third time, giving the wires another twist. The wires dug into his fingertips, sparking on contact, and the slight shock sent a charge of excitement up his arms. The speeder hummed to life, a gentle purr that didn't even alert anyone to the theft that was about to happen.

Han quickly familiarized himself with the console, his fingers dancing over the switches. He slammed a lever, and underneath him the repulsorlift engine flared, lifting the speeder. It wobbled briefly and then steadied. Han reached into his jacket pocket and produced his two lucky golden dice attached by a chain. The moment he took to hang them from the windscreen was not wasted time.

He ignited the rear thrusters and was gone. The speeder was his, now.

The theft was masterful, clean, and swift.

Masterful and swift, yeah, but *Han* wasn't clean at all. His face was coated in ash, stuck to his skin with sweat and the blood smeared around his nose and lip.

His left eye throbbed from Kilmo's recent punch. But nothing could diminish the utter elation he felt as the speeder took him away from the gang that still searched for him, hoping to finish what they'd started.

He drove into the dawn, urging the engine faster, ignoring the shouts of protest behind him. They soon dissipated, and he hit the bridge, luxuriating in the wind in his face, the smell of brine on the air, the breakneck speed he reached. This was the life he needed. Not skulking around tunnels doing errands for a crime boss.

He thought of the only place that deserved the word "home" despite how dubious. Han had grown up in the lair of the White Worms, placed a favela in the underbelly of Coronet City.

Where Coronet City was the gray of ship hulls and circuit boards, coated with the grime of any industrial or manufacturing area, the favela was the gray of filth and despair, with a metallic tang of danger. The place he wanted desperately to drive away from.

But then there was Qi'ra. He smiled wryly, the drying blood on his lip cracking, picturing the look on her face when they were free. He couldn't leave her here. He just couldn't. If she'd been in the same position, she wouldn't leave him.

He didn't listen to the small doubt in his head that said he wasn't entirely, 100 percent sure if that was true. But Qi'ra was like all the kids the White Worms had raised: a survivor. They had to be. Still, he wouldn't have been able to face himself if he'd left her. With a sigh, he changed course and headed in to the favela.

He slowed a bit, trying to look less like a thief getting away with the best lift of his life and more like a respectable man heading to work in the factories, building a respectable Star Destroyer for the respectable Empire.

Never mind that he looked nothing like a respectable man right now. He wiped his sleeve across his nose to try to clean up some of the blood, but he couldn't tell if the blood transferred to the sleeve or if he'd just wiped more dirt on his face.

Forget respectable then, it was boring. He revved the engine again and picked up speed, dodging sleepy merchants carrying barrels of fish and bolts of cloth. He wove in and out of traffic, leaving the slower-moving vehicles behind him as if they were standing still. He couldn't help but let out a whoop of joy. Speed was life. Speed was *everything*.

The city became more decrepit as he got to the outskirts. The buildings were broken down, some roofs collapsed, some slums built from only metal struts and canvas walls. He thought he spied some feet sticking out from a trash receptacle, and sped on, frowning. It wasn't his problem, and he hadn't recognized the feet anyway.

The area got poorer and dirtier as he neared the Den. *For the last time,* he thought. Maybe he'd be lucky. Maybe the gang had already gone to bed. Nocturnal beings tended to do that when the sun rose, after all. And the White Worms hated the sun more than they hated being cheated out of coaxium payments. He still needed a plan to get out of that problem.

The speeder slowed to a stop, and Han jumped out. He regarded the vehicle briefly: He had already destroyed the installed security system, so at this moment anyone could steal it from him fair and square. He could cobble together his own security, eventually, but not right now.

If the gang saw this, they'd take it. Nothing belonged to you when you worked for the White Worms.

All loot belonged to Lady Proxima.

A group of scrumrats, little kids as grimy as Han if not as bloody, ran by with their take from the evening clutched in their fists.

"Hurry up!" a teen boy shouted. "Or Proxima's gonna have your hide!" Two teens a few years younger than Han came into view, herding the kids. They pushed them and threatened them, accompanied by their growling sibian hound.

Han despised the creatures. Hulking and huge, white as the Worms' Grindalids leader with fewer legs and more slobber. He hated their affection, which was inevitably drenching, but their animosity was worse. He sneaked into the den after the kids, not wanting to be seen by anyone. They turned down one tunnel, looking for a safe place with a little bit of light to examine their treasures, take a moment to eat something stowed in a pack, or greet friends.

Most of the tunnels into the den were completely dark. Humans were not the dominant species of this area, and the photophobic Grindalids hated any natural light. Han had learned to maneuver in the dark thanks to it, but it wasn't a skill he was proud of having; it was a necessity. He passed the younger 'rats, hoping they wouldn't notice him.

A boy, maybe eight years old, pulled something shiny from his bag. He showed it to the older girl with him, a girl Han knew as Lex.

"Look what I got. I bet Lady Proxima'll give me an extra portion for this!" he said.

Immediately Lex snatched it and examined it. "No, no, she's gonna give that extra portion to me, now!" she said, and laughed.

The boy grabbed at her but she held it out of his reach. "No fair, give it back!"

Han left the cruel game of keep-away with a boy's dinner hanging in the balance. Kids had to learn to fend for themselves down here. He'd had to.

He passed a furnace, glowing golden in the otherwise dismal depths of the tunnels, and jumped when a pair of hands seized his shirt and pulled him behind the furnace. One hand went to his pocket to protect what he had there, while the other balled into a fist, ready to fight. But the assault never came, and instead, lips landed on his and kissed him for all he was worth.

Qi'ra. The only person he ever wanted grabbing him.

His free hand went to her bobbed brown hair and pulled her closer, forgetting his adventure, his throbbing face, and the desperate need to get out of the tunnels as fast as possible. This was what he had come back for. Qi'ra and freedom were the only worthwhile things in his world.

She pulled back for air first, her brow creased with worry. "You were gone too long, I knew something must have gone wrong," she said.

Her blue eyes shone in the light of the furnace as they searched his face, taking in the blood and swelling. She frowned and touched the skin around his eye.

Han grinned slyly and puffed his chest out. "This? This is nothing. You should see them." He pulled her closer, and then, at the skeptical look on her face, amended his statement. "Actually, they're fine."

She smiled, his easy tone soothing her as he'd intended.

"Listen, Kilmo stiffed me on the deal right in the middle of the exchange. I'm handing over the coaxium vials when his goons jumped me!" He grinned again. "But I showed 'em."

"Yeah? How?" she asked, centimeters from his face, catching on to his urgency and excitement.

Han grinned. Wasn't it obvious? "I ran away. Then I boosted their speeder."

Qi'ra smirked as if going along with a joke. "We going somewhere?"

Han pulled her closer. "Yeah, anywhere you want." He pulled his hand out of his pocket and showed her a metal cylinder, the seventh cylinder Kilmo had been asking for. Inside was a protected glass vial, full of a blue, glowing liquid.

Coaxium: a rare and expensive raw hyperfuel. A large amount could power starships through the galaxy. This small amount could power two scrumrats out of the sewers.

Qi'ra gasped. "You held on to one of the vials!"

Another group of street kids ran by. A voice floated to his ears, "Han's back." He groaned. Now word would spread and the Worms would be coming for him. He had to act. Qi'ra pulled him deeper into the alcove and held his hand in front of the furnace light to closely examine their prize.

"Careful!" he said.

"This is worth—" she said.

Han answered her, picking up the conversation in the

comfortable manner of old friends. "—five, six hundred credits. More than you said we'd need—"

Hope bloomed on her face. "—to buy our way out of the control zone!"

Han nodded. "Finally get away from Proxima—"

"Off Corellia! This could work, Han!" Her face was a picture of joy, and at that moment, Han felt like he could do anything.

"It will work. You always said one day we were gonna get outta here. This is it."

She looked into his eyes. "What are we waiting for?"

He kissed her again, quickly, and they were off.

CHAPTER TWO

Qi'ra had four plans ready to go depending on Han and his success or failure with this deal. In a flash she decided to implement a new, fifth plan.

Han managed to look adorable and charming even with his dirty, bloody face swelling up like Lady Proxima on a sunny day. He had opened his mouth for some clever retort or other, but they didn't have time. The 'rats had already been talking about how Han was back, so Lady Proxima's goons would be looking for them shortly.

She grabbed his hand and ran. She knew he would follow; they'd built up a trust and didn't question each other much anymore. She felt her heart swell as they ran, feeling like this time, maybe, this time would be their chance to get free.

Qi'ra veered away from the tunnel occupied by more scrumrats, who definitely would have sold them out for an extra quarter portion. She turned down a disused tunnel that she had mapped out looking for fast exits.

It was not a tunnel that humans would like to spend a lot of time in. She had wondered if this was by design, or if the Grindalids simply didn't care. This one didn't have the warm glow of a furnace. It did have a particular and significant odor: waste and rot, blood and brackish water. The damp ground squelched unpleasantly under their feet and she pushed on, not thinking about what they were running through.

She turned her head to tell him why they were traveling down this particular desolate path when his face switched from excited hope to despair. She stopped suddenly and Han immediately crashed into her back, banging his face on the back of her head. He stepped back, swearing and rubbing his already swollen eye.

The shape that had stopped them in their tracks let loose a guttural laugh.

Qi'ra groaned. Moloch. The hulking brute who sat at the right hand of Lady Proxima. Unlike most of the Worms, he was dressed for the elements in an envirosuit, his pale, wrinkled body draped in brown robes bleached white in patches by the foul toxins that lingered in the lair. He had his vaporizer, the mask that kept his face constantly hydrated and out of the sun, pulled back, and his white face and wrinkled beak squinted at them.

Beside him stood Rebolt, a boy who had grown up beside Han and Qi'ra, with the ambition to become Head of the scrumrats. He had been thwarted time and

again by Han and Qi'ra—the latter becoming Head
Girl, favored by Lady Proxima. But that was a blessing
she couldn't exploit today; the Lady was too smart for
that.

Rebolt, unfortunately, was Moloch's favorite, probably for the exact reason he couldn't win points with
Lady Proxima. He wasn't smart, lacked initiative, and
blindly followed orders. Rebolt would never turn on
Moloch simply because he wouldn't be able to figure out
how. Currently he helped Moloch bully whatever "'rats
needed correcting," as Moloch would say. He loved correcting Han and Qi'ra the most.

"Han. Just the scrumrat we were looking for," Moloch said, his mouth turning into a dreadful imitation
of a smile.

Han stepped in front of Qi'ra nonchalantly, his trade-
mark grin pulling at his mouth. "Moloch, hey, how are
you? I'm just on my way to see Lady Proxima. That's
where . . . right now, actually." He took a step back to
where his body bumped Qi'ra's. His hand brushed hers,
the deft fingers delivering the vial. She shifted to match
his movements and dropped the vial into her pocket.

"You have our credits?" Moloch was never one for
pleasantries.

Han winced ruefully and indicated his bruised face.
Qi'ra thought it was a waste of time to try to elicit sympathy; it would never work. But Han always had to try.
"Wait till you hear about the night I've had, you won't
believe it. I mean, you will believe it, but—"

Moloch had heard enough. He turned to Rebolt.
"Search him."

Rebolt had pale, acne-scarred skin and a perpetual

frown that made even his smiles look menacing. He snarled at Han to hold still.

Qi'ra took a step back as Rebolt roughly patted Han down, pulling at his clothes and squeezing the hemlines to see if he had any secret pockets anywhere. Han tried to go with it, placidly letting him search his jacket and trousers, yielding when Rebolt pushed him around. He found Han's tools and tossed them to the ground.

Qi'ra slid the vial deeper into her pocket and tried to look properly concerned but not guilty. The good news was that most of the Grindalids had never really gotten good at reading human body language. The humans were sharper, though, so she edged quietly backward into the shadows, hoping that she would go unnoticed.

Rebolt frowned, confused. He'd found no vials and no credits when he'd been sure he'd find one or the other on Han. He looked at Moloch for further instructions. "Lady Proxima will know what to do with him," Moloch said, gesturing at Han. Rebolt grabbed Han by the arms. Qi'ra tensed, ready to run down the tunnel, but Moloch's eyes found her unerringly—the bastards could see in the dark, after all—and considered her. Then he grunted, shrugging her off, and she smiled in the dark, free. She had something worth hundreds of credits in her pocket, and Moloch and Lady Proxima were preoccupied with Han!

She could run. She could take the vial, leave this planet, and never look back. But Han had returned when he had a speeder and coaxium. He could have been halfway off the planet by now! She cursed to herself. The bloody noble fool. He had come back for her and gotten caught. Now Lady Proxima was going to sell him, or eat him, or worse.

The coaxium was her ticket to freedom now. Her fingers stroked the cool metal in her pocket and she sighed and turned around. She owed him. She hated owing people.

Well, at least Qi'ra got away, Han thought. She had gotten away with his treasure, which hadn't been in the plan, but he would rather she had it than Lady Proxima. He tried to ignore the hurt he felt that she had left, and focused on the goon dragging him along.

Rebolt squeezed Han's arms harder than he had to. "I'm going to enjoy this," he whispered in Han's face.

Han winced. "Your breath, Rebolt. It's legendary."

Rebolt spat in his face, ensuring Han would take a fraction of that scent with him wherever he went.

The lair was built out of abandoned and outdated habitation cubes salvaged from an abandoned Corellian building project. They were connected by massive, rusty desalination pipes. But neither the Grindalids nor the humans they raised were clean people. The whole lair smelled of raw sewage, a foulness that was oppressive and nearly impossible to get used to. The scent only intensified nearer to the center, which was Lady Proxima's den.

The den was a foul pit in the middle of the disused warehouse. Machinery and tools still lay about, shoved to the side to make room for the watery pit at the center, where Lady Proxima and her young lived. Long ago her goons had blackened all the windows and befouled the place just so, making it a sweet nest for their queen. Han

remembered having to help clean the pool Lady Proxima lived in. The cistern extended deep into the ground
with branching chambers reaching who-knew-how-far
beneath the city. Any efforts Han had made to skim filth
from the water had been immediately undone the second Lady Proxima resurfaced in the murky pool.

The water remained brackish and muddy with a thin
oily sheen that glowed in the light of the weak bulbs
lighting the lair. They filched the electricity from one
of the power grids nearby, which made the lair livable
for the humans. The depths of the pool remained dark,
though, and you could smell the tainted water down the
hall. The worst insult to a scrumrat would be to tell
someone to go off and drink the Lady's water.

One did not use this insult when she was within earshot.

Rebolt shoved Han into a puddle of sewage water
outside the diameter of the Lady's pool. Other 'rats had
gathered to see the show, and Han scanned them to see
if there was a friendly face. He found none. His captors
loosened their grips, focusing on their leader, who was
rising from the water like a legendary sea snake.

Hideous she was, but also their queen. Lady Proxima
was a thick, wrinkled worm, with pale, glistening white
skin and a beakish face, and twelve arms: some spindly
and some stronger, all ending in claws. She was draped
in metal and chains like a worm who had rolled in metal
shavings and then claimed itself royalty.

As she opened her beak, the smell in the room got
slightly worse. Han winced—even after years of practice, he couldn't hide his visceral reactions to some

things. One young 'rat screwed up her face, too, and was swiftly slapped by one of the older kids.

In front of their queen, her servants bent their heads as one, and some of the 'rats followed. Han simply stood, waiting.

Lady Proxima didn't pay attention, looking at Han. She surveyed him up and down, and finally said, "You're looking worse for wear, boy. What happened?"

Han widened his eyes, trying to look indignant on her behalf. "I'll tell ya what happened, they double-crossed you and tried to kill me!"

Lady Proxima made the hissing, huffing sound that indicated laughter. She didn't believe a word. "*Did* they? What about the credits?"

Han worked to keep his voice steady. "They kept them."

Lady Proxima nodded. "And my coaxium vials?" she asked, her voice tense, foreshadowing a coming storm of rage. The question was rhetorical; she knew her goons would have delivered any returned coaxium that they'd found on him.

Han shrugged. "They kept that, too. But—" he added, seeing her swell with anger. He searched around for something to say after the "but" and came up with "—we learned a valuable lesson: We can't trust those guys." He smiled, satisfied he'd firmly laid the blame at the feet of the gang who had jumped him.

Lady Proxima's volume was rising, the rage surfacing from the depths just as she had from her pool a moment earlier. "You expect me to believe you walked away with nothing?"

"Well, I . . . ran away with my life. I think that's something," Han said, expanding his arms and showing her that he was trophy enough, her good little soldier scrum-rat. "I mean, to me that's a lot."

Lady Proxima finally looked away from him, meeting Moloch's eyes to confirm.

The hated Grindalid stepped forward and cleared his throat. "He didn't have anything on him," he said, reaching over to pat Han's pockets again to prove they were empty.

Lady Proxima's tense overlay was starting to crack. She drew herself up. "I trusted you with a simple task and all I'm hearing are excuses!"

Pain exploded in Han's midsection as Rebolt hit him in the stomach with a rod. He doubled over, fighting back the sudden nausea, his diaphragm protesting violently at having been attacked twice in one hour. Han didn't even see Lady Proxima signal, so for all he knew Rebolt was showing initiative by hitting him. *Rebolt had a thought on his own for the first time in his life,* Han thought. *Good for him.*

Han fell to his knees, landing on all fours in the sludgy puddle. One of his fingers got wedged in between two rocks, distracting him from the pain for a moment. He pulled it free and focused on getting his breath back.

Lady Proxima was talking, addressing the crowd that had gathered. "Pay attention, children. I will give you all my love and protection as I have given it to Han since he first came into my embrace. But there must be *consequences* for disobedience or else you never learn."

Han spied Qi'ra in the crowd near the back, watching

him with a stony look on her face. He couldn't read her expression, but she had *stayed*. That was enough.

Rebolt hit him again, across the shoulders, and he nearly went face-first into the water. He struggled to bring his head up and look at Lady Proxima, who was watching this beating with satisfaction.

Han had taken enough beatings for one day. He spat blood into the vile puddle. "You know what?" he said. "I don't think I'm ever gonna learn."

Lady Proxima's ugly face screwed up like a pale fist. "What did you say?"

Han pulled himself to his knees, finally getting his breath back. "I said—"

Rebolt decided then to take more of that initiative he had been attempting and swing at Han a third time, this time toward his head. Han caught the rod in wet hands and twisted it free from Rebolt's grasp. He turned it around, standing. Now *he* had a weapon. The shock on the other boy's face before Han hit him with the club was something sweet he would remember for a long time.

"—next time somebody hits me, I hit 'em back," he said, dropping all pretense of trying to grovel and placate. He was done.

Lady Proxima roared with fury, and before he could deliver some more deserved strikes to Rebolt, Han found himself looking down the barrel of Moloch's blaster.

"I wonder what you will do when I shoot you," he said, and for once Han couldn't think of a clever retort. Moloch's finger tensed, and Han got ready to eat hot blasterfire, but then a slim hand rested on the barrel, pushing it gently from Han's face. Qi'ra had appeared beside him.

"Moloch, wait. Don't," she said. She was speaking to Moloch, but her eyes were on Lady Proxima.

Around them scrumrats gasped to see someone openly defy the queen. Even Moloch wasn't sure what to do, and everyone looked at Lady Proxima for guidance.

Lady Proxima looked down at her new irritation. She smiled, and there was nothing kind there. Han knew she had a soft spot for Qi'ra. "Qi'ra. You poor misguided thing. Remember the Silo? We pulled you out of that horror, gave you a home. Don't throw it away for Han. He's not worth it."

Han was worth a lot, he wanted to interject, but figured this was between Qi'ra and Lady Proxima, and he should just stay out of it.

Qi'ra put her hand on his shoulder, declaring that she was in this, too. "But he's worth more alive than dead. Whatever he lost on the deal, we'll earn it back, double! We will make it up to you."

Moloch laughed, his blaster barrel still in Qi'ra's hand. "Coaxium is valuable. Scrumrats are cheap."

Around them most of the 'rats nodded, having been beaten down to understand their lack of worth in the eyes of those who raised them. A spare few looked sullen or outright angry at the statement. Those might be the ones to get out someday.

Lady Proxima nodded along with Moloch. "Too late for haggling. I have no choice but to kill him." She looked at Qi'ra thoughtfully. "Maybe I'll sell you. You may still be worth a few credits."

Qi'ra opened her mouth to say something she probably couldn't take back, and Han took that opportunity to raise his hand above his head.

"All right, everybody, stand back!" he shouted. He brandished the thing in his hand.

Everyone around him shrank back, wise to the variety of weapons one might hide on their person. Even though they all should have probably remembered he'd been searched.

Lady Proxima, unfortunately, remembered. She didn't flinch. "What's that supposed to be?"

"This is a thermal detonator," Han said, his voice confident and strong. He moved his thumb and made a subtle clicking noise. ". . . that I just armed."

Lady Proxima was having none of it. She crossed her nondominant arms. "That's a rock."

Han grasped his rock tighter. "No, it's not."

Lady Proxima twitched in her pool, losing patience. "Yes it is. You just made a clicking sound with your mouth. Is that all you've got, child?"

"Please tell me this isn't your plan," Qi'ra said, her voice low.

Found out, Han did the only thing left he could think of. "No," he said. "This is—" and he threw the rock at one of the blackened windows.

The rock sailed up and through the glass with a satisfying crash. Black shards showered some of the scrum-rats below, causing them to scream in surprise and pain. But those screams were nothing like the sound that came from Lady Proxima.

In the time Han had been in the tunnels, the sun had risen to show its full glory on the gray city, and it even managed to force its way into the slums. Now with the black barrier gone, it flooded into the room that it hadn't touched in years, illuminating Lady Proxima like a halo.

Her white Grindalid skin, and that of her subordinates not dressed in enviro-suits, blistered immediately, sizzling, popping, and oozing. She shrieked louder than Han had ever heard, writhing to escape from the light piercing her skin. She finally dived into the rusty water, getting away from the light in the solace of her lair, leaving white blood blooming in the dark water behind her.

The odor of cooking Grindalid, something Han had hoped to never smell, burned his nostrils. He coughed once and didn't wait any longer to see who else was badly injured. He grabbed Qi'ra's hand and they ran.

CHAPTER THREE

At first, Qi'ra thought they'd lucked out and no one was following them. The 'rats were too frightened, and the uninjured Grindalids would be seeing to their mistress and their fallen comrades. Light had flooded the room, and nearly all of the photophobic beings had been hit by the beam.

Except Rebolt was human. And Moloch had immediately activated the enviro-suit mask, which rapidly covered his face. And both of them would be intent on killing Han and Qi'ra. If you betrayed the White Worms as they had, you didn't expect forgiveness. No one who injured the Lady had ever lived.

"You stayed," Han said, looking over at her and grinning.

They pushed past a young 'rat walking the tunnels,

counting his night's take and completely unaware of the chaos in Lady Proxima's vicinity. He shouted in protest when they made him drop all the items he'd pocketed.

"Yes," Qi'ra said. "And I'm wondering if that was smart. Do you have an exit planned?"

"Of course."

"Is it anything more complex than run to your lifted speeder and get out of here?"

"You know me so well," he said, and actually winked at her.

They didn't have time for any side tunnels or sneaky ways out this time. They headed straight for the outside door, shouldering the current guard, Syke, aside. He and Rebolt were the keepers of the massive white hounds, creatures that would attack anything with such gusto that their teeth often broke—which was fine with them because their teeth regenerated, as if the hounds weren't terrifying enough.

Syke's hound, asleep on the ground beside him, woke up with a snarl, but Qi'ra slammed the door in their faces and turned over a barrel to slow their movement. Whatever was inside splashed to the ground and covered it, and Qi'ra hoped the rising stench would be enough to distract the hounds.

Han pointed to the speeder. It was obviously lifted; nothing that nice would be seen in their part of town. The paint was a deep purple, almost blue, and it was unmarked. She wanted to ask how he had managed to lift it from under Kilmo's nose, but they heard the hound snarl behind them. Questions later, then, she decided, and they hopped in.

She took a moment to run her hand over the console, almost stroking it. "An M-68. Not bad."

"Nice, right?"

"I love it. But you know we'll probably have to sell it, right?"

Han started the engine and winced as if she'd hit him right in the heart, but didn't contradict her. Two seats on a transport off the planet would be expensive enough. Vehicle transport was out of the question if they wanted to eat wherever they ended up.

Qi'ra saw his golden dice hanging from the windscreen and smiled. "We'll enjoy it while we can," she said, and Han hit the accelerator. The speeder turned 180 degrees and shot forward, slamming them back in their seats. Behind them, shouts and barking hounds receded in the distance, and they were away, their cheers of victory whipped away by the wind.

"There's a starliner leaving from Coronet Spaceport, we're gonna be on it," Han said over the sound of the engines. "We can bribe our way through the checkpoint."

Good. They had a destination. Qi'ra was honestly surprised he'd thought that far ahead.

She pulled the vial from her pocket and examined it, turning it in her fingers. It was hard to believe that something so small would fetch such a high price. "This'll have to be enough to get us through the Imperial checkpoint without ID chips," she said doubtfully.

Han snorted. "You kidding? That's grade A refined coaxium, worth at least seven hundred credits!" He grinned, all cocky confidence again.

She glanced sideways at him. "You said five or six hundred," she reminded him. "So, what is it?"

Han shrugged. He never was one for precise measurements. He got a faraway look in his eyes even as he expertly maneuvered around the trash, vehicles, and droids in their way. "Once we're through, we're free." He said the word like it was a precious gem on the tip of his tongue. "I'm gonna be a pilot."

Qi'ra nodded, taking up the thread. "We'll get our own ship, go anywhere we want, and never have to take orders or be kicked around by anybody—"

"Ever!" Han finished, then turned a sharp left and swerved to avoid a protocol droid, who chattered something disapproving at them as they left it in the dust.

"Ever," she repeated, and smiled at him. The kiss in the hallway had been impulsive, and she and Han had always lived for the moment, but now, maybe, she could actually consider that she and Han might have a tomorrow. His cocky grin turned to something wider, and he looked happy for a moment.

Then Moloch's truckspeeder hit them from behind.

"Damn!" Han said through clenched teeth. "Thought we'd get a little more of a head start." The speeder wobbled from side to side from the collision before he could steady it.

Qi'ra turned around in her seat, dark hair whipping past her face. "Moloch!" she said. "Faster!"

Moloch, Rebolt, and Syke had jumped into Moloch's modified, oft-in-need-of-repairs truckspeeder—a vehicle that didn't have the best acceleration, but its anti-gravity generator was a lot stronger than the classic landspeeder's. And it certainly could pack a punch when it got to full speed.

Han slammed on the accelerator, but the road widened and Moloch pulled up beside them. Beside the engine, Moloch had created a custom-made pen for the hounds. Right now it was even with Han's head, and the beasts snarled and leapt at their bars to get at him. Moloch yelled something at them, but the sound of the wind and the hounds drowned him out. Moloch bumped them again, knocking the speeder to the side. Han swore and gripped the controls harder. This thing was meant for street racing, not demolition competitions. He looked around for a place to lose Moloch.

He veered down a tight alley lined with boxes and machinery. A perfect needle to thread to lose the huge truck behind them, he thought. They were actually gaining ground and edging away from Moloch . . . until they caught the interest of an Imperial patroltrooper as they sped past.

Han's luck was wearing thin, but he could handle Imperial patroltroopers. They just wanted to arrest you, while thugs like Moloch and Kilmo wanted you dead.

They would be fine.

He checked behind him after they passed the trooper, hoping they wouldn't notice. But they did. Now he and Qi'ra had two tails, one a large truckspeeder he was fairly sure he could lose, and a nimble, swift speeder bike that would be a little harder.

Still, the speeder couldn't dodge what it couldn't see. Ahead of them, droids were unloading a cart and stacking their material in the street. If someone had been moving at a reasonable pace, they could easily have avoided it, but these poor droids were on Corellia and it was foolish to think the street was a safe place for, well, anything.

Han edged to the left. Qi'ra looked ahead, then at him, and then back to the obstacles in the road. "Han?" she asked. "Do you know what you're doing?"

He slammed a lever to throw the speeder into a lower gear as the trooper sped up behind him. The Imperial waved at him to pull over, and he obliged, swerving to the right at the last moment to clip the edge of the rubble in the road but leaving the patroltrooper no time at all to dodge. The speeder bike went straight into it, flipping several times in the air before landing on the road, with Moloch roaring by after it landed.

Han relaxed a fraction, one threat down. The road widened again and he took a moment to appreciate the speeder's handling. Now that he had room to drift into turns and let the vehicle accelerate, he felt a lot more confident.

Han gunned the engine, but Moloch still managed to roar up behind them.

What had they put in the engine of that truckspeeder? It shouldn't be able to move like that! It bumped them again as if to remind them they weren't free yet.

"That stinger's fast," Han grumbled, fixated on the road.

Qi'ra turned to look over her shoulder again. "But we're faster, right?" she asked, the wind almost taking away her voice.

Han searched the console. He hadn't driven this model speeder before and hoped it had some features he hadn't found yet. He fiddled with a switch. "I hope so."

"Han!" Qi'ra grabbed his shoulder; he was about to intersect with a fish market. He swerved hard to the left. He hoped he would hear the sound of the truck plowing into liters and liters of fish, but Moloch made the turn easily.

He gritted his teeth. "It's okay, I know a few tricks Moloch hasn't seen." He tapped the console, hoping the answer would appear in lights. It cheerfully told him that engines were running at 95 percent and at this speed he would be due for more fuel in approximately one hour. Not the information he needed right now.

The road narrowed again as they approached an intersection of bridges, one of them heading toward the Santhe shipyards. A half-built Star Destroyer hovered in the construction antigravity field on the far end, huge white sensor globes suspended by cranes in the nearest factory.

"Good thinking!" Qi'ra shouted. "We'll lose them in the shipyard."

Qi'ra grabbed his arm to get his attention back on the road. They'd reached the hub where most speeders slowed down to avoid horrific, fiery death. Another larger speeder was barreling toward them, but Han decelerated a fraction, then jerked the controls to the left and hit the accelerator again, making a sharp turn and heading for the shipyard. Qi'ra held on tight, her hair flying.

Once he had made the turn, he let out his breath. "Yes, that's exactly what I was thinking before you said it!"

bounced off to hit the other side. Sparks flew out behind them, and he struggled to keep it at the correct angle without tipping them completely over, but it was too tight. With a lurch the speeder stopped, fully wedged in the gap.

Han and Qi'ra sat for a moment, stunned. Then the repulsorlift engine died and the landspeeder dropped, screeching as it slid down to the floor.

Qi'ra looked at him with a stony gaze. "Am I still supposed to be watching?"

Han frowned at their situation, hearing Moloch behind them. He'd ordered the hounds set free and was going to follow on foot.

Qi'ra unstrapped herself and climbed out of the wedged speeder. Han followed her and took a moment to look up at the prize he had to abandon so soon. It was still a beautiful vehicle, but it was essentially useless now. The golden dice still hung from the windscreen; he reached out and snagged them before they escaped.

Qi'ra looked over her shoulder and snorted derisively. "For luck?" She sounded like luck was the last thing they would find that day.

He grinned. "Hey, we need all we can get."

Han. That troublemaker. Moloch had wondered why Lady Proxima hadn't just let him kill the kid—he surely had caused more pain for the White Worms than he had given benefit. Now he'd injured the Lady, stolen from the gang, and forced Moloch to chase him when he really should be going after Kilmo and doing the job Han had failed to do.

Han had also injured the Lady *in front of the entire gang*. The Lady couldn't appear weak; she was strength and power incarnate. Moloch wouldn't be surprised if she ordered the execution of everyone who saw the incident.

If word spread about Lady Proxima's failure, her rivals might be tempted to eliminate her altogether. And then there would be a power vacuum. Moloch could make use of that.

He smiled inside his enviro-suit. He would kill Han when he found him, but he'd have to remember to thank the boy's memory if this whole day ended with him taking over the White Worms.

He shook the thoughts from his head. Right now, he had to catch those two kids and take them back to Lady Proxima. Or what remained of her, anyway.

He approached the speeder in the gap, shaking his head. That kid never knew when to quit. And now he'd messed up a perfectly good speeder. Through the gap Moloch spied a hangar door, and beyond it a crumbling seawall. He could just see Han and Qi'ra running in the distance, following the seawall toward the fish market.

He looked over his shoulder to where Rebolt was standing, fuming. He hated Han more than Moloch did. Back at the truckspeeder, Syke stayed with the hounds, soothing them through their metal grate.

"Get Syke and the hounds," Moloch said simply.

Rebolt's face lit up with glee, glad the chase wasn't over. Syke handed one leash to Rebolt, who flinched as he took it. Syke seemed to be the only human who liked the hounds. The snarling beasts ran straight to Moloch, dragging their minders behind them. Moloch took the leashes and led the hounds to the speeder.

Han's morning adventures had caused him several small injuries, and his blood was smeared on the seat and the speeder controls. Moloch let them get a good long sniff.

"Feed," he said.

CHAPTER FOUR

Qi'ra thought she was quite stupid to trust that Han had a plan. She wondered where they would have ended up had she not suggested the shipyards.

Admittedly, the shipyard hadn't exactly worked out for them. They'd lost their speeder, but they had gotten a lead on Moloch. Perhaps he would give up at this point.

But Qi'ra knew better. Moloch would never let them go.

They headed down the seawall toward the bustling Coronet City Spaceport. As the Empire grew in power, the port had been taken over by Imperial soldiers, who managed all traffic by sea and by space. There was where they could get their tickets off this world.

She glanced back and saw something that made her

heart drop into her shoes. Moloch, Rebolt, Syke, and some pretty angry-looking hounds were following them. They could lose the bipedal pursuers in a crowd, but those hounds could track them anywhere.

Except for maybe through a fish market.

She sped up, darting in front of Han and taking the lead, heading straight for the market. Fish of all sizes, from the long and slender fleek eels to the huge bluevev glider that was longer than a human is tall, hung from hooks at one stall. Han and Qi'ra had to sidestep the fish guts thrown on the ground underneath the glider.

Another stall had tiny scalefin fish on a string like lights, the merchant selling them by the line. Qi'ra had eaten some of those fish before, after stealing a meal from an inattentive visiting Imperial. It had been a dare, and she had demanded to keep whatever she got. She'd never tasted anything as good as that fish, and her gaze lingered on them as they ran by.

She led the way farther into the market, weaving around barrels of fish, cooking pots both in use and for sale, and piles of nets that she avoided nimbly. Han stumbled behind her, and she slowed briefly, looking around for a solution.

Qi'ra pointed. "Now we're gonna do it my way."

Snarling dogs and cursing sounded behind them. Rebolt, Moloch, Syke, and the hounds had reached the docks. The hounds were in a frenzy, torn between wanting to smell all the fascinating smells and their duty to their master to find Han.

Qi'ra found what she was looking for and approached a barrel behind a merchant's stall. It was big enough for both of them. She pushed the lid off and checked the black water inside. It would do.

"Get in," she said.

Han stared at her. Then he looked at the black water, its smoothness broken by something moving within. Then he looked back at her like she was joking.

Qi'ra made an exasperated noise. "Trust me!"

The barking was getting closer, and some people were screaming in fear as the hounds lunged here and there, looking for the scent, finding it, and losing it again.

Han glanced back at them, and then into the water. A battle was clearly waging inside his head, and he finally—wisely—went with the lesser of the two terrible things.

He braced his hands on the edge of the barrel and swung his legs over. He grimaced the moment his feet hit the cold water, and then he stiffened.

"Nngh," he grunted. "Eels are . . . not my favorite."

Without the drama, Qi'ra followed him, pulling the lid back up to balance on the lip of the barrel. She sank, submerged to her neck, and then slid the lid over as the hounds' snarls and barks got louder.

They stayed like that, breathing shallowly in the brine-saturated air. Their eyes met in the sliver of daylight that penetrated the barrel, and she raised her hand to her lips.

Outside, the snarling hounds were very close, and they could hear the echo of Moloch's enviro-suit humidity breather. The barrel rocked gently from a hound bumping it with its nose, but then it moved on.

"Stinks like fleek and scale fin," Rebolt complained,

standing right next to the barrel. "It's throwing off the pups."

"They aren't here. Keep moving," Moloch said, sounding agitated. If he lost his prize, Lady Proxima would punish him. And Qi'ra knew what Lady Proxima's punishments were like.

Qi'ra was focusing so hard on the movement outside, she forgot about the fleek eels. One slithered past her neck and she flinched, jerking forward. Han caught her in his arms, steadying her. She got her footing under her again, but he didn't let her go. She could just see his quirk of a grin in the dim light as he leaned over her.

She pulled away. "What are you doing?" she demanded in a whisper.

His voice was hesitant, not believing she had rejected him. "I was . . . gonna kiss you."

She could not believe him. Was there a less romantic location for a kiss than up to your neck in live eels? "Not the time," she said through clenched teeth.

He nodded once. "Right. Later."

He was incorrigible. She smiled slightly in spite of herself. He had distracted them from the very real threat of being captured by Moloch, and she could at least appreciate that. Seeing her smile, he opened his mouth to probably say something else clever, but she moved a finger over his lips. "I think they're gone. Should we get out?"

He took her hand and kissed the finger covering his lips. "Maybe a little longer, just to be sure," he said softly. Then he dropped her hand. "Did you just squeeze my thigh?"

"No," she said firmly, hoping he would finally see

they were in the worst place in the world to have a romantic moment.

All flirtation gone, Han said quickly, "All right. Let's go."

Qi'ra started pushing the lid back, squinting against the light and keeping an eye out for their pursuers. Beside her, an eel popped its head out of the water and looked at Han, who shot out of the water as if he had been propelled.

Come on, they're just eels, she thought. She climbed out more slowly, as if one could be dignified while exiting a barrel of live fleek eels.

"Let's find a place on the way to clean up," Qi'ra said. "We need to show a good face when we bribe our way through, not covered in blood and smelling like eels."

They headed toward the looming spaceport, and freedom. She took his hand, feeling vulnerable all of a sudden.

They were doing it. They were getting away.

Lead Transport Security Officer Falthina Sharest adjusted her cap and looked in the restroom mirror. Her hair was knotted at the nape of her neck. Her brown uniform was immaculate. Her face was schooled in a stern, no-nonsense mask. Her lipstick was one shade redder than regulation because she wanted to see if her boss would get that pedantic with cracking down on "rule-breakers."

Still, she tried to treat each day like it was the first on the job. Comfort led to sloppiness.

It would help if the job were more comfortable,

though. They were short some officers, and the increased Imperial traffic had made her superiors extend her hours. Of course they offered no increase in pay for these hours; such was the plight of a civilian workforce under the Empire. It was enough to make you bitter, if you were the bitter type. And she definitely wasn't. At least, that's what she told her boss.

The spaceport had been a cushy job, once. She'd been there for years before the Empire came, greeting travelers and her neighbors going in and out of the port. But when they took over, there had been a tightening of security. They'd brought in new, elevated duty stations for officers to watch the travelers carefully, able to signal a stormtrooper at the slightest indication of trouble. They'd erected a much larger wall separating the boarding areas from the entrance, and the ID-reading technology was greatly improved.

All those credits they'd spent on taking the beautiful port and transforming it to function under Imperial control, but they couldn't pay the officers more.

Falthina took her job seriously, of course. She'd detained and brought about the arrest of shady types trying to get away from responsibilities, or steal Imperial secrets, or worse. Still, she had dreams, like anyone. Finally get a ticket off Corellia, see some other planets, only come back to visit her sister on the other side of Corellia. Maybe. And one couldn't do that on an officer's salary. Especially when the Imperial supervisors took more and more of her day away.

She held the border tightly. Unless, of course, the travelers had something for her to make her life a little easier. She'd gotten pretty good at hiding the presents

(They were always "presents" in her mind, not "bribes." She was receiving presents to make up for her increased unpaid hours. Only shady officers accepted bribes.) and would quickly relocate any underlings that noticed her behavior.

Corellia had always been home, and dear to her even though it was a dingy shipyard planet with a population desperate to get away from Imperial control. Which was ridiculous; the Empire had brought jobs to this planet floundering in fleek eel guts. They should be grateful. The Imperials did work her for unpaid hours, but it was still better than cleaning fish or working to death in the shipyards.

She thought about her future travels, and the contraband presents she had sold last week to make some good credits. She'd stashed them in an untraceable savings account just in case, which ate up a bit of her extra income, but one had to spend credits to make credits, she'd once heard. She stopped her daydreaming and hurried out of the restroom, passing a wet girl who smelled horribly of fish. Why were other Corellians so disgusting? Had they no pride?

The spaceport was large, lit by the morning light streaming in through windows high up the walls. Motes of dust, probably floating metal detritus from the shipyards, glittered in the air, but no one stopped to admire them. The port was clogged with travelers, some Imperials on official duty offplanet, some harried families looking as if they were leaving on a vacation, and then there were those with haunted eyes, those desperate to get away. Falthina would have to watch out for those.

She hurried to her post to relieve the morning customs officer, a man she hadn't met before.

He greeted her with a nod. "Falthina Sharest," she said, saluting. "I'm your relief."

"Oh, is it that time already?" he asked, glancing at his terminal. "You're early."

"Better than late," she said.

He shrugged, and she suppressed a disapproving frown. He didn't seem to care much about protocol. He saw her standing at attention and grinned. "Is everyone here so uptight? Relax, Sharest. This isn't the Senate or the deck of a starship. This is customs of a dirty, broken-down planet and you're here for the same reason I suspect the rest of us are." She raised an eyebrow. "You angered a superior, didn't you?"

She felt the color rise to her face. "I have always lived on Corellia," she said tightly.

"Oh, then you know what a punishment it is to live here," he said, standing and stretching. Seeing her face, he grinned to show he was kidding. "It's okay here, I mean. It's a pretty easy job. It smells like fish and grease and burning metal, but at least we're not getting blown up by terrorists, right?" He gave her a sloppy salute. "I'm out of here." He gestured at the terminal in front of him. "Pretty busy day today, and that's just the scheduled traffic."

She was determined to do a better job than this lazy newcomer who didn't even button his uniform properly. They briefly exchanged glances that showed they were judging each other: She judged his slovenly appearance, he judged her as a tightly wound type, probably reminding him of the person who had sent him here.

Was the Empire now using Corellia as a dumping ground for Imperial bad boys? She groaned at the thought, then got to work.

She surveyed the crowd. Most of the travelers queued peacefully and patiently, but a scuffle had erupted near the doors. She raised a hand to find the button for the alarm, but saw stormtroopers hurrying to the job.

That's what a well-oiled machine was supposed to do. Not ignore duty.

She settled in and turned on the light, indicating her queue was open to receive travelers.

The job was, as her grandmother used to say, dull as an old milk knife. She scanned ID chips, read the results, and waved people through the checkpoint where they hurried on to shuttles and ships. She began eavesdropping on other discussions to keep herself awake. Unfortunately, the conversations of travelers were as dull as the job.

One couple was arguing about the seat assignments on their shuttle. He wanted to sit together and she was telling him not to upset the ticketing agent with pointless requests. One girl was crying that she didn't want to leave home and go live on Coruscant, and she didn't care that Mommy had gotten a promotion. One Imperial official berated another, threatening to report him for the incident at the pub the night before.

Farther down the line, two teens held hands, looking vulnerable and out of their depth. They both looked poorly used in shabby clothes, damp, and the boy had bruises blossoming on his face. The girl looked around nervously as if keeping watch for something. She whispered something to the boy and he looked over by the door, where troopers were speaking to two humans and a very large person in an enviro-suit.

The boy slouched and looked bored, exactly like someone who didn't want to be noticed would look. She had seen it all.

A notification appeared on her terminal. LOCAL AU-THORITIES SEARCHING FOR SCRUMRAT HUMAN BOY AND GIRL. KEEP ALERT.

CHAPTER FIVE

"Han, they're here," Qi'ra said, watching Moloch and his cronies fan out among the crowd, looking for them.

He glanced over and then shrugged like it was nothing. "We're almost there. Just hold on to me and don't look back."

She grabbed his hand, and he hoped she wouldn't notice his anxiety manifesting in his sweaty palms.

"Once we're through, we've got to be smart and figure out where we're going," she said, always planning several steps ahead.

All he wanted to do was get off the planet. He'd figure out what to do afterward. But he would play along. "Anywhere the Empire isn't," he suggested. "Wherever we go couldn't be worse than where we've been." He indicated their clothes, still damp with eel water.

She wasn't buying his light banter. "Yes, it can. Out there we've got no protection. We could get snatched up by traffickers, sold to Crimson Dawn or the Hutt cartel."

He shook his head. "That's not gonna happen. I won't let it." He rooted in his pocket until his hand closed on the gold dice. He handed them to her.

She held them in her palm and smiled. "For luck?"

"Damn right," he said, and grinned back.

This was going to be easy.

"Next!" barked the emigration officer, a stern, pale Imperial woman. He wondered if you could get a job as an Imperial officer if you didn't look like someone had ratcheted your spine straight and plugged your bowels permanently.

They stepped up and she stared down at them. Did this woman ever smile?

"ID chips," she said through the smoky glass that separated them.

Han slouched to the side and smiled up at her, summoning easy bravado. "Funny story, we don't have 'em."

The woman scowled at him and looked around, presumably for a trooper. Would arrest be worse than being taken back to Lady Proxima? What if the troopers just handed them over to Moloch?

Qi'ra stepped forward. "But we do have this," she said quickly, holding up the vial. She lowered her voice so the people behind them couldn't hear. "Refined hyperfuel. It's worth at least eight hundred credits. Maybe more."

The officer paused. "You could be detained just for having that." But that hesitation told Han everything he needed to know. She had a taste for greed and power, and those kinds of people were easy to manipulate if you had the right tool.

"What good would that do anybody?" he asked. "Let us through, it's all yours."

She'd made her decision in that hesitation, Han knew, but she made a show of considering the bribe, and then looked around to see if anyone was monitoring her.

A security drawer opened in front of them awaiting the vial. They had done it.

Falthina eyed the vial, calculating the value and what it could get her. She could use it the way these kids were: to get the blazes off this planet. Or she could save it, building enough credits to invest in the life she'd always wanted. The options were huge.

She slid the drawer open. "The coaxium. Now."

The girl shook her head sharply. "As we're going through. Not before."

Falthina frowned. They didn't trust her. She didn't appreciate that. She was not calling the troopers on them; she was doing them a favor!

A scuffle sounded closer to them, and the boy looked around, tense. "Just do it, do it," he said, but the girl held her eyes, not backing down.

What if she was caught, Falthina thought, hesitating. If they found out about this, they may find out about the other "presents." Bribery and letting undocumented children through: The response from her superiors would be huge . . . She gathered herself. The prize was too valuable not to risk it. "You're a sharp one. Sharper than him by the looks of it."

The boy went through the gate, pulling the girl by the hand.

"The coaxium," Falthina ordered. "Now."

The girl put the vial in the drawer as the boy made it through the gate. As Falthina snapped the drawer closed, hands landed on the girl's shoulders. A larger boy and a Grindalid in an enviro-suit pulled her back.

Falthina thought fast. If she didn't act officially here, the bribery could be discovered when the authorities came over to investigate the disturbance. She had to control this chaos. She hit the alarm and the gate slammed shut between the teens. "Security, security," she said calmly into the intercom.

Lights flashed along the barrier, gathering the attention of the troopers sitting on gate turrets, their barrels swiveling to seek out any threat.

The girl struggled against her captors. The boy who had made it through the gate pounded on the glass between them.

"Han, go now!" the girl yelled. The boy holding her dragged her away, still struggling.

The boy pounded again. "I'll come back!" he shouted. "I will!"

He stepped back from the glass and watched her retreating figure, looking like he'd been cut off from life support.

Footed troopers had reached the gate and looked to Falthina for information. "The boy made it through," she said, an edge of command to her voice. These troopers always responded to a commanding voice, she had discovered. "Find him before he gets offplanet."

They nodded to her and bustled toward the officials-only door. She smiled, feeling the comforting weight of the coaxium vial tucked into her boot. "Thank you for your diligence," she said as they went searching for the boy.

CHAPTER SIX

Han staggered as if he had been cut free to swim in vacuum. If he went back for her and got caught, then if Lady Proxima didn't kill him, Qi'ra would for not at least taking advantage of her capture. He sank into the crowd, his throat tight and his eyes blurry. He had to get away before the troopers started looking for him on the other side.

He stumbled over an open pack. Nearby, some parents were fussing with a small child, trying to force it into a sweater. Their backs were to him. Han spied a brown cloak among the clothes and snagged it. Then he lifted a floppy hat from the head of a passing kid and darted behind a column, panting.

Han went still, the gravity of the situation hitting him.

He'd lost the coaxium and he'd lost Qi'ra. No credits, no ID, no support. He had only his wits.

However, that had been his situation for most of his life. And he was still alive, wasn't he?

He couldn't help Qi'ra as he was now. He had to take care of himself and then come back for her. He took a deep breath and looked around. The spaceport wasn't as crowded on this side, as people had dispersed toward their specific gates. Across the way he saw an Imperial recruitment office.

It was a way off the planet, even if it wasn't the ideal way.

He threw the stolen clothes on, hunched over, and headed toward the recruiter. Lady Proxima couldn't touch an Imperial soldier, after all.

Another queue. He stood among other recruits, some looking haunted and hungry, like he was sure he did, others looking eager as if this was their dream job.

Actually, in a way, it was. He had dreamed of being a pilot; this was one way to do so.

Officers were meeting with recruits and sending them down a windy tunnel toward the tarmac and shuttles. Han watched the other recruits go down the tunnel, straight to freedom.

Another Imperial officer, this one an older man with the same pale, pinched face as the woman at the gate, was processing the recruits. He waved at the tall, lanky boy in front of Han. "Approved, proceed to IDT-28," he said in a bored voice.

He looked at Han, looking like he'd rather be on a break than talking to new recruits. "Name?"

Han stepped up and looked around him. "This where you sign up to be a pilot?"

The man smirked at his confidence. "If you apply for the Imperial Navy," he allowed. "But most recruits go into the infantry."

Han shook his head impatiently. "I'm gonna be a pilot. Best in the galaxy. How long will that take?"

The officer gave him a bit more attention, sizing him up. "Depends on how good you are at following orders."

Han looked around, checking to make sure that Rebolt hadn't delivered Qi'ra and then come back to grab him, too. Or sent stormtroopers after him. Or Moloch wasn't coming for him himself.

The officer tapped on his desk to get Han's attention. "Why? You got somewhere to be?"

Han focused back on him grimly. "Yeah, back here as soon as I can be."

The man chuckled. "I don't hear that much. What's your name, son?"

"Han."

The man waited, but Han didn't say anything else. "Han what?" he asked.

Han frowned, confused. Han was his name. It had always been his name. He didn't have another.

"Who are your people?" the man pressed.

His people? His family was gone. The White Worms hadn't been family. The closest thing he had was Qi'ra and he didn't know her people's name, either. Neither seemed to be the answer the officer was looking for.

He shrugged. "I have no people. I'm alone." The words hurt more than he had expected.

The man made a note on a keypad. "Han . . . Solo.

Approved. Proceed to transport ID-83 for the Naval Academy at Carida."

Solo. It would do as well as any other name. Better, maybe, as it described him pretty well. He looked back at the gate one last time, at Corellia and his old life. He turned his back on it and headed through the turnstile and down the tunnel to the shuttle that would get him, finally, off this planet.

"Good luck, Han Solo," the officer said as he departed. "We'll have you flying in no time."

Captain Nettic Whain slammed the file on his desk. "Another demerit, another loss of weekend leave, another three cases of insubordination, and that's this week. Will you explain to me why exactly this recruit Solo is still in the Academy? We have kicked out more obedient recruits for less."

Sergeant Triosa Broog shifted uncomfortably under her superior's gaze. "It's his flight record, sir. He is useless at everything, except that when we get him in a ship he's, well, I've never seen anyone with his reaction time or innovative problem-solving skills."

Captain Whain looked at the file again. "You say 'innovative problem-solving skills' but here you wrote down, 'reckless and responsible for one, possibly two, destroyed fighters.'" He raised his eyebrows. "'Possibly' two, Sergeant? How can you 'possibly' wreck a fighter?"

She grimaced. "Other recruits want to follow his tricks. One tried to perform one of his more reck— innovative maneuvers. But no one flies like him, sir. No one. The recruit lost control of his fighter, destroying it. We almost lost the recruit."

Whain sighed. "I would much rather have one hundred soldiers who follow orders and don't think for themselves at all than the best pilot in the galaxy who thinks he knows better than his commanding officer."

"One more chance," Broog said. "I think I can get him to follow orders this time around."

"Why is this one pilot worth so much?" Captain Whain asked.

Broog pointed to a statistic in the file. Whain read it, and then read it again. He sighed. "Take away his flight privileges for a week," Whain said. "If he improves, reinstate them. If not, send him to a place we can use a reckless soldier who doesn't follow orders."

Broog winced. She knew where that was. "Yes, sir."

"And get me the name of the recruiting officer who sent us this maverick."

She relaxed visibly. She'd clearly been waiting for her own punishment. Whain dismissed her, deciding that if she couldn't get this recruit to get in line, she might be joining him in the infantry.

The Empire had no room for rebels, after all.

As the years went by, Han would measure them not by time, but by the number of parsecs away from Qi'ra. It hadn't been three years; it had been thousands of parsecs. Wherever in the galaxy he was, he always considered his distance from Corellia.

Imperial training had been laughably easy, except when he was expected to do what he was told. Every time he got in trouble, his flight record made his superiors hesitate to kick him out of the navy, and he got harsher and harsher punishments.

He wasn't perfect, of course. He had never claimed to be. Hardly ever. No more than once a day. If the other squadrons would just accept he had the best reflexes and knew best what to do when things got dicey, things would be so much easier. But none of his fellow pilots had grown up like he had. No one had had to think quick when a pickpocketing went wrong and you had to make your way through a crowd in the fastest, yet stealthiest, way possible. And those kinds of skills were just what he needed when his squadron ran across raiders like these.

The raiders were certifiably insane to start chasing Imperial ships, but the brand-new tech built into Han's squadron of Infiltrators must have been too tempting to ignore. The "TIE brutes," as they were called, might not have been much to look at, but the heavy armor, twin laser canons, and integrated droid intelligence would fetch a good price on the black market. Two of the raider Headhunters expertly cut through their formation, with Onyx 2, their second in command, veering away to avoid collision. The rest of the squadron struggled to re-form, and a quick command came through Han's helmet.

"Onyx Squadron, maintain formation!"

Han knew that voice, and it always made him grind his teeth. Flight Officer Ubbel was always demanding they play it safe. Han privately thought that if Ubbel had been in charge, the Empire would have encompassed one of the smaller skyscrapers on Coruscant instead of half the galaxy.

"I can take them faster than the squad can!" Han shouted.

"Negative, negative, Onyx Nine, return to formation!"

Han actually liked Onyx 2, his friend Cadet Lyttan Dree. The number of other cadets who liked him was frankly diminishing. His natural charm always drew them in, and then most people would quickly figure out that being close to him would probably reduce their chances for advancement. Dree, or Onyx 2, managed to be a good pilot, Han's friend, and still follow the rules. Han had always meant to ask him how he did that, and now he might never get the chance.

He peeled off from the formation and chased the Headhunters down, feeling much freer now that he could fly where he wanted to and not worry about the others in formation. In theory he could understand the need for a formation, but in practice he always preferred to worry only about himself and his own ship.

He accelerated, watching the raiders flank Onyx 2 as he tried to outmaneuver them. Han's helmet squawked again, and he turned down the audio as Onyx Leader was shouting at him to return to formation. Then his droid started fussing at him.

Imperial droids were the worst. The White Worms hadn't had much use for droids, so Han hadn't grown up with them behind doors, underfoot, and always politely, infuriatingly, telling him how wrong he was.

His ship's intelligence, MGK-300, was such a droid. It thought that since it was integrated directly into his ship, it knew more about the ship than he did.

He'd already long since had enough of MGK's so-called guidance, but it still beeped furiously at him that they were making the squadron weaker because of his actions.

Han ignored it. If the droid wasn't telling him something was wrong with the ship, he didn't see a need to listen to it.

He got one of the raiders in his sights and fired, nearly missing, but clipping a wing. The ships separated, one keeping up with Onyx 2 and one turning to pursue Han.

Now he saw the point of the squadron formation. He wheeled and turned, heading back, and met head-on his own fellow cadets flying toward them. He ducked to slide under them and they fired. He cheered them on, but then felt the ship heave under him as something behind him exploded.

His Infiltrator went into a spin. Han fought for control, trying to tune out the squeals and beeps coming from behind his head.

"Yeah," he said, "I know we lost the reverse thrusters! Thank you!" The ship started to spin, the universe whirling madly around him, the Star Destroyer's docking bay a rapidly moving target.

MGK beeped what Han knew was standard emergency protocol at this point—which was essentially giving up. He shook his head. "Not ejecting! I can make it back to the docking bay!"

The droid made known its firm disagreement, beeping and booping faster and faster as it began to panic.

These machines were distracting, irritating, and useless. How did anyone fly with this nagging going on? "You know what?" he asked, flipping an emergency switch to power down the droid. MGK couldn't distract him now, and he could finally focus.

As if the droid were trying to get the last word in, the control panel sparked and spit when he touched the switches. Pain flared in his hand and he yelped, shaking it. Had MGK done it on purpose? He couldn't tell. It was pointless to wonder, because the docking bay was suddenly much, much closer.

He struggled to maintain control and decelerate. At the last possible moment, he yanked the control yoke upward, managing to slip through the artificial atmosphere of the docking bay cleanly, without clipping any of the sides—which Han thought was pretty impressive. His ship hit the floor and bounced, careening him into three tethered TIE fighters. His chin hit the control panel and he saw more stars, wondering briefly if he had flown straight through the ship and back into space. Then he heard the alarms and remembered where he was.

No one was impressed with the fact that he'd saved Onyx 2.

Commodore Almudin's round face seemed to eclipse the rest of the tribunal. Other high-ranking important types were there, but Han could only see the ridiculous round face, even as he struggled to take the man seriously. The commodore outranked him (actually, everyone on the tribunal outranked him), and rumor had it that he'd had an amazing flight record in his day. But right now he flew a desk and had the exciting job of sentencing real pilots in military tribunals.

Han's chin still throbbed from the quick work the medical droid had made of his gash, and he ignored the other aches from the crash as he stood straight.

But the officer's face really was irritating.

The other officers on the tribunal, two women and a man, looked both bored and annoyed, as if in their minds Han was already sentenced to death and they were just waiting for lunch.

"Cadet Solo," the commodore said, like he had before, with that tone of less than disgust, "I still can't decide if you're brave or stupid."

He shrugged. "I like to think I'm a little of both, sir." He paused. He could never get the ranks right. Was this man a moff? He'd better cover all of his options. "I mean, Moff." The man's face didn't change. "Sir Moff."

That finally broke him. He scowled at Han and said, "It's 'Commodore,' and if you think having a smart-ass attitude is the way to go here, you're sorely mistaken.

"Why don't you tell us what allegedly happened here?" he continued, indicating a screen that had lit up. It was flanked by two Imperial guards, Lieutenants Tag Greenley and Bink Otauna. Once upon a time, Han had attempted to befriend them, but they turned out to be such colossal screwups, Han started to avoid them before they got him or themselves killed. Still, he needed all the friends he could get. He gave them a little wave and a grin. They looked back at him wryly and said nothing.

The screen lit up, and Han saw his own ship, leaving formation to pursue. He felt a surge of pride as he always did, seeing from the outside how free he looked. He realized he was just admiring himself, and he cleared his throat and pointed in the general direction of where Onyx 2 was being pursued.

"Onyx Two was flanked by Headhunters." He'd reported all of this. He had no idea why they needed his comments again since he'd already given them all the information in his report. "If I'd followed Command's directive and returned to formation instead of going after 'em, he'd be dead now."

This tribunal was ridiculous. Couldn't they see that he'd saved their second in command?

"There is no place for maverick heroics in his Emperor's navy."

Han held his hands up, as if fending off praise. "Trust me, I've got no interest in being a hero, Commodore, what I—"

The commodore cut him off abruptly. "Well, congratulations. You're not one. This tribunal, me in particular, finds you guilty of disobeying a direct order, and you are hereby reassigned to the infantry. Report for immediate transfer to Mimban."

He wasn't getting kicked out. Relief flooded him. He smiled. "Okay. I thought it was gonna be way worse." He cocked his head and inquired, "And roughly, when do you think I'll be flying again?"

Commodore Almudin smiled, and there was nothing friendly about it. "Oh, we'll have you flying in no time."

CHAPTER SEVEN

As soon as Han landed, he understood the play on words the commodore had used. Imperial mudtroopers definitely did fly on Mimban. Usually after some sort of explosive device had launched them into the air, often in several pieces. They would land, splattering mud, and not get back up.

Han flew now, luckily still in possession of his limbs. An explosive's shock wave slammed into him, pushing him head over heels backward, the only thing saving him being the trench he tumbled into. Face-first, naturally.

He looked up, eyes wide, spitting mud. Han still wasn't entirely sure what they were fighting for, or even if they were on the correct side. In theory they were here to suppress a hostile uprising against the Emperor and bring the peace and prosperity that Imperial support always supplied, but near as he could tell, *they* were the hostiles that were invading an already peaceful planet. They were probably trying to take the planet for its resources, although Han couldn't guess what the Emperor needed with all this mud.

He lay in the trench, panting, coated from head to foot in Mimban mud. It was inescapable. It smelled of rot, of blood. It wasn't clean mud; someone was always getting a skin fungus from the stuff. He finally gathered his senses and sat up, pulling off his partially demolished, mud-covered face guard and goggles.

Visibility wasn't much better. The smoke and flame from the battle turned the already dense fog a dismal dark red, making the action just half a klick away invisible. The enemy could—and did—appear out of the fog, attack them, and then slip back into it.

Han had no idea how he'd stayed alive so long. He had seen countless fellow soldiers die on the battlefield. The casualty reports were updated so often that he couldn't even follow. More troop transports arrived every week, more blood for the fields. Still, the Mimbanese and their trenches held off the Imperials. Han figured the dead were the only ones who won this nightmare battle, because at least they could stop fighting. However, dying was not the way he wanted to win anything.

Major Staz gave him a nod. Han had seen the nod before. It meant, *Glad you're not dead, rookie, now get back in there.*

"Your Empire needs you! Troopers forward!" he shouted. "Solo, get up! We're almost there."

Hadn't he just seen the explosion that sent Han back

to the trench? "Almost *where*?" he said. "Where are we going?"

The major heaved himself out of the trench and ran forward, calling over his shoulder and pointing. "Just over that last ridge! Victory is—"

Han ducked as another explosion sounded, dodging the shrapnel. The major hadn't been as lucky as Han had just been, and this one was a direct hit. The man flew into bits just as Han had seen happen time and again. Han ducked back into the trench, panting. Still reeling from the first bomb, he felt stunned and confused. He'd lost superiors before and knew quite well that this didn't mean you got to ignore your orders, even though common sense said that you shouldn't head into the place where someone else had just been vaporized.

Around the battlefield, Mimbanese rebels materialized in and out of the mud, picking off infantry with their blasters. Imperial AT-DTs entered the field to meet them, trying to overtake them with sheer numbers. Chaos reigned, and Han saw more mudtroopers taking refuge in a crater made by a previous battle. Gathering with a larger number seemed safer than following in the major's deadly footsteps.

He jumped out of the trench and ran toward the crater, ducking low and sliding as his boots squelched in the murky mess. He landed in the crater on his back and just stared at the gray sky of Mimban, wondering how he had gotten here.

Another explosion sounded, the bright flare silhouetting a lone humanoid figure. Han thought it was someone other than an Imperial, because his body language was casual instead of military, and his blasters looked a lot less like Imperial issue and something a lot more like what Han would have preferred to use over the Imperial rifles.

The figure used the blaster to casually pick off some attacking Mimbanese. He shot to the left with his left hand, the right with his right hand, expertly twirled one of the blasters and shot straight ahead, and then gestured to three other troopers.

Han stared at the Mimbanese falling all around this casual soldier. Over the ringing in his ears, Han could hear the man yell as he gestured. "Come on!"

His companions dived into the crater as another bomb hit, showering them with mud and a few limbs of their fallen comrades.

The three sat up, one of them moving in an odd kind of way Han couldn't quite place. Was he injured? He swiveled his head and looked at the commander. "When you said, 'We'll just pop over to Mimban, skirt the battle,' was this what you meant? 'Cause it kinda feels like we're right in the meat of the battle."

More mud rained down on them, and a boot—still with a foot inside—landed on the lap of the second trooper. She lifted her face mask, picked it up, and tossed it to the side casually.

"It kinda reminds me of home," she said.

The woman had dark skin and a steely look in her eye. She looked nothing like Qi'ra, but her mannerisms, her casual acceptance of a strange (or violent) situation, struck him as very like what Qi'ra would have become in a few decades. He shook his head, trying to rid himself of the nostalgia.

The third member of their group got stoically to his

feet. He was a large man, his uniform straining across his shoulders. He didn't speak.

The captain held a pair of macrobinoculars up to his face. He leaned over the edge of the crater.

In the distance an AT-hauler hovered in the air, its large arms lowering another AT-ST onto the battlefield. Once its tethers were released, it rose out of enemy range and flew back to the Imperial Camp Forward.

The captain, with bright-blue eyes and light but weathered skin, laughed and lowered the scope. "Ha! See, I told you they'd have 'em."

The first member of their party, the one who hadn't removed his mask, clambered to his feet. "Congratulations. Remind me to give you some kind of reward later." The voice was tired and sardonic.

The captain ignored him and pointed to the direction the AT-hauler had gone. "That means Forward Operations must be that way."

Shouldn't they know where Forward Operations was? Had their minds been addled by the explosions, too? It was possible; Han had seen a lot. "It is," he told them, "but the major said we're supposed to go that way." He pointed toward the major's current place of rest.

The other man looked where he pointed and then looked at him like he was a stupid child. "Go that way and die," he said.

Han nodded. "That's exactly what happened to the major," he said.

The man looked around as if to find someone to take this annoying infantryman away from him. "Well, who's the ranking officer now?"

Han tried to puzzle out the mud-coated insignias on the man's worn and blaster-scarred uniform. "You are, Captain."

His three companions burst out laughing, startling Han. "So what's the plan, *Captain* Beckett?" the woman asked.

The other talkative one crossed his arms. "Yeah, *Captain*, we'll follow you anywhere, apparently."

Han had laughed at a superior officer once. He'd cleaned latrines for a month afterward. But Captain Beckett merely glared at his companions and climbed to the top of the crater again.

No one else was paying any attention to this man or his companions. They had ill-fitting uniforms that had seen a lot of action. Their weapons were nothing close to regulation, and Han stared hungrily at their blasters. He was beginning to doubt these were Imperial infantry. He could call them out. He might even be a hero, revealing infiltrators. Or he could follow them in whatever they were doing.

Yeah. That sounded much more interesting.

Captain Beckett returned. He addressed the woman. "Val."

"Yeah?"

He pointed to a few of the mudtroopers beyond Han. "Take Rio and those four mudskulls and flank them on the left." He pointed to Han. "I'll take this mouthy scooch and Korso around to the right. Maybe we'll get lucky."

She smiled, her steely gaze softening. "There's a first time for everything."

Captain Beckett laughed. Han saw the way they were

looking at each other. No officer looked at a cadet that way. There was nothing of the chain of command here. His look held respect, trust, and affection, and she followed him for the same reasons, not for any insignia.

She left to gather the other mudtroopers, who looked eager to follow anyone willing to take control of this bloodbath.

Han jogged to keep step with Captain Beckett and Korso. "Can I just ask—" he began.

Captain Beckett rounded on him and looked at him with those blue eyes. Korso moved on ahead. "You wanna live, Sparky?" Beckett asked.

No officer had ever called him Sparky. Han thought of Qi'ra and nodded. "Very much."

"Then shut up and do what your captain tells you," Captain Beckett said. "And drop that equipment. It just slows you down."

Han's infantry specialist backpack fell to the ground without another word.

Similarly obedient, the four other mudtroopers had followed the new soldiers from Captain Beckett's team—he had called them Val and Rio. Han didn't much care about the chain of command, and he had learned that in a muddy hole with people dying all around you, the others didn't question it, either.

Captain Beckett was a questionable Imperial but a damn good soldier. Han tried to cover him, but he didn't really need it. Korso, the tall, silent companion carrying a rotary blaster cannon, took point as they ran into the fray.

"Korso, you and the kid watch the left, I'm on the

right!" Captain Beckett called. They ran into the battle, and for a moment, or two years (it was hard to tell), all was blasterfire and explosives. Han tried to catch the heat signatures in the mist to fire at the Mimbanese, but he found it better to just shoot once he could actually see the bright-red skin and bulging eyes of the enemy.

Korso was a large man, and he shielded Captain Beckett, unleashing a barrage of lasers when he could and blocking when he needed to. The enemy Mimbanese, hiding among the mud and behind their primitive woven-reed armor, were much better with stealth than the mudtroopers and seemed to be everywhere. They moved through the mud as if it were water while the mudtroopers staggered, slipped, and fell.

Beckett took out a group on the right, blasting a trench of soldiers as they popped their heads up to fire back at him. Han wanted to take a moment to appreciate his skill, but he had his own problem to worry about, the Mimbanese making use of the low visibility to attack from the left. He took a moment to focus his rifle, aiming not just haphazardly at shadows in the mist but focusing to spot flashes of red skin or bulbous black eyes. He fired three shots in quick succession, the enemy falling and not getting up again.

Korso was a force of nature. Any Mimbanese who decided to engage him close up would be nearly liquefied by the cannon's point-blank blasts, and if they ran to get out of the way, they were vulnerable to Beckett's or Han's blasters.

Han held his own, inspired by a leader he could finally respect. Beckett was someone who was a straight talker, who wanted his soldiers to get the job done but do it strategically and not run straight into death. He took down a few more fighters who jumped at them from the mist, ducked, and ran to keep up with Beckett, keeping an eye on the battlefield. Korso was grappling with a large Mimbanese and sliding backward in the mud.

Han saw the shooter emerge from the mist, taking aim at them, and he shouted and ran for Beckett and Korso. He couldn't get purchase in the mud, however, and didn't reach them in time. Multiple blaster shots hit Korso and the Mimbanese man he struggled with, and they both went down.

Han reached Korso and pulled the Mimbanese off him. He looked up at Han, dazed eyes not recognizing him, but still alive. Beckett appeared beside Han and they both struggled to lift Korso. Han looked at Beckett for guidance, and he pointed to a trench nearby. They stumbled, for once glad of the mud that made it easier to drag the big man. Blaster shots hit the area around them, sizzling and raising a rancid burning smell of coppery blood and befouled mud.

They tumbled into the trench with Korso, and Beckett laid him on his back to look at him. But now his eyes were sightless and blank. With a heavy sigh, Beckett carefully closed them, letting his shoulders fall for a moment. It was a brief moment, but Han saw more emotion there than he had ever seen an Imperial show for a fallen soldier.

Beckett straightened and gave Han a look. Without a word he headed off, and Han followed, not even questioning what the look had meant.

They had finally gotten out of range of the battle

and were nearing the Camp Forward. They were able to walk without constantly watching for the next blaster shot.

"I'm Han," he offered, trying to distract the man from his grief for only a minute.

"Nobody cares," Beckett said, his voice harsh.

Han looked back over his shoulder at the trench. "Sorry about your friend."

Beckett looked down for a moment. "Me too, he risked a lot to help us."

Han wondered what Beckett meant, but he had learned enough about this man not to ask for information not freely given.

"Thanks," he said. "For saving my life."

Beckett looked up and smiled slightly. "You did all right," he said. They walked a little farther, and Beckett turned and faced Han, looking serious. "You want some real advice?" Han nodded. "Get the hell outta here. Any way you can. As soon as possible."

Han now had serious doubts that this man was a captain. No Imperial would advise another to abandon the battlefield. It was good advice, though, and Han continued to follow Beckett. They reached the base of forward field operations at last. The domed tents sat on the muddy field like boils. Droids modified to handle the planet's mud trudged from tent to tent carrying medical equipment, caf, and other provisions.

Other troopers fresh from the battle hurried past Han and the rest to carry fallen fellows to medical tents, and Han thought briefly of poor Korso. If only he'd been able to make it a few more meters.

No. Han had seen his body. There had been too many

blaster hits. He was surprised Korso had taken that many before he fell. He must have been a formidable soldier.

The patrolling troopers and vehicles took no notice of Beckett and Han as they entered the base. Perhaps Beckett was legit after all. Han had to uncover the truth.

"Which company do you command, Captain?" Han asked. Maybe he could get a transfer.

Beckett checked around, looking for his other soldiers. Val and Rio headed their way, no longer trailing the two confused mudtroopers they had left with. Rio still wore his helmet firmly on his head.

"None-Of-Your-Business company. And we're full up," Val said.

As if to make the dismissal complete, Val cut between them and pointed to the airfield. Beckett nodded and they headed off. Han noticed that none of the departing troopers' uniforms fit terribly well. Rio's trousers were sagging, and as Han watched closely, a blue hand snaked out of the back of his jacket and hitched up the trousers. Rio hadn't removed his hands from his blaster as he did so.

Definitely not Imperials. And yet, Han took a step forward, wanting to follow this leader more than he'd wanted to follow anyone. Maybe Beckett could be his ticket out of the infantry, out of the Imperial military altogether.

He had told Han to get off the planet any way he could, after all.

"Attention!" came the shout behind him. The other mudtroopers straightened, and with one last look at the departing trio, Han took a moment, and then stood up straight, too.

"In three hours we move out for the southern marsh-lands." Han saw that the speaker was Lieutenant Bo-landin.

He sighed audibly.

Bolandin's head snapped up. "What was that?" he demanded.

"I'm just wondering what our objective is, Lieuten-ant," Han said.

"What it always is, Cadet," Bolandin said, a look of disbelief on his face. He looked as if Han had missed the first day of basic training. "To bring peace and prosperity to the planet. To install a regime loyal to the Emperor and eradicate the hostiles."

"But it's their planet," he objected. "We're the hos-tiles."

The lieutenant got close to his face and squinted his eyes. "You got a problem, Trooper?"

Han didn't meet Bolandin's eyes, but looked toward the airfield where Beckett, Val, and Rio were nearly out of sight. "No problem, sir," he said.

The lieutenant gave Han a warning look, the I've-got-my-eye-on-you look that he'd become very familiar with, and then headed toward the tents.

Han stood at attention until Bolandin was gone, and then he turned and headed for the airfield as non-chalantly as he was able.

Tobias Beckett was trying not to think about Korso. He wasn't a friend, not a companion like Val and Rio, but they'd had a deal: He'd get Beckett access to uniforms and help him infiltrate the army, and he'd get Korso off this miserable mudball when they left. Korso had done his part, and instead of freedom he'd gotten a grave.

Beckett didn't like failing to uphold his end of a deal.

He shook his head and surveyed the airfield. Troopers were active, but most of the vehicles and soldiers were still on the battlefield. They could still hear the explosions behind them.

"Looks like they're running sorties every half hour," Beckett said.

Val took her own lay of the land. She pointed at the edge of the airfield, and then at the vehicles. "I can take out the guards at the perimeter, and the pilots, the signalmen." She squinted and appeared to be counting under her breath. Then she sighed impatiently. "Here, I'll just take them all out." She got her blaster ready and checked its power cells.

"What are we looking at?" came a young voice behind them, and Val swore quietly.

The kid—Han, he'd said his name was—had come up behind them and was eagerly watching them plot.

Beckett clapped his hand on Han's shoulder hard enough to send a message. "You got a talent for sticking your nose where it doesn't belong."

Han smiled slyly at him. "And you're wearing a uniform picked fulla laser burns, a uniform you took off a dead man. You're not Imperial Army; you're thieves here to steal equipment for a job."

Beckett could feel the anger rise within him. He didn't have time for this.

"And I want in," Han finished, as if he had anything useful to give to the plan.

Beckett ground down on the chakroot held between his molars. He *really* didn't have time for this.

Val sighed. "Now we've gotta shoot him."

"No," he said, shaking his head.

"Yes," she said, flipping the safety off her blaster.

The kid looked uncertain but edged closer to Beckett, still sporting that cocky grin.

"No," Beckett said, a bit more forceful. "Snap his neck. Less mess."

Rio stepped forward, his two dominant arms outstretched, and approached Han.

The kid took a step back hastily, raising his hands. "Hang on, I came up running scams on the streets of Corellia! I've been boosting AV-21s since I was ten. I'm a driver, I'm a flier, and like you said"—he turned his rueful, hopeful grin on Beckett—"I've *gotta* get out of here."

Rio dropped his hands but didn't step back. "What's a flyboy doin' down in the mud?"

"I got kicked out of the Academy at Carida for—" He paused here, looking slightly embarrassed. "—having a mind of my own. But trust me, I'm a great pilot, and I need to get home!"

Rio laughed. "Back to Corellia? You *are* nuts."

Han drew himself up. "I got a reason."

Val dismissed him with a wave. "We've already got a pilot."

Han looked at Rio. "The Ardennian?"

Beckett sighed, annoyed now at Rio, who had promised he could keep his disguise up this time.

Rio sputtered. "*Ardennian?* You got a lot of nerve, pal. I'm an Imperial trooper!"

Han smirked. "A couple of your arms popped out of your butt and hiked up your pants, 'trooper.' "

Rio moved his helmeted face centimeters from Han's, two hands raised as if welcoming a fight, trying to hide the other two behind his back. "You've got a very vivid imagination," he said.

Val jabbed her rifle barrel into the kid's stomach, her threat a bit more insistent. He still didn't move. He knew she wouldn't shoot, not here. It was too public. Beckett was surprised they hadn't attracted attention yet.

Han's face looked desperate now, his eyes wide and pleading to Beckett. "I'll do whatever I've gotta do to get back to Corellia. I've already been away too long. Please. Just give me a shot!"

As one, Beckett, Val, and Rio turned away from him and went back to surveying the airfield. Maybe if they ignored the kid, he would go away. He looked to be the kind who liked attention.

"Well," Han said behind them, "if you're not interested in me, I think the lieutenant might be *very* interested in you."

Beckett straightened his jacket and turned around. He eyed the kid and noticed the lieutenant in question a few meters away, his back to them. "Blackmail, huh?" he asked. Han nodded as if he didn't want to do it, but he would if he had to. Beckett laughed. The kid had guts, he had to give him that. He raised his hand and shouted. *"Lieutenant?"*

"Captain," the lieutenant said, trotting through the mud upon seeing Beckett's insignia.

Beckett grabbed Han by the elbow. "We've apprehended a deserter. Take him in."

Han looked shocked, as if the sudden shift in power had given him vertigo. "That's . . . Wait, no!"

The lieutenant sneered at him. "I should have known. This one's a troublemaker." He signaled to two storm-troopers on guard, who came forward and pinned Han's hands behind his back. They started to pull him away.

Rio raised his voice as they left. "He's delusional, too!"

"And a liar!" Beckett added. "I wouldn't believe a word he says!"

"Don't go anywhere without me!" Han called over his shoulder. Like he was already part of Beckett's group and this was a minor hiccup. The gall of that kid. He was a piece of work.

"Feed him to the beast," the lieutenant said as he moved out of earshot.

The last thing Beckett heard was Han finally focusing on his captors. "The beast?"

CHAPTER EIGHT

The Wookiee dreamed of Kashyyyk, and of his family. The hungrier he got, the more he dreamed. Compared with his smooth-skinned captors, he was ancient. Their life spans were mere seasons to a Wookiee. He could wait, if need be, until these humans dropped their guard. Or until they died. He was good at being patient.

A crash disturbed his meditation, and he had to leave the trees and swamps of his memories and return to the present, which was only mud, darkness, and thick, dried mats of fur.

The mud coated him. The humans hadn't allowed him anything with which to groom himself, and they had pelted him with the thick, foul stuff. He had tried to comb it out with his claws, but it was no use. The mats pulled at his skin whenever he moved, pushing him closer and closer to raging.

A human had fallen into his pen, landing in the mud on his back. The guards had been throwing him scraps of meat every few days, but had talked about wanting to find someone alive to feed to him. He hadn't gotten that hungry. Not yet. But he resented being used as entertainment, resented this small, smooth thing that they threw at him to taunt him.

He took a step forward, and the mats pulled at his skin, and the simmering rage began to boil.

"There's a beast?" Han asked. The troopers had finally gotten his attention. None of his charm—or threats—had worked on the fake captain, and now he had a beast to worry about? This was starting to be a pretty bad day.

Without explanation, the troopers muscled him forward toward a pit. Han tried to resist, but they clapped a shackle on his ankle and gave him a push. He slipped on the mud and tumbled into the pit, landing roughly on his back.

He'd thought the battlefield, with the blood and the burning and the dead, had smelled bad. But at least that had been in the open air—or open mist, considering the planet he was on. Now he was in a roughly twelve-by-twelve-meter hole, with a lattice grate above him supported by a wooden beam in the center of the pit, with chains wrapped around it. One chain snaked into the shadows of one corner.

Around him lay discarded bits of droids and bones. A refuse pit with a beast? This was where he was going to die?

Han heard a low growl come from the corner. It sounded angry. Hungry.

I guess that's the beast, he thought, and got painfully to his feet. He backed up until he hit the wall.

"I haven't fed it in three days," a voice said above him. The guards who had tossed him in had stayed around to watch the slaughter, it seemed.

"Should be fun," the other responded.

The beast lunged from the shadows and, unable to back up any more, Han leapt to the side and landed painfully on the bones that littered the floor. He tried to get a good look at the shape above him.

Han had never seen such a filthy Wookiee. The thing had been slathered with mud, and his fur was all matted. He had to be miserable. And if he was filthy, miserable, and starved, this wouldn't be fun.

The Wookiee was at least two and a half meters tall. Han scrambled to his feet and took a step back as it stepped forward, growling. He dragged a chain connected to his ankle, like Han. No, actually, it was the same chain. He took a moment to glare up at the watching guards. They'd chained them together? Seriously?

Focusing on his opponent, Han put up his hands nervously and said, "Whoa, big fella . . . this doesn't have to get ugly. Got something for ya. It's right here—" He made to go into his pocket and look for something, wishing he could come up with another throw-a-rock-and-get-free plan. Instead of finding anything for the growling creature, he reached down and found a clod of mud. He swung it as hard as he could, upward, and hit the Wookiee in the face. Probably a mistake. Even though Han had a moment of hope as the beast roared in surprise and pain, the Wookiee recovered and swung back at Han, connecting and sending him backward into the wall again.

He was slower getting up this time. He blinked and tried to remember what he knew about Wookiees. He felt his side. Badly bruised, of course, but he hadn't been ripped open. And Wookiees had frighteningly sharp claws. The Wookiee wasn't trying to kill him, not right away, anyway. Han dashed forward again and ducked when the Wookiee made a grab for him and ended up behind him. He gave a push with all his might, and the Wookiee took one step forward and whirled on him, growling.

The air left his body as he slammed against the wall again. Gasping, he leapt to his feet again and jumped, grabbing the Wookiee's matted coat and scrambling on top, holding on for dear life. This was not a dumb creature to buck and jump to unseat him. The Wookiee spun around and slammed his back into the support beam. Again and again he slammed Han against the beam in order to scrape him off or crush him.

"This is even better than I thought!" said one of the guards with relish.

"We needed this," the other said, as if he were sliding into a hot bath and not watching two sentient creatures fight to the death.

The Wookiee's slamming attacks worked. Han fell off. He lay on the ground, trying to figure out if his spine was still intact or if it had come out the front of him. Perhaps now the Wookiee would give him a quick death. That would be preferable at this point. Time seemed to slow as he saw the guards laughing eagerly, the Wookiee above him, roaring, and the support beam. The *cracked* support beam.

Perhaps he wouldn't die today.

Cheating death would require some communication, however, and that wasn't his strong point. But what did he have to lose?

He climbed to his feet and sneered at the Wookiee. "That all you got?" he taunted.

With a roar, the Wookiee picked him up and threw him at the beam, which gave a little more when Han slammed into it.

This can work, he thought. *If I can live through it.*

The Wookiee advanced on him, roaring as he pinned Han to the muddy ground. As mud filled his mouth, Han grunted, and then wheezed something out, a coughing roar.

The Wookiee stopped mid-roar and cocked his head. He gave a roar back, one not of rage, but of communication.

"I know enough," Han said. He added another roar, and then a grunt, hoping he had said, "You're not the first dumb Wookiee I've tangled with."

The Wookiee roared with rage and threw him roughly to the ground.

He fought for breath, realizing he should probably table all the insults he had learned and try other words. He painfully pulled breath and roared, or wheezed, the words, "Listen, me have plan of break out." Or hoped he said them. Han could understand Shyriiwook well enough, but speaking it was another matter. Beyond insults, his vocabulary was hardly robust.

Even though he hadn't insulted the Wookiee this time

(he was pretty sure, anyway), the fact that he was speaking no better than a Wookiee toddler apparently enraged the beast more, and he roared in Han's face.

The world was growing dark with a red halo. He fought for just a little more air and wheezed, "You and I freedom make . . . by secret battle of pretend . . ." He flailed his hand so it slapped the support beam behind him. "Look . . . big stick . . ." That made sense, right?

Something lighted in the creature's eyes, some kind of sudden understanding. Han wasn't sure how his rudimentary language skills had gotten through, but he knew that the Wookiee understood him, even past their simple discussion.

The Wookiee dropped him, which wasn't comfortable but better than getting flung to the ground. Han got up cautiously and motioned his opponent forward, hoping against hope that he had communicated successfully.

"Now, come on, you mangy Kashyyyk moof-milker!" he yelled, and the Wookiee took an exaggerated swing backward and Han found it simple to duck so that his opponent could focus all of his great strength on the beam.

Han dodged each blow as the Wookiee focused his roaring rage on the beam, shouting for help from the onlookers to help the ruse. He blurted a surprised yelp when the Wookiee's hands landed on his shoulders, lifted him, and hurled Han into the support beam with all his strength (or what Han figured had to be all his strength). Ears ringing from the roaring beast, Han rolled as he hit the mud, the Wookiee leaping to land prone beside him, just as the beam cracked fully and gave way.

The grate above them collapsed, tumbling the guards into the pit and knocking them unconscious. The spike holding Han and the Wookiee's chain to the beam slipped out, and they were free.

Han laughed in triumph. He slapped the Wookiee on the shoulder. "See what happens when you listen to me?"

The Wookiee groaned, low in his throat. Han reflected how it was amazing that he could tell the difference between a roar of rage and a communicating roar. No longer fearing for his life probably had something to do with that.

"That's the next part of the plan," he said, pointing to the top of the pit. "I can't fix everything at once."

The Wookiee stood, shaking his head, seemingly baffled by this small person. He put his hands on Han's shoulders again, and Han had a panicked moment, fearing he had completely misread the entire situation.

"Hey, wait, what are you doing?" he said, and then yelled as the Wookiee launched him upward and out of the pit.

Bloody and swollen and wishing he'd come up with a less painful plan, Han climbed to his feet. A ship's engines grumbled overhead as an AT-hauler passed above them. Han pointed at it and then yelled "Follow me!"

He dashed off without looking back. Han figured he had already proven himself to be the brains of this duo, and the Wookiee would be right behind him. They'd communicated and worked together well (albeit painfully), and as soon as they got out of this he could go his way and the Wookiee his own.

The Wookiee clearly felt differently, as Han's leg was nearly ripped from his hip when the chain between them went taut and the Wookiee's greater mass pulled Han to the ground.

"Hey, we're going this way!" he said, yanking on the chain.

The Wookiee yanked harder, trying to run in the opposite direction, and Han stumbled forward. Han would not win this test of brute strength.

"I have some very good friends of mine at that airfield and they are leaving right now. It's our one shot at getting off this mud ball. If you wanna live, we go that way. After that, you can go whichever way you want, I don't care, but right now that's the way to go." He pointed toward the airfield just in case the Wookiee needed more information. "Trust me!"

The Wookiee looked in the direction he had been running, and then the direction Han was going. He made a chittering sound then nodded once. They ran toward the airfield just as stormtroopers arrived, attracted by the sound of the pen collapsing.

The Wookiee, now freed, roared at them, and they stopped in their tracks. He pushed a nearby trooper to the ground and pulled his blaster out of his limp hands. He tossed it to Han, who caught it with surprise.

And they were really and truly off, this time going the same direction.

Val and Rio tossed the last dead pilot onto the tarmac, clearing out the Imperial AT-hauler. Rio climbed aboard, pulled off his helmet, and took a deep breath, stretching his lower set of arms.

"I couldn't breathe in that thing!" he said, tossing the helmet to the floor as he got settled in the pilot's seat.

"No wonder they're such lousy pilots. They can't turn their heads, they can't breathe, they can't hear each other." He shook his head at the bodies littering the ground below, as if they would never learn. They wouldn't, now, but that was beside the point.

Beckett came up behind him and checked the cockpit as Rio got set for launch. He was about to close the door when he caught movement in the distance.

"I'll be damned," he whispered.

The eager kid who simply would not go away was running toward them, waving, coated head-to-foot in mud. At first Beckett thought the kid was being pursued by something large and very muddy, but the way the two ran, holding the chain that bound them together, it was clear they were cooperating.

Rio followed his gaze and laughed. "Unbelievable!" He squinted his bulbous eyes, and then widened them. "Is that a Wookiee with him? I'll say it, I don't care. This kid's growing on me." The two figures continued to wave, jumping up and down. "You know we could use some more muscle on the team."

It felt wrong to be considering a replacement for Korso so quickly after his death, but Beckett couldn't ignore the truth in Rio's words.

"Don't even think about it," Val warned, reading the look on Beckett's face.

"I'm telling you," Rio continued. "You will never have a deeper sleep than when you're curled up in a Wookiee's lap."

Beckett couldn't help but admire the way that the kid had doggedly pursued them. There was something special about a kid so persistent that he had survived a battle, been thrown into a cage with a Wookiee, and apparently *convinced the Wookiee to break out with him*. The kid was a pain, but Beckett found he'd rather he be on his team than working against him. And adding a Wookiee to the team . . . that might be worth it. Beckett smiled.

Val made a disgusted noise and pointed Rio toward the pilot's seat. "Let's get out of here."

Beckett watched the unlikely pair run a moment more. Troopers had broken out of the misty haze and were chasing them, some pausing to take aim and fire blasters, others just running to get in range.

He had to bring friends, didn't he? Beckett shook his head and punched a button. With a joyful whoop, the pair ran forward toward the plank that had just lowered.

The troopers had started to fire on them, but the hauler was armored enough that mere blasters weren't a problem. The human and Wookiee wouldn't be having any fun, though, so Beckett made sure they were inside before he signaled for Rio to move.

The Wookiee was roaring when they came into view, and Beckett drew back a moment, startled. That didn't sound grateful, but the Wookiee wasn't looking aggressive. Perhaps it was relief?

Han grinned at his companion, his white teeth and bright-blue eyes the only non-muddy things about him. "See?" he said to the Wookiee, punching his shoulder. "Told you I'd think of something. They're very good friends!" He looked around, admiring the ship.

"And I knew you were thieves but I didn't know an AT-hauler was your goal. That's a bold move. What could you want where you need this kind of lifting power?"

"Nobody asked you," Rio said, but his voice was friendly.

"Fair enough," Han said, matching Rio's tone. "So where are we headed, Captain?"

Beckett sighed. They were now part of it, like it or not. "Vandor. The Iridium Mountains."

"That's exciting," Han said, digging some dirt out of his ear. "What's the plan?"

Beckett smiled. "Kid, you keep your mouth shut and your eyes open, I guarantee you'll have all the excitement you can handle, very soon." He looked at the mud-caked relics in front of him. "Now you two go get cleaned up before Val sees you." He nodded toward the copilot's seat, where Val sat rigid and obviously ignoring them. Beckett dropped his voice. "We're in enough trouble with her as it is."

Han tried to wash every moment of his time on Mimban off his body. Under the newly acquired mud, he had layers of dust, more mud, some blood, and general body odor. Or at least that's how it felt. He couldn't remember the last time he had showered.

He would use all the hauler's water supply if he wasn't careful. He needed to leave some for the Wookiee.

The water around his feet turned black all of a sudden, and he turned in surprise to see the Wookiee entering the shower with him. His bulk blocked the stream of water, and Han glared up at him, mud sliding off both of them in rivulets.

"We couldn't have done this like maybe one at a time?" he demanded.

The Wookiee growled like it was no big deal. Easy for him to say; he had hair covering everything. And mud. The poor guy.

Han shrugged. Of everything he had dealt with today, this was pretty low on the list of things to be upset about.

The Wookiee lifted a bottle of something Han was pretty sure wouldn't be found in an Imperial ship. He squinted at it. "Where did you get detangler?"

The Wookiee grunted a few times. Han laughed. "The woman? Val? Did she go from hating us to pitying us?"

He gave Han a pointed look. Han sighed. "You. She pitied *you*. Still hates me?"

The Wookiee made a noncommittal grunt and went back to getting the mud out of his thick coat. Han left him to it.

The hauler headed toward the sharp, snow-covered mountains of Vandor-1. Han and the Wookiee stood on an observation gantry slung beneath the fuselage of the AT-hauler, the wind whipping their hair around and stinging Han's eyes.

He still didn't know exactly what they were here for, but stealing this ship had gotten him away from the Imperials, and that was all right with him.

Han glanced up at the Wookiee. "Thanks for helping me get outta there," he said.

The Wookiee moaned low in his throat.

Han waited a beat, then added, "And you're welcome, by the way."

The Wookiee roared, and Han turned on him. "No, they only took *you* because of *me*. This is a sweet deal. We do this one job with them, make some real money, and then we're free. When's the last time you could say that?"

The Wookiee shrugged and made a sad sound.

"Been a while for me, too," Han said, looking back over the mountains. "What's your name, anyway?"

The Wookiee groaned and made a complex sound of grunts. Han chuckled. "*Chewbacca?* Son of *who*?" Before Chewbacca could repeat it, he just shook his head. "We're gonna have to come up with a nickname, 'cause I ain't saying that every time."

Chewbacca thought about it, then shrugged and nodded.

Han peered over the railing, straight down to the jagged peaks below. Snow was a rare sight in Coronet City, and Han had never seen anything like the icy crests spread out before the hauler, glittering in the sunshine. He wondered how deep the snow was. The sharp cold that stung his skin was exhilarating. It was truly beautiful here.

"Do you think if we spit it'll freeze before it hits the ground?" he asked.

The Wookiee nodded and growled deep and wet in his throat. He let loose a giant ball of phlegm, and they watched it drift down to get lost amid the snow.

They camped deep into the Iridium Mountains. They'd hit a supply depot before arriving, and Han now sat in a very thick, fur-lined coat. He'd had to reassure Chewie that it wasn't lined with Wookiee hair.

Chewie remained as naked as before, needing only his now-clean natural coat to keep him warm.

Han was still cold, of course. He could feel the hypothermia squeezing in between the seams of his clothing layers, like the mud had on Mimban. He watched his breath puff out in white clouds.

Val and Beckett were in the distance, watching something through a scope. Their voices traveled over the cold, dry air.

"It is still a bad idea. They're going to get in the way," Val said.

"They'll be useful," Beckett said. "The Wookiee will be, anyway. Even Rio isn't as strong as he is."

"It's pointless to argue about it now," she conceded. "The only way to get rid of them is to shoot them. And even I'm not that desperate yet."

Han decided it was time to interrupt this train of thought. He got up and approached them, and they stopped talking. "How much longer?" he asked. "I'm freezing."

"Here it comes," Beckett said as if he hadn't heard Han. He handed the scope to Val. Over their shoulders, in the dusk, Han could barely see the streak of an armored freight carrier pulled by a heavy-duty drive chain. It had three sections: engine, supply cars, and caboose. Han could just tell there was a turret-mounted cannon atop the caboose. It had an over–under design, with cars both sitting on top and hanging beneath the tracks. As the train snaked around the mountain, it shuddered and thundered on high trestles, knocking loose snow and rock as it passed close to the cliff edges.

Beckett pointed, his hand on Val's shoulder. "We hit the conveyex between the tower and the bridge, Rio drops us in, we separate the payload container, hook it up to the AT-hauler—"

"Rio jams their distress signal," Val said, taking up the narrative, "I blow the bridge, the payload slides off the track, and we sail away." She spoke casually, as if she were giving directions to the cantina.

"Sounds simple enough," Han said.

Beckett gave him a withering look. "Nothing about this is simple. See the depository?" Han squinted but shook his head. All he saw was the conveyex tearing across a bridge before it entered a tunnel through the mountain. Then he realized it wasn't a tunnel; it was the entrance to a fortress built right into the mountain for maximum security. Now that he knew what he was looking at, he could spot the probe droids guarding the depository from anyone intending harm.

"That's Crispin Imperial Depository," Beckett said, and then turned to Val. "If we trip that security beam and wake up those vipers, things are about to get real spicy, real fast."

She put the scope away. "Well, I'm not the one you should be worried about," she reminded him.

Beckett frowned. "What? Enfys Nest?"

Val nodded and sighed. She looked like she was about to face a rancor or something.

"What's an Enfusnest?" Han asked.

"I told you, we're way ahead of the competition

on this one. There's no way Enfys Nest even knows about this shipment. Only my guy has the intel."

"You'd better be right," Val said, "because sometimes you put your faith in the wrong people. Our one chance to bring in a huge score and you bring in amateurs."

Beckett spread his hands. "In case you hadn't noticed, we're a little shorthanded."

"So we get who we need! The Xan sisters! Or Bossk. But instead you're putting our lives in the hands of morons." Val turned her back on him and walked away.

Han shrugged. He'd been called worse.

They set up camp near the hauler, which Rio had set down among snow-covered trees. They were far enough away from the conveyex tracks that the Imperial forces wouldn't be able to detect them with scopes or their viper droids.

The evening was homey in a completely unexpected way, with warmth, food, and stories. Chewie stoked a campfire while Rio prepared dinner, the pilot showing gourmet skills that amazed Han. But as he watched Rio deftly chop and sauté, his four arms moving in an almost dancelike fashion, he admitted to himself he shouldn't have been surprised.

Beckett brought up the previous conversation, finally acknowledging that Han had been witness to Val's ire. "You guys morons?" he asked Han and Chewie.

"No," Han said.

"There, see?" Beckett said, as if it were finished.

"We're not morons," Han said. "I've waited a long

time for a shot like this, I'm not about to screw it up, all right?"

"Oh, come on, Val, he looks so sincere!" Rio said from his spot by the fire. "Plus, have you ever tried to disinvite a Wookiee to anything? Not a good idea!"

Chewie chuckled at that, but Val was unmoved. "That doesn't prove anything."

"Look, I've got good instincts about these guys, and besides, do you see any other options?" Beckett pointed around at the snowy mountains around them.

"I just hope you know what you're doing," she said.

"Look, we're gonna clear our debts," he said, touching her cheek. "Go back to Glee Anselm. And I'm finally gonna learn how to play that valachord."

She smiled for the first time that Han had seen. "Babe, you're never going to learn how to play that valachord."

"She's right," Rio said. "You are tone-deaf."

They all laughed at Beckett, who glared at them, but the tension had broken. They all settled by the fire, and Rio and Beckett started telling adventure stories.

Even Val relaxed a bit, laughing and rolling her eyes at the obvious exaggerations. She didn't tell many herself—just one that she tried to bring up, but Beckett steadfastly refused to participate. Val didn't have to go into much detail—something about a queen and explosives and gladiators?—but clearly the memory was deeply personal to both of them—and deeply humiliating for Beckett. Even the mention of it made Rio laugh so hard he fell off the rock he was perched on.

As Han listened to the tales, he felt sure that the Imperial infantry time on Mimban was only a hiccup on his journey from Corellia to a life of adventure. He was with the right people, at the right place, at the right time. Life was going to be more interesting and more lucrative than ever before.

Chewbacca stayed quiet, too, going through the team's equipment and finding an old bandolier that fit him nicely. He held it up to Val and Beckett with an inquisitive grunt.

"Go ahead, it don't fit any of us anyway," Beckett said, and Val nodded.

With the bandolier around him, the Wookiee somehow looked a little more decent, the illusion of nudity banished by the simple strap of leather and ammunition.

Han and Chewie ate with the group, Han taking sips of the cooking sherry and brandy that Rio passed around afterward.

Val leaned against Beckett, the light of the fire playing gently on both their faces. For a moment they looked like a happy couple camping on a pristine, unexplored world, not seasoned thieves about to attack an Imperial complex.

Val regarded Han. Her face hardened again. "Don't you think we should tell these two what we're up against?" she asked, waving her hand at Han and Chewie. "It's not going to be easy."

"They may not know a lot, but he's street smart," Beckett said, jabbing a thumb at Han, "and he's a Wookiee," he added, pointing at Chewie as if she needed reminding. "They don't need to know who Enfys Nest is to spring into action if we're raided, right, kid?"

Han nodded. "I grew up on the streets, running scams

and lifting speeders. Current events and politics aren't my strong point, but I have gotten out of tons of scrapes."

Chewie didn't bother defending himself. He was a Wookiee, after all. That's all they needed to know about him.

"So are you two finally going to settle down after this job?" Rio asked Beckett and Val.

Val laughed derisively. "Him? Never."

"Well now, I've always got my dream," Beckett drawled, sounding hurt. "I really want that valachord."

"Your lifelong dream," Val said, smiling at him with a little more tenderness this time.

"A valachord?" Han asked, trying to remember what instrument that was.

"Yeah, I've always wanted to learn," Beckett said wistfully. "I think I'd be good at it. And this deal will finally get me credits to do it. Retire, buy a little cottage, buy a valachord."

"Are they expensive?" Han asked, still not sure what one was.

"Well, they ain't cheap, I'll tell you that," Beckett said. "But what's driving you, kid?"

"Yeah, what's your sob story, flyboy?" Rio asked.

"Who, me?" Han asked. "Well, I'm on a team that won't tell me what we're stealing—" he began, but Rio shook his head.

"That's not what I mean. You're after something, I know the look. Why'd you defect? Revenge?"

"Nah, it's not revenge," Val said, looking at him with something other than malice. "Look at him. If anything, it's a girl."

"Oh, a *girl,* tell us about the girl, Han, is she nice?" Rio asked, jumping from his rock. He leaned forward and gave an exaggerated grin. "Does she have sharp *teeth*?"

"There was a girl," Han said reluctantly, staring at the fire. "But, uh, I got out. She didn't. Swore to myself I'd become a pilot. Get a ship. Go back and find her. So that's what I'm gonna do right after this job."

"How do you know she'll still be there?" Rio asked.

"I just know," Han said.

"Personally, I refuse to be tied down by anyone," Rio said, pouring himself caf from the pot by the fire. "Though many have tried."

Val chuckled. "Come on, Rio. You can't fool me. Everybody needs somebody." She leaned forward and smiled at Beckett, moving his blond hair off his forehead. "Even a broken-down old crook like this one." She kissed Beckett, and Han was torn between wanting to look away to give them privacy, and wanting to look and see what love was like when you were allowed to have it.

"What about you?" Han asked Chewbacca. "What are you gonna do with your share?"

Chewie glanced at Han, who figured Chewie was asking for translation. He nodded.

Chewie let out a long groan, mournful and low, and Han listened intently.

Han swallowed as everyone looked from Chewie to him.

"What's he saying?" Rio asked.

"He said the Wookiees were enslaved by the Empire,

taken off Kashyyyk. Now he's searching for his—" Han stopped, trying to translate the word. "Not sure if he's saying 'tribe' or 'family.' "

"What's the difference?" Beckett asked, staring into the fire and twirling his DG-29 blaster thoughtfully.

Chewie groaned again and Han listened, then translated. "He was fighting to free his homeworld. He's fought the Empire for . . . a long time. He was captured . . . they called him a monster . . . drugged him." He stopped translating and looked at him in disbelief. "They were taking you somewhere to sell you as a pit fighter?"

Chewie nodded and waved his hand for Han to continue. "He wants to help his world. Free Kashyyyk. Also there are enslaved Wookiees out here like him."

Han sat back and looked impressed. Freeing an entire world was a noble cause. He just wanted his own ship and to go back to Corellia for Qi'ra. He hadn't even thought about the rest of the galaxy. Nobody on those planets had ever done much for him, so he wasn't sure why he should stick his neck out for them. But Chewie was a part of something Han had never experienced. The closest he had come to a tribe or family was Qi'ra.

Han watched Beckett twirl the blaster. He felt like a kid, wanting to copy all of Beckett's smooth habits and talents. "Show me how to do that," he said.

"Kid, the only thing you need to learn to do is do what I say, when I say it. By this time tomorrow you'll have more than enough to buy your own ship." He twirled the blaster in his hand once more, and holstered it. He picked up a rifle and stripped off the stock and barrel with quick twists. What was left was a slim blaster, lethal and quick. He gave Han an appraising look and then tossed it over the campfire to him. Han caught it in surprise. "You'll need a good weapon tomorrow," he said.

The blaster felt right in his hand. A DL-44 blaster—a *modified* DL-44, he reminded himself.

"Get some sleep," Beckett said. "We have a train to rob tomorrow."

"Do you really hate him that much?" Beckett asked Val in the dark.

Val sighed and rolled over to face him in his sleeping sack. "I can see the Wookiee replacing Korso," she said. "We're hurting without some muscle. But the kid, he's naïve and is likely to make a stupid mistake or four. We can't afford it."

"I think he'll come in handy," he said. "You didn't like Rio at first, either."

She laughed. He loved that sound. It meant she had finally let her guard down, showing the side only the people closest to her saw. "Rio was obnoxious and tried to steal our speeder before he joined the crew."

"Yeah, but that's how you find a good pilot."

"Only if he doesn't succeed in lifting your vehicle," she reminded him. There was a pause. "Do you really think you'll be content with settling down after this?"

"Do you really think I won't?"

"I've known you a long time, Beckett. You're not happy if you're not scheming. How much scheming do you do playing the valachord?"

He stroked her face. "I scheme a lot with this one," he said. "And I'm pretty happy."

She was silent in the dark. He wondered if she had gone to sleep. Then she said, "All right, then we'll retire."

CHAPTER NINE

They had a solid, well-thought-out plan. And Han had a secret suspicion that the detailed plan was where they had gone wrong.

Stealing the AT-hauler had been a good move. It was strong enough to lift one of those cargo sections full of whatever Beckett and crew had wanted to steal. It was fast enough to keep up with the speedy conveyex. And Rio proved immediately that he was skilled enough to keep level with the train despite the twists and turns in the track.

It was when they left the hauler that things started to go sideways.

Beckett went first. Goggles in place and jaw set, he opened the hauler's gantry and stood at the edge for a moment, wind whipping his hair. He waited for Rio to get a little closer and then leapt to the roof of the conveyex below them.

There was no turning back now. If Han lost his nerve and failed to jump, Val would be completely justified in tossing his useless carcass from the hauler to land wherever she and Rio wanted him to splatter. They'd already dropped her off at her spot on the bridge, several klicks away, to place the charges that would blow the bridge at the right time.

Chewbacca jumped down after Beckett. The goggles held down the hair on his head while the wind whipped the rest of his coat, making him look twice his size.

Han could do this. No question. He thought of the times in his childhood on Corellia when he had jumped from large Imperial shuttles onto speeding monorails, except he had never done that, so he tried to imagine that he had done something remotely similar. He gripped the edge and panted, seeing Beckett and Chewie below him, waiting.

His earpiece crackled, and then Rio's voice was there offering support. "Hey, don't think, *I'm gonna die.* Think, *Hey, I might live.*"

Rio needed to work on his motivational speaking, Han thought. But then he realized Rio's advice, as absurd as it was, had broken through his terror. He took a deep breath and jumped, feeling everything fall away from him for an eternity. He slammed down on the roof of the conveyex behind Beckett and Chewie, convinced they had been more graceful than he.

He failed to get his balance and for a terrifying instant he stumbled and slipped toward the back edge of the car. He reached out to grab something, anything, and gripped the sharp edge of the car before he fell to a very long, painful death. He held on, panting, and then pulled himself up with a grunt. He had to prove himself to this team. With a deep breath he finally got adapted to the movement of the train, and stood up.

He waved to Beckett and Chewie. "I'm okay!" he assured them, and Chewie turned with a grunt. Han suspected the Wookiee hadn't been worried about him.

The cold wind was a hundred times worse than the general creeping cold he had felt the day before. It cut through everything, making him feel as if the clothing he wore had been stripped away already. His nose and ears immediately began to get numb.

We couldn't have stolen something from a tropical planet? he thought miserably.

Beckett and Chewbacca were already at work ahead of him, carefully walking along the roofs from car to car, counting the containers and attaching safety cables to the pipe that ran along the roof of the tanker car. Beckett then dropped the shoulder bag he carried and pulled out a large fusioncutter, a tool with a laser bit designed to cut through almost anything.

He crouched down and got to work on the lock securing the hatch. It parted easily with clouds of sparks flying off and away downwind to die quickly in the cold air.

Han reached Beckett as he set the tool aside and yanked the lock off, another piece of detritus to fly away and litter the wilderness below. He put his hand on Beckett's shoulder to steady himself and peered inside to see what the grand prize was for this little adventure.

He nearly didn't recognize it; it was *too* familiar. In

his mind, the contents of the containers belonged in small stolen cylinders, not a mobile vault containing countless glowing glass vials. The very same substance that had saved him and damned Qi'ra.

"Coaxium," he said aloud. "That's enough to power a fleet."

Beckett nodded, surprised Han knew his stuff. "Or blow us all straight to hell," he said, grinning.

The AT-hauler had kept pace with them, and now Rio dropped down winch cables for them to attach to the heavy U-bolts at the four corners of the car's roof. Two steps done, and it was going smoothly. All they had to do was attach the cables, wait for Val to blow the bridge, and lift the car from the tracks as the rest of the train plummeted to the valley below, and they would be off with a Hutt's ransom worth of coaxium.

Han was party to a massive theft, part of a crew that knew its stuff. He felt again that he was in the right place to learn exactly what he needed to know. This was the one job that would change everything.

That confidence lasted about two or three seconds.

With the wind screaming around them, they felt rather than heard the sharp *thunk* of magnetized boots on the train behind them. Han looked back and recognized the uniform of range troopers, covered head-to-toe in synthetic-fur-lined armor.

He had no love for any of the Empire's troopers, but the range troopers were some of the worst. They had served in tougher climates than most, and their jobs included guarding high-speed trains. With such flashy jobs, they saw themselves as elites, looking down on all the other Imperial soldiers, troopers and infantry alike.

The range troopers moved with confidence, warm in their armor and secure with their magnetized boots. They were also steady with their aim, trained to ignore the swaying train and icy elements as they shot.

Distracted by the troopers, no one was watching the track ahead. They were surprised when the track twisted to accommodate a shift in the landscape, and the train twisted with it, turning nearly ninety degrees sideways. Beckett and Han found handholds, but Chewbacca flew over the edge with a howl.

"Chewie!" Han yelled in alarm. The Wookiee hadn't agreed to the spontaneous nickname, but they weren't really in a position to debate it. The Wookiee's hairy hand barely managed to catch hold of one of the cables. While Beckett tried to distract the troopers with blasterfire, Han leaned over and caught Chewie's free arm. The Wookiee howled again and started to pull himself up slowly, Han doing more to steady his weight than anything else.

A trooper fell to Beckett's attack, crumpling where they had fallen, still attached to the train by magnetic boots. Beckett let out a whoop and worked to focus on the other one.

Still holding on to Chewie, Han glanced up and saw a large rocky outcropping The snaking train passed within centimeters of the jagged rocks—close enough that Chewie would be scraped off the conveyex like a bug on a landspeeder windscreen. "Come on, Chewie," he shouted, starting to pull at the Wookiee's arm.

Chewbacca howled again and Han yanked, trying

not to look at the approaching rock or notice how his numb fingers weren't grasping as tightly as he wanted them to.

Then the train tilted again, back the other way, which allowed Chewbacca to scramble back on top as they slipped by the rock. He and Han lay panting for a moment, then Han touched his arm.

"You all right?" he asked. "A little close there, buddy!"

Chewie grunted, a relieved sound.

"Han! What's the holdup?" demanded Beckett, ducking a blaster bolt.

Han nodded. "We're on the clock," he said. Chewbacca gave an affirming growl.

With Beckett trading fire with the troopers, Han and Chewbacca dropped down between the cars toward the mechanism that coupled their car with the ones behind it. Han took a moment to enjoy the respite from the wind that the side of the train gave, and then he motioned to Chewie for the next step. It was easy to separate the cars, pulling opposing levers up in unison, and the back half of the train sped away from them, making Han laugh and wave at the troopers who fell behind as their half began to decelerate.

A blaster bolt hit the door between them, and Han stopped waving and jumped back, flattening himself against the wall beside the door. Better wait until they rounded a bend before they celebrated.

This might work out. He shouted to Chewie as the wind hit them again, "Now all we gotta do is—"

He stopped speaking as speeder bikes appeared beside the train, matching its speed just like Rio was doing with the hauler. The bikers were protected head-to-toe from the elements like the range troopers, but in unique, angular armor. They each had a flag attached to their speeder, and the one with the largest, most frightening mask stared right at their car and their loot—or perhaps they were staring directly at Han, Beckett, and Chewie.

"Who's that?" Han shouted into his comlink.

Beckett's voice, low and resigned, crackled as he spoke. "It's Enfys Nest."

"*That's* the—"

The air erupted into a volley of lasers and harpoons, the blaster bolts heading for Han, Chewie, and Beckett while the harpoons *thunk*ed directly into their tanker. Two more bikes headed for the AT-hauler and began harassing Rio.

The raiders were surgical with their attack, some of them focusing on defense, some on taking out Beckett's team's cables, some attacking the hauler, and others dedicated to hitting the car with their own harpoons to secure it for removal. Instead of one large hauling ship, they had many small swoop bikes. Han didn't think they could carry the weight of the car among them, but he wouldn't have guessed they would attack with such planned precision, either.

It was as if they were being attacked by something with the technology of a Corellian fisher and the sophistication of an Imperial grand admiral.

If their team didn't act fast, these raiders would efficiently and effectively destroy Beckett's plan.

Han couldn't keep track of the different directions the raiders were attacking, so he and Chewie crawled back up to Beckett, dodging the fire and looking to create a combined attack. Something with at least a fraction of the focus that Nest's group had.

Han took aim at a speeder bike close to him and fired, but the shot went wide as Han dodged a more immediate threat and fell onto the roof of the train. The hauler had banked sharply and swung so close to them that they all had to roll to avoid it. He looked up at it, weaving and narrowly avoiding the side of the mountain that rushed by.

Something was wrong. Han knew that Rio wouldn't fly like that normally. He was too good. Even if he was being evasive, he wouldn't put the rest of the team in danger to do so.

Han looked up and saw blasterfire lighting up the hauler's cockpit.

"Chewie!" he shouted, pointing at the hauler. "I'm going up there!"

The Wookiee made a frantic gesture toward his ear, and Han realized he had heard him through the comm; he didn't need to deafen them by shouting. "You'll have to uncouple the rest on your own," he said in a normal voice.

Without waiting for confirmation, he looked up and watched the hauler tilt and weave and nearly hit the roof of the monorail again. It dipped close, threatening to scrape them off the top, but Han jumped at the ship, hands extended, and caught hold of the open gantry, climbing aboard.

Once inside, he ran, legs bent to manage the rocking, boatlike movements of the hauler without falling. When Han reached the cockpit, he realized that he was now in charge. They needed a pilot.

Rio had put up a good fight. He'd killed the raider who had boarded the hauler and attacked him. The raider was on the floor, rolling limply as the hauler tipped back and forth. Rio hadn't gotten away uninjured, however.

The floor was covered in streaks of blood, and only some of it was from the raider. Han sucked in his breath when he saw Rio. Two of his four arms were completely limp, scorched with blasterfire. The wounds were too large to cauterize as blaster injuries sometimes are, and the guy was bleeding out. He looked up and met Han's gaze dully.

"Did you . . . hear from Val? Did she blow the bridge?" he asked, one of his good arms gesturing weakly toward the track ahead of them.

Han swallowed past his dry throat. "N-not yet. Soon." He tried not to stare, but his brain had frozen. He knew he should help Rio but realized it was much, much too late.

Rio had enough awareness to notice Han's discomfort. "What's the matter?" he asked. "Does it look bad?"

Han snapped back into himself and approached Rio. "No," he said, shaking his head. "It looks . . . all right."

"Need you to take the yoke while I patch this up," Rio said, gesturing again as if he had a few cuts and bruises. "Glad you're here, kid. It's no good to die alone." He sighed, falling limp over the control board and out of his chair. With its old pilot gone, the hauler tipped again and went careening toward the mountain.

Instinct finally took over Han's senses and he jumped into the other chair, grabbing the tiller and pulling up sharply to get the vessel steady and away from the mountain. He realized at once the skill Rio had brought to the team; with his four arms and nimble body, he could serve as pilot and copilot, something Han couldn't do no matter how good he was. He stopped thinking about the scent of charred flesh and the body slumped in the copilot's seat. The only important thing was keeping the hauler airborne. He looked to the conveyex to see how Beckett and Chewie's fight was going.

Not well.

Chewbacca and Beckett were still fighting marauders on the conveyex, Chewbacca firing on the swoop bikes from where he was about to decouple the other end of the car, and Beckett grappling with Enfys Nest. Chewie was good, but the raiders were skilled at flying in un-expected patterns to avoid his shots, almost as if they could see where he was going to shoot before he had decided.

Beckett was having much more trouble, though. Nest had gotten in too close for rifle fighting and was attack-ing with an electrified staff. She fought with a swift, bru-tal efficiency, the staff and the power behind it more than making up for whatever body weight advantage Beckett had on her (which was hard to tell as her armor covered her entirely). Beckett tried to block with his rifle, but she drove in directly and hit him in the mid-section. He went rigid and flew backward, tumbling over and over with electricity snaking around his body. He landed at the edge of the roof, still twitching as his muscles spasmed from the electrical charge. He didn't get up.

Nest was done with Beckett; the next item on the list

was to slice through the cables they'd attached from the hauler to the container. And Han could do nothing to stop her theft of their stolen goods.

He heard a crackle in his earpiece.

"Beckett, what's your status?" It was Val, with blasterfire in the background.

Val's part of the job had gone smoothly. She'd used her grappling gun to get to the bridge, deftly swinging underneath so she could place the bombs at the weakest points. She was the first to see Enfys Nest's Cloud-Riders come over the mountains. Time was running short now. She just hoped they were ready.

Now the train was close enough for Val to see Enfys Nest's raiders show up and ruin things. The hauler was tipping and swerving as if Rio were drunk, and she watched helplessly as Beckett fell to Enfys Nest's electro-ripper staff.

The safest thing to do would be to abort, get out of there with the hauler intact, and try again.

But the safest thing to do would have been to never take this job in the first place, and that hadn't stopped them. She couldn't help them. So she focused on placing explosives, watching the timer, the tracks, and the position of the train.

As the train neared, it looked like Enfys Nest had the upper hand. Val swore, placing the explosives faster. She had to trust Beckett to get rid of Nest, since she had the bridge and the viper droids to worry about.

They hadn't found her yet, though. She wired the explosives with a practiced hand, working methodically at placing the charges, checking the connections, checking the timers, and then moving to the next one. She'd have to place the charges, fire the grappling gun to a safe part of the bridge to be far enough away from the explosion and the droids while the bridge blew, and then rappel down to meet the team on the ground.

"Val," Beckett shouted into the link, and relief surged through her. He was all right.

"Val! Keep your eyes open, we just tripped the sensor," he said, regret and panic in his voice.

A buzzing sounded in the distance, and she looked up. "Viper droids, heading your way!" she shouted.

And there were many, many more droids than initial recon had indicated there would be.

Five, six, eight. Far too many to handle on her own. They buzzed officiously down the tracks, drawn to the action on the train, but they were programmed to deal with the first threat they encountered. She could be that threat and keep them off Beckett and the crew.

"What's your status?" she added over the comm. As she spoke, she stashed her remaining bombs in her pack and got her blaster and grappling gun ready.

Beckett grunted, distracted.

"Think you can take care of them?" the kid said, butting in like always. "We've got a few things to deal with here."

"I didn't ask you," she snapped. "Beckett, what's your status?"

"Beckett's been hit with an electroripper, I've taken over the hauler from Rio, and we've got about twelve raiders to deal with," Han replied.

"How many droids?" Beckett asked, sounding drunk.

"Ten, maybe twelve." She fired her blaster a few times.

"Fewer, now." She fired again, backing down the track. She found limited shelter in a sensor array and backed into it, trying to make herself small. "I don't think I can take them all."

"Val!" Beckett had more energy now. "Get out of there!"

"And go where?" she demanded. He really could be dense sometimes. She'd backed up past her explosives. Currently she was on the part of the track that would be obliterated in moments. If she went back, she would be blown to bits; if she moved forward, she'd be out of the minimal shelter and the droids would cut her to pieces.

"I know, just hold on a little longer!"

The droids floated around her protective sensor, firing when they saw her. One bolt missed her but hit her grappling gun, knocking it off the bridge. She dodged another attack and her blaster went flying. Now all she had left was the trigger for the bombs. She took in the vipers' menacing advance, the train's proximity, and Nest's speeders buzzing around her team like wasps.

Things became slow. Calm. She felt sure of her next movements.

Beckett wouldn't have retired at the end of this job. She knew that. She wouldn't have let him. She loved the rush of the job, the thrill of getting away with whatever was needed at the time, the satisfaction of working with a team where all of the pieces clicked into place like a reassembled blaster. She liked the credits, she liked working with people who had become her family. People who would die for her.

The places the group had visited! The snow here was

beautiful; she'd never touched anything so cold, growing up on Solarine. She'd swum in vast oceans, dodged
sea creatures bigger than anything living she knew ex-
isted. She'd seen Rio get eaten by such a sea creature,
and thought he was dead until he blasted his way out of
the creature's throat in a fantastically bloody mess.
Beckett had helped drag him back to shore, and they
had all laughed themselves sick about it over the fire that
night.

She thought of the time someone had kidnapped
Beckett. A queen from a planet so far on the outskirts
of the galaxy that even the Empire hadn't started stripping it. But this woman had come on a quest to find
herself a husband, and had been looking for years. Val,
Rio, and Beckett had been in a bar celebrating a job.
Val had gone to the washroom, when she came back
Beckett was gone, and Rio was holding a bloody gash
on his cheek. It seemed Beckett had done the queen a
small kindness: Opened a door for her? Picked up something she had dropped? Val couldn't remember anymore, but the queen had decided that the blond-haired,
blue-eyed Beckett was good enough to end her search.
She'd pushed a button on a bracelet and two security
droids whooshed in, grabbed Beckett, and efficiently
took down Rio.

Val had had to bribe, bargain, and eventually get
scheduled to fight the queen's champion to win Beckett
back. She hadn't fought fair—a fair fight would have
been pointless. She'd smuggled some explosives into the
castle with her and blown up the gladiatorial arena, stolen several weapons, and with Beckett blasted her way
out of there.

That night he had told her never to leave him. She had agreed. They'd sealed their promise, drinking a whole bottle of rare Toniray wine that Beckett had lifted from the queen. They figured that was the closest they would come to actually settling down, and things had been good since.

He was yelling at her on the link now, pointless pleas to do the impossible and somehow get out of it alive.

"Not going to happen, love. It's been fun, wouldn't trade it for the world," she said, and as the droids converged on her, she closed her eyes, hit the trigger button, and thought about the taste of wine on her tongue.

Beckett's comlink was off, but even over the wind and the roar of the train, Han could hear Beckett scream as Val's connection abruptly went silent and the bridge erupted in flames ahead. Then the shock wave hit them.

All conscious thought left him, and instincts took over. He would have been grateful for it if he'd been thinking clearly. As it was, he didn't think at all.

His hands steadied on the controls as he struggled with the hauler, finally feeling it speak to him, ship-to-pilot. The train shook below him, the inevitable dive into the canyon coming soon. Chewie had to uncouple it or they'd all be dead.

Enfys Nest had abandoned the cargo, joining her raiders on their bikes, leaving Chewie and Beckett alone on the car. Beckett was stunned, staring at the smoking track in front of them. Chewie had leapt down to decouple the other end of the car with a roar. Han separated from his instincts for a moment to assess who was left in their adventure.

Val, probably gone. Rio, gone. Who would be next? He shifted uncomfortably in the chair, still soaked with Rio's blood. Beckett had struggled to his feet and watched Enfys Nest leave. She had managed to sever all but two of their cables, and she'd kept a few of her own. These were not enough for either to secure the payload once the train left the tracks. They'd lose the payload, and if Chewie and Beckett didn't get inside, they'd be lost with the train.

He had less than a minute before everything went very, very bad.

Instinct took over again, and he got on the comlink. "Chewie! Grab the cables! Grab the line!" he shouted.

The end of the track was coming up, and he struggled to stay steady as the train shuddered beneath him. He watched them from the cockpit and saw Chewbacca looking back up at him. He pursed his lips and nodded once to the Wookiee, who nodded back. Without needing to elaborate any further instructions, Han focused on flying as the end of the track approached. Chewie wrapped one long arm around Beckett and grabbed the cable with his other hand.

Beckett's screams changed timbre as Chewbacca grabbed him and lifted him bodily off the train. "No!" he shouted, struggling in Chewie's arms. "Val!"

Beckett wasn't thinking clearly, Han realized, and he didn't care if he took the rest of them down with him. But it was too late to let him. Han pulled up sharply to gain altitude as the train began to plummet off the trestle into the valley below. The hauler and swoop bikes struggled with the weight of the car, both of them pulling at it as they headed for a cliff.

Han had known they couldn't carry the car with only two cables attached, but he was willing to try. Now, while dealing with the added complication of Enfys Nest's bikes, he knew he couldn't clear that mountain peak, and Nest wouldn't let them maneuver around it.

In a deeply modulated voice, Enfys Nest shouted, "Release your cables, or die!"

How did the raiders think they could take the car with only a few cables when the hauler definitely couldn't? Well, it didn't matter; they were beyond discussion.

The cliff face was looming over them now, the hauler refusing to gain altitude. "We're too close, I gotta release."

"Don't you drop it, Han!" Beckett screamed from where he dangled with Chewie. They had to see the cliff coming up, didn't they? Their death was staring them right in the face.

"Chewie, grab the line!" Han commanded, then waited a moment for his friend to comply. As Han had recently told Beckett, he wanted very much to live. He released the cables and felt the hauler immediately gain altitude. He chanced a look down: The raiders had clearly realized that sticking with the coaxium was death, and dropped their own cables.

Freed at last, the car tumbled into a ravine.

"No, you coward!" Beckett screamed as Han struggled to get the hauler high enough to pull away safely.

The raiders sped away, and Han had a suspicion they knew what was coming, so he accelerated as fast as he dared with Chewie and Beckett still dangling below.

When the car landed, the force of the bright-blue explosion lifted the hauler and pushed it forward. Han could see the mountain peak blossom slightly as if it were a bubble made of rock; then it caved in on itself.

The hauler danced around on the shock wave like a leaf in a storm. Han had no chance to see if Chewie and Beckett had made it inside or if they had been vaporized by the blast—handling the hauler was all he could focus on. It tipped and veered, something clearly offline due to the blast. Tall, ragged peaks loomed, and Han wasn't sure they would clear them.

"I can do this, everything is fine, I can do this," he muttered, keeping the mantra going as he struggled with the controls and did just clear the closest peak. Well, almost. They would have cleared if the hauler hadn't tipped again and scraped its left side against a jutting rock. At this point, all was lost. Han heard Chewbacca roaring, and was relieved he had at least made it inside.

"Hang on!" he managed to shout, leaning on the controls and cutting the left engine to see if that would stop the unmanageable wobbling. It started to smoke inside the cockpit, and he blinked and coughed, still wrestling with the vessel.

They hit a snowbank with a spine-rattling *thump* and slid several meters, tearing up trees and rocks around them. Han gave up trying to control the crash, and merely braced himself as the hauler finally slid to a stop in the middle of a snowy field.

He opened his eyes, unaware that he had closed them. He took a long, shaking breath and rubbed his face. A heavy hand landed on his shoulder, shaking it gently. He looked up into the face of Chewie, who was growling softly. He blinked and grinned. "We made it."

CHAPTER TEN

They gave Beckett some time to himself, staying aboard the hauler while he created small memorials for Val and Rio. Han had wanted to argue that Val could still be alive; he'd been holding on to an illogical hope that she had somehow used her grappling gun to get away before the bridge blew. But Beckett was sure. He stayed out there for several hours, letting Han and Chewie wonder over their next step: Mainly, how would they get off this planet with no ship and no loot?

As Beckett hunched over the little graves, Han and Chewie approached slowly and stood a respectful distance behind him until he realized they were there.

Beckett turned, his face still ravaged with grief over Val and Rio, and rage regarding the loss of the coaxium.

"Listen," Han said. "I know—"

Beckett interrupted him with a punch.

Han fell back into the snow and stared openmouthed. "What the hell?"

"Val was right. I never should have brought you on the job," Beckett snarled. "You can't follow orders! Do you have any idea what you've done?"

Grief slashed cruel lines across his face, making him age ten years in an afternoon. "We weren't stealing for ourselves!" he continued. "We were hired by Crimson Dawn!" He nearly spat the last words, making Han's spine go cold.

Behind him, Chewie made a distressed roar. Han echoed him in Basic. "Crimson Dawn?"

Crimson Dawn was a crime syndicate, one of the top five in the galaxy, and very likely the most powerful of them. Rumors and stories and more circulated about them: their cruelty, their wealth, their brutality. Working for them could be very lucrative, and failing while working for them could be deadly. Losing something as valuable as a fleet's worth of coaxium—well, they might as well commit suicide now and save Crimson Dawn the trouble.

Maybe Val and Rio had gotten off easy.

"Now we owe them," Beckett said, "a hundred keys of refined coaxium, and when they find out we don't got it, they're gonna kill us."

Chewbacca snarled low in his throat.

Han pointed at the Wookiee, nodding. "Right. We run. I'm already a deserter. What's the difference?"

Beckett looked at him as if he were a stupid child. "Difference is the Empire don't send a team of enforcers to hunt you down as a deserter. Dryden Vos will. You got any clue what that's like? Having a price on your head?" Han didn't answer, and Beckett continued. "Only thing to do is go to them. Dryden and I go back a long way."

His voice dropped, like he was trying to convince himself instead of Han. "Maybe I can figure a way to make it up to him."

"Okay," Han said, brushing off his hands. "Then that's what we'll do." He had something to prove to this man: He had to prove that he was worth the trouble, that he was worth teaching. He couldn't claim to replace the people Beckett had lost, but he could sure as hell work hard to make up for the lost job. And he could form the nucleus of a new team.

Beckett watched him, relaxing a bit. He seemed to finally take Han at his word. "No. He knows me, not you. If you come with me, show your face . . . if they don't kill you, you're in this life for good."

"If we find some way to square this, do we still get our money?" Han asked.

Beckett smiled wryly. "Maybe."

"Then for me it's worth the risk." He glanced behind him at the Wookiee watching them. "How about you?"

Chewie gave a short barking roar.

Han turned back around to Beckett. "That's 'yes,'" he relayed, smiling.

Beckett looked at him for a minute. Perhaps he saw himself in Han, his own younger days when he was eager to prove himself to anyone who would give him a chance. He seemed to come to an internal decision, and started walking.

"Look, kid. Sorry I punched your face," he said.

"Happens more often than you'd think," Han said, shrugging. "I'm sorry about Rio."

"Yeah, we squeezed our way outta some tight spots together, but we both knew that someday one of us would bury the other. I really thought he'd be burying me, though. He'd be faster with the shovels, you know."

Han swallowed, unsure of how to say it, just sure it had to be said. "And Val. She was your . . ." He trailed off. There hadn't been a specific relationship stated, but they were clearly more than teammates.

Beckett got a look of bittersweet tenderness on his face. "Actually," he said, "I think I was *hers*."

Han nodded, uncomfortable at the sudden look at the man's naked love and grief. Again he thought of Qi'ra and understood immediately what Beckett meant.

He turned and looked at the wrecked hauler and then at the expanse of snow around them. The sun would be going down soon. "So," he said. "We going to find Dryden Vos and talk to him? How?"

"He's nearby, on his yacht."

Han looked around, seeing nothing but snow, mountains, and the large horned beasts Beckett had told him were kod'yoks, who stood at a distance in their great shaggy coats and watched them, chewing thoughtfully. "How are we going to find him?" Han asked.

Beckett snapped out of his nostalgia and grinned at Han. "Shouldn't be hard."

A long slog through the snow followed. Han had been cold before—dunks into cold water during winters on Corellia, working nighttime jobs with little more than a shirt and pants during a storm, sleeping without a blanket in the tunnels of the White Worms. And just today, hanging off the end of a train, the icy wind chafing his exposed skin.

But this was a different cold. Chewie marched on, noticing nothing, the snow beginning to gather in little balls at the ends of his hair. Beckett was lost in his grief, or perhaps his fear of the Crimson Dawn's Dryden Vos, but he walked with purpose. Han, however, could feel this cold, this close-to-ground, buried-in-snow cold, seeping through the furs and through his skin to settle in his bones.

Beckett was leading him to his doom, he was fairly certain. He would simply fall over and freeze solid. It didn't seem like a bad way to go, especially since he'd just escaped violent death by splattering on rocks or exploding with the train.

"There," Beckett said suddenly, and Han looked up, peering through the ice that had formed on his eyelashes.

They'd walked several klicks, he thought, around and down the mountain pass. Han hadn't noticed much except for the cold and wondering if he still had toes. When he finally paid attention to his surroundings again, he gazed with wonder at the vehicle in front of him.

Standing like a beacon in the middle of a snowy plain was a tall star yacht moored at the rugged outpost of Fort Ypso. It was as if someone had taken a small Star Destroyer, etched it with gold, and tipped it on its end. It looked more like a floating building than a ship, with a slim keel nearly reaching the ground and gradually sloping up to form a much larger shiplike structure near the top.

"What is that?" he asked.

"That is Dryden's star yacht," Beckett said.

They walked the rope bridge that connected the fort to the gangway to the ship. Han felt out of place in this gilded castle built to signal how much wealth the owner had. Beckett approached the entrance and nodded at the guards, who let them pass. They entered an antechamber that had a window in one wall, beyond which was a uniformed attendant waiting at what looked like a coat check. He looked at Han expectantly, and Han looked at Beckett. Han started to remove his fur coat.

"Your *weapons*," the attendant said.

Beckett slammed a large knife on the table between them. "Only one I got left," he said. This was his fusioncutter, the knife that had cut the seal of the conveyex car. He accepted a claim token, an oddly sterile exchange for rendering oneself completely vulnerable in a strange place.

After hesitating one more moment, with Beckett looking pointedly at him, Han reluctantly handed over his already precious DL-44. The attendant took it and opened a large case behind him, placing it with an impressive array of blasters, blades, and weapons Han had never even encountered before. The attendant put a tag on the blaster and handed Han the matching token.

Once they were free of all ways to defend themselves, the window to the weapons check closed and the antechamber began to rise. Han realized the chamber was actually a lift—an ornate golden room that already looked fancier than anyplace Han had ever been. And it was only the lift. They rose swiftly, and Han's ears popped as they got higher and higher. He glanced at

Chewie, who stood patiently, and then at Beckett, who ignored him. He was still wrestling with his inner storms, and Han wasn't sure when would be a good time to interrupt the process.

"So, this Dryden Vos. Any hints as to what I should do?" Han asked, the silence starting to unnerve him.

"We are going to Dryden's cocktail party, which is pretty much a permanent event," Beckett said. "We go in. Get a drink. Wait till Dryden sees us. And don't piss anyone off in the meantime."

Han ran a hand over his snow-dampened hair. "Great," he said. He looked at Chewie. "You got a comb?"

Chewie made an injured sound and indicated if he'd had a comb, he would have used it on himself.

"Yeah, makes sense," Han said.

After what seemed like an hour, the lift stopped and opened to an even more opulent room. Han was officially, completely out of his element. And this element was gold.

Directly ahead of them, in dusky, filtered light, humans and nonhumans mingled dressed in their finest, the cocktail party proving to be *the* place to be in the galaxy. They moved about and chatted in the foreground, while in the distance was a dais where a tall woman danced and sang. Her dark skin contrasted beautifully with her gold dress and mask, which caught the light around her and seemed to drink it in and then reflect it as a more brilliant light, somehow.

She sang into a mike, the melody drifting around the room in a haunting lilt. She sang in a language Han recognized as Huttese, and he watched her in awe. Behind her levitated a vat holding a critical-looking fleshy creature whose giant head crooned backup into a mike inside the vat.

Han thought he looked familiar from an old holovid, but he wasn't sure. Probably not.

Closer to the stage, people swayed and danced slowly along with the singer, but most eyes were focused only on her. Above the dais was a platform where a few people stood, chatting quietly with their heads close together, some surveying the room.

Below them on the floor was the large symbol of the Crimson Dawn, a horizontal line with a half circle depicting a rising sun.

"Come on," Beckett said, leading him away from the partiers. He'd already spotted a tall man on the balcony above the stage. He had pale skin and reddish-brown hair, and wore draping black clothing that had to have been stitched to his measurements within a millimeter. He watched the party as if he owned the room, which he clearly did, but also everyone in it, which Han assumed he didn't. There was a potential energy to the man, as if something were coiled within and ready to strike, should he call it forth. This had to be Dryden Vos, their boss.

People seemed to want to be close to him, and yet once they entered his orbit they kept a safe distance, as if they wanted his passive attention but hoped to avoid active, direct attention at all costs.

The man sighed and nodded to someone, left the dais, and exited through a door in the back of the room, leaving it slightly ajar.

A lithe woman with a bald, angular head and an ashen complexion came up and greeted them. Han flinched when someone else removed their coats without asking. The woman greeted Beckett in a language Han didn't understand, but Beckett nodded to her. "We're here to see Dryden. He's expecting me."

"He will be with you shortly," she replied in Basic. "He's just finishing with the regional governor."

The song ended, and in the brief moment of quiet Han heard a cry of pain followed by a heavy *thump*.

"So," Han said, focusing back on Beckett nervously. "I'm just gonna mingle."

Beckett relaxed a moment. "Listen, kid," he said, frowning. "These people are not your friends and they're never gonna be. Don't talk to any of 'em. Don't even look at anybody. Just keep your eyes *down*."

Han nodded once, looking at Beckett's shoes. "Got it."

"I'm gonna get a drink," Beckett said, and his feet wandered away.

Han sighed and looked up at Chewie. At least there was someone he could look directly at without worry. "Sounds like a good idea," he said.

The pair stuck out like people who brought rocks to a blaster fight. Wealth, fashion, style, opulence, and more words that were beyond Han's vocabulary were on display around them. People took no notice of him, as if they couldn't be bothered with the scruffy human and Wookiee who had clearly gotten lost on the way to the gambling den in the fort below. He surveyed the room more closely. From the glittering party guests to the ethereal music, the blatant wealth on display, and the clear vein of corruption, the atmosphere was almost dizzying. He wanted this; he wanted to be one of these people, who were the kind that took what they wanted from those too stupid to hold on to it. This was the dream of kids who grew up cutting purses and hot-wiring speeders—that someday you would steal enough to live like this.

He wasn't there yet. But he was among them, and that was an important step. If they managed to keep Dryden Vos from killing them, they might be able to do more jobs and get paid an amount that would buy more than dinner.

That was a big "if," though. He had to leave that part to Beckett.

The singer began a new song, swaying in a sinuous fashion, her song nearly lulling him to sleep. Chewie grunted and pointed to the food.

Han nodded. "Sure, yeah, whatever," he said, and ventured farther into the crowd.

He made it to a set of large round windows giving a spectacular view of the mountains. He was watching the plume from the still-burning fire when he felt a hand on his shoulder.

"Hey, Chewie, would you please—" he started, then realized the hand was not large and hairy.

Had he already offended someone? Were they going to start a bar fight at a cocktail party? He clenched his fists and turned.

All the oxygen seemed to leave the room. The woman who had touched his shoulder had perfectly coiffed brown hair, a long, slim black dress with a slit up the side, and a wide, half-circle necklace with a matching brand on her wrist. She did not have on torn, filthy clothing, and she didn't smell of eels.

His brain ceased sending messages to his limbs. Han

wanted to say something, to hug her, to grab her by the shoulders and ask her where she had been, to clutch her hands and apologize for not coming back like he'd promised. He wanted to kiss her, plunge his hands into her hair, breathe in her smell. But his eyes were locked on hers, and he simply struggled to breathe.

Qi'ra gave Han a slow look, and then smiled. "Remember me?"

CHAPTER ELEVEN

Years later, his first words to Qi'ra would still bring a horrified blush to his face. The detail would burn itself into his memory no matter how much he wanted to forget it.

He found his words, opened his mouth and said, "You're . . . not a Wookiee." He winced the moment the words were out there.

Her lips quirked into a small smile. "Neither are you. But I never held it against you."

He finally grabbed her and crushed her in a hug, his brain short-circuiting and unable to say anything. She laughed and hugged him back. Was that it? Was he forgiven?

He let her go and stared at her. "What are you doing here?" he finally blurted, looking around as if she didn't fit in, either—but clearly she did. She was gorgeous now, clean, refined, elegant. Nothing like the beautiful and rough scrumrat he had grown up with.

"Could ask you the same question," she said, looking him up and down. "I work here."

"Qi'ra, I was, I was . . . coming back for you," he said, words failing him.

Grief flickered briefly over her face. "It's in the past," she whispered.

He shook his head. "Not for me. The only reason I'm here is to do this job, get a little money, and I was going to come back and find you."

She hadn't changed her expression, which was slightly amused, but calculating. She didn't look angry. "Well, now you don't have to. I'm right here."

"That day," he said, shaking his head to clear the memory. "So many times I think I should have—"

"If you'd stayed, they would have killed you," she reminded him. "I'm glad you got out. You've got to survive, Han. When somebody falls, you keep running. It's how you stay alive."

No, that wasn't what he had learned. You stick by allies on the street, if not for loyalty's sake, then to make sure someone always owed you a favor. But that was mercenary, too, and he closed his mouth on the argument.

Still. It felt wrong.

"How did *you* get out?" he asked. He feared the answer, but had to know.

"I didn't," she said simply. That brief look of grief again, quickly hidden by a sip of her drink as he felt his face grow hot.

"What . . . ?" he asked. Was Lady Proxima here? No, that was ridiculous.

But she couldn't mean she worked for the Crimson Dawn. Because if she did, then that meant Lady Proxima had made good on her threat to throw Qi'ra to the crime syndicate, that she had been sold like stolen goods. He tried to swallow back the guilt that threatened to overwhelm him. *This is my fault,* he thought.

She smiled, all poise and charm again, and looked him up and down. She took in his dirty, torn clothes, his small injuries here and there, and then nodded with a smile. "You look good. A little rough around the edges, maybe, but good."

"You too," he said, eager to get on any other subject.

She laughed. The illusion of wealth melted and for a moment it was as if they were ten years younger. She was his ally, his friend, his—*his* again. He found himself nostalgic for the horrid times in the White Worms' lair, when he'd done nothing but wish they could get away.

A tall server strolled past carrying a tray of rose-colored drinks in fluted glasses. Qi'ra took two and handed one to Han. She held her glass up, and he mirrored her toast. Tiny bubbles crawled up the sides of the glass, jostling free to float to the top when their glasses clinked together.

"What shall we drink to?" she asked before they sipped.

"Let's start with two, and then go from there," he said. She laughed, and he smiled his sideways grin, feeling comfortable with her again. She may have gotten out of poverty and into this pampered life, but he could still make her laugh.

Several meters beyond Qi'ra, Chewbacca stood looking at them, having just come from the buffet. He held
two steaming cups of liquid—caf, maybe?—and stared
at Han, one hand stretched halfway toward him. When
he saw Han was busy toasting Qi'ra, he shrugged and
downed both cups, smearing his fur with liquid and
causing a few horrified observers to turn away from the
unrefinedness of it all.

"So," Qi'ra said, pulling Han's attention back. "You
ever get that ship we were gonna fly away on?"

Han nodded. "Yeah." He paused. "Sorta." A knowing glint shone in her eye as he backpedaled carefully.
"I'm about to. That's actually why I'm here, working on
a very big deal."

Qi'ra seemed interested beyond polite conversation.
"How big?"

"Enormous," he assured her.

She chuckled, seeing straight through his boasting
evasion. "So when are you going to close this 'enormous
deal'?"

He grinned. "Any minute."

"You know," she said, "I thought about you a lot. Off
somewhere on some adventure, and I imagined myself
with you and it always made me . . ."

"What?" he asked, leaning forward with interest.

She was about to answer, but they were interrupted
by a sharp "Hey!"

Beckett approached them, stepping unceremoniously
between Han and Qi'ra to face Han. "What did I say?"
he asked, sounding for a moment like Lady Proxima
talking to an offending scrumrat.

"Look, I can't keep my eyes down the whole time, I'm going to bump into something," Han said.

"Look, but I told you—" Beckett said.

Qi'ra interrupted him sharply.

"Beckett!" He turned quickly to face her. "Wait. You two work together?" she asked.

Beckett's reply was interrupted when a jovial voice called, "Tobias!"

Beckett and Qi'ra's body language changed immediately, Han noticed, both of them turning paler, standing a little more at attention, and looking around to make sure nothing was out of sorts and everyone was acting the way they should. It was the look of prey when a predator joins it at the watering hole; was it here to drink, or was it here to feed?

Dryden Vos joined them jovially, spreading out his arms like he was greeting a brother. He grabbed Beckett in a huge hug that looked less like affection and more like a capture. He drew back from him, but Han could see one viselike hand was still attached to Beckett's shoulder. "You all right? You hurt?" Dryden asked, appraising the man.

"I'm fine," Beckett said firmly.

"I'm so sorry about Val," Dryden said, leaning close. He didn't look sorry at all, but instead looked like an actor reading hurriedly through a script to get to a good part.

"So am I. I'm just so—" Beckett began, but Dryden turned away from him to take in Han and Chewie, who had just joined them. Han noticed Dryden wore a large ring with the same symbol as Qi'ra's necklace, the symbol on the floor and even on the napkins: the symbol for the Crimson Dawn.

Dryden's face split into a welcoming smile. "I don't believe we've been introduced," he said, looking from Han to Chewbacca.

"This is Han Solo and Chewbacca," Beckett said, pointing needlessly at each. "They're with me."

Dryden was facing away from Qi'ra, and she had already relaxed a moment, watching Dryden in a calculating manner. She looked momentarily startled when she heard the name Solo but didn't say anything.

"I'm Dryden Vos," he said, and then gestured at Qi'ra. "Seems you already know my top lieutenant." He smiled at Qi'ra. Han wasn't sure if it was a look of ownership or romantic love or fatherly affection. It was complex, and all Han knew was that he didn't like it. He made himself look away, feeling his emotions scrawled too obviously on his face.

"Han and I grew up together on Corellia," Qi'ra said, looking at Han.

"A fellow scrumrat," Dryden said, nodding. "I admire anyone with the tenacity to claw their way out of the sewer, particularly one as putrid as Corellia."

Qi'ra smiled, and Han forced his jaw to unclench and smile at the backhanded compliment. Dryden had moved his attention onward, however, and hadn't noticed his discomfort and jealousy. "Something really must be done about the poverty there," he mused, as if talking to himself. "In fact, I've considered establishing a fund to do just that. In any event—" He grabbed Han's sweaty hand and shook it, his grip tight and his handshake a precise three pumps. "Good to have you!"

he said. He didn't shake Chewbacca's paw, but nodded at him. "You too, Chewbacca." He nodded to the door in the back of the room he had previously come through. "So let's eat a little, drink a lot, and talk privately, shall we?"

He led them into the room, not looking back. Han gave an uneasy look to Beckett and Qi'ra, but they were following Dryden without question. Only Chewie seemed as uneasy as Han as he fell into step beside him.

The Wookiee grumbled something as the group entered the study.

Did he really want to talk about this *now*? "We're just friends, all right?" Han said.

Chewie grunted again.

"You're touchy," Han snapped.

If Dryden's party lounge was stylish luxury, his private study was blatant in-your-face, up-your-nose, and into-your-brain wealth. While it did have a desk and a sitting area like offices were supposed to, it also had display upon display of curiosities from all over the galaxy. Treasure, ancient artifacts, weapons, a suit of old Mandalorian armor, even taxidermied creatures posed in glass bells. He had books, tablets with alien writing, jewelry displayed on black velvet, exotic furs draped over sculptures, and a glittering crown set in a display case that had caught Chewbacca's eye. Han wanted to ask if he had recognized it, but figured it wasn't the time.

"Like what you see?" Dryden asked, clearly proud of showing off his wealth. "Never be ashamed of your appetites, Han. It's good to stay hungry."

"He's definitely that," Beckett said, taking a seat on a plush white sofa.

"Look around," Dryden said, as if Han weren't already doing that. He ran his finger over a crystal vase with flowers carved deep into the surface. "Spoils of war. I appreciate beauty. But *building* something, that's what I want. This is our time, but it takes hard work. Determination. No room for carelessness."

At first his voice was thick with greed and pride, but as he spoke it became harder and found an edge. Han could feel himself tensing up but he wasn't sure why.

Dryden kept walking around the room, seemingly ambling, but he was getting closer and closer to Beckett, who watched him carefully.

"Beckett," Dryden said in a clipped, businesslike voice. "I know that Rio and Val were more than just your crew, and as your friend, you have my sympathies, but as your *employer,* you've put me in a terrible position."

"I know, Dryden," Beckett began, "and I'm sorry—"

"Excuse me? You're *sorry?*"

Beckett scrambled to explain. "Dryden, there were complications, there were factors—"

"Enfys Nest," Dryden said, spittle flying from his tongue. Han watched in alarm as dark red striations rose on his face, almost as if someone had dumped paint on his head and it ran over his skin in rivulets. His face pulsed, the red lines growing darker, and Han didn't know if they fed on his anger, or his anger fed on them. He had clearly said this name before, and didn't like the taste any more then than now. "Has been a constant irritation forever, one that you should have anticipated and one you should've dealt with."

But we did anticipate it. And they killed Rio anyway.

Han wanted to point this out, but felt it probably wouldn't have added to the conversation.

"Trust me, I know I made a mistake, but when you hired me you told me no one else had this inform—"

"*Test* me. Test me one more time and you'll see what happens," Dryden interrupted, teeth clenched. His voice was rising in volume, and Han imagined he could hear the music from the cocktail party increase in volume, as if part of its job was to drown out any unpleasant sounds coming from the office. Dryden had lost all composure, and any illusion of kindness and friendship had dissolved to show the true cruelty underneath the surface.

Dryden's face was growing dark, but not red as if he were enraged; red striations appeared as if his blood had turned inky and ran close to the surface. *What's wrong with him?* Han wondered.

With a roar, Dryden turned his hideous, reddened face toward the crystal vase and pushed over the entire pedestal. The vase toppled and shattered when it hit, splattering glass in all directions. Han winced and Chewbacca let out a startled moan, but Qi'ra just closed her eyes as if this was something she witnessed all too frequently.

Beckett's afraid for his life, but Qi'ra looks like she's dealing with nothing scarier than a toddler having a tantrum.

Dryden was panting from his outburst, and Qi'ra appeared at his side, guiding him to a couch and putting her hand on the back of his neck. She held him gently, as if he were a rampaging beast and she the only thing that could calm him. Which, Han thought bitterly, didn't seem too far from the truth. This intimate scene played out with Dryden relaxing, turning from rancor to human again, and he took a deep breath and all the tension left his body.

"I think what Dryden is trying to say," Qi'ra said, "is that we're not interested in why you don't have it."

"No, I'm not interested," Dryden said softly, as if he had taken a sedative but still wanted to be part of the conversation. "I'm not interested at all." The markings on his face slowly returned to their usual soft, red color.

Beckett watched him closely, silently. Han marveled that he seemed to know when to speak and when to keep quiet. Finally, he said, "Dryden, what can I do to make this right?"

"Make this *right*?" Dryden said, eyes wide. "There is no making this right. You know who I answer to, and you know what he'll expect of me. He'll say there have to be consequences, or else people will start to think they can get away with . . . anything. So here is what I need from you. I need you to give me a reason not to kill you all. And I need it. Right . . . now . . ."

Han could see the rage coiling up inside Dryden again, and he looked from him to Beckett, panic rising in his own throat.

"Because I will make it up to you," Beckett said patiently.

"No, no, no," Dryden said, holding up a hand. "*How?* How will you make it up to me?"

"By delivering what was promised," Beckett said.

If anything, the promise startled Dryden out of his rage buildup, and he laughed.

Qi'ra was less impressed. She leaned forward and

said, "One hundred k-grams of coaxium? *Refined* co-axium?"

"Yes," Beckett said. "We will simply steal it from somewhere else."

"From where?" Dryden demanded.

Qi'ra nodded. "You'll be hard-pressed to find that anywhere outside an Imperial vault. Scarif? Maybe Mercy Island?"

Dryden shook his head. "That's impossible."

"So!" Qi'ra said positively. "Let's come up with some other options. Other ideas that we might—"

"What about *unrefined*?" Han blurted out.

Everyone stared at him. No one spoke.

What had he done?

Qi'ra read the room quickly: Chewie, the Wookiee who had attached himself to Han (or probably the other way around) looked at him as if he were speaking a new language. Beckett looked shocked but disbelieving, as if Han were a child who'd offered to go on a diplomatic mission to the Emperor. Which was pretty close to the truth. Most important, there was Dryden.

Here was a man who hated being interrupted, especially when he had a good rage going. Qi'ra could do it, of course, but she did it with touch and soft statements. Dryden looked at Han like he was already in the crosshairs, and he just had to decide exactly where to shoot him to obliterate him.

No one spoke, and Han sat there looking uncertain, like he had said something out of the blue without any planning behind it. Qi'ra sighed inwardly. Actually, he had done exactly that. *Just like old times.* She cleared her throat and spoke up to save his sorry butt, hoping to keep Dryden's attention from burning Han to a cinder.

"The only known source of astatic coaxium is the fissure vent discovered beneath the spice mines on Kessel," she said thoughtfully.

Han eagerly grabbed the lifeline she had thrown him and acted as if the plan had been there from the start. He nodded eagerly and said, "Yeah, Kessel . . . that's the one I was thinking of, a very, very good one."

Behind Beckett, Chewie was shaking his head, clearly begging him to stop going down this black hole from which there was no escape. Han shrugged slightly—she knew that shrug. He had started in a direction and there was no going back. Nothing to do now but charge ahead.

He probably thought it was his only chance, and was trying to save Beckett in a stupid, clumsy way. In all fairness, Dryden had been about to kill Beckett, and he probably would have taken care of Han and Chewie soon after. However, Qi'ra would have been able to stop Dryden. Beckett was completely safe.

Probably.

Dryden was watching all of them. Was he waiting for more insights from her? Beckett to tell Han his plan was crazy? Han to continue piecing together an impossibility? She calmed slightly; the fact that Dryden was considering this as a reasonable plan meant he hadn't really wanted to kill them. Of course, when he was in a rage he didn't always do what his logical mind wanted. But he was calm now, tapping his chin and thinking.

He finally shook his head. "The Pykes control Kessel," he said. "Crimson Dawn has a fragile alliance with them. We can't jeopardize that without risking another war among the syndicates, which I will not do."

Dryden had made his decision, and plucked his laser-bladed knife off the table beside him. He stood and loomed over them, waiting for their last words.

"But we don't have any alliance with the Pykes," Beckett said quickly.

Han picked up the thread. "—and nobody's ever gonna know we're working for you."

Dryden turned to Qi'ra as he had done so often in the past few years. He raised an eyebrow. "Possible?"

She had to give it to Han for innovation, but she had to be honest here. It was a crazy notion. "Risky," she finally said. "As soon as the raw coaxium is removed from the thermal vault, it'll start to destabilize unless . . ."

"Unless!" Han said, urging her on. "Unless. . . . ? Work with me here."

"Unless you find somewhere to process it, fast," Qi'ra continued.

Qi'ra had taken some time to learn more about the substance that had ultimately separated her from Han and put her on the path to working with the Crimson Dawn. If she knew about anything, it was coaxium. It had been her idea for Dryden to hire someone to rob the Imperial conveyex, after all.

The men stumbled for a moment, trying to think of coaxium refineries not under Imperial control, but then the Wookiee made a moaning barking sound.

"He's saying 'Savareen'?" Han translated.

"Savareen! There's an old refinery on Savareen," Beck-

ett said. "It's remote, doesn't fall under Imperial juris-
diction yet."

Dryden knew the place. "Very cooperative people,
the Savarians. But Qi'ra's right. You won't have time to
make it there before those canisters explode. You'd need
an incredibly fast ship and a brilliant pilot."

Han shrugged. "We'll get the ship." Then he pointed
at himself and grinned. "We've already got the pilot."

Qi'ra struggled to keep her face straight. She'd grown
up a lot in the previous years, and she thought Han
might have. However, it seemed he was just as impetu-
ous as always. But showing her disbelief wouldn't help
at all.

Han was a good pilot, even when he misjudged the
size of a space to slip through, Qi'ra thought as she remembered the escape from Moloch on Corellia. She was
prepared to defend his piloting skills if Dryden asked
her, but instead he burst out laughing, suddenly delighted at this young pilot's clearly unearned confidence.
The entire room relaxed a bit as the murderous glint left
his eyes.

Beckett laughed, too, a bit nervously. Dryden turned
to him and said, "He *is* hungry. And arrogant. I like
that." Beckett nodded like he had brought Han to
Dryden on purpose. Dryden turned to Qi'ra with a
thoughtful look on his face. "What do you say, my dear?
Do you think your friend can do what needs to be
done?"

Han glanced her way, silently pleading. They had
exchanged this look so many times as children. *Come
on, bail me out. And when you need something, I've
got your back.* Only she'd interrupted Lady Proxima's

wrath, allowing them to escape, and he had left her on Corellia. He already owed her.

But they didn't keep score. He had gotten her out of her own numerous scrapes. She nodded slowly and smiled. "Yes, I believe he can."

"Good," Dryden said, clapping his hands together once, as if shaking his own hands on a deal with himself. "Then it's all settled." He got up, looked sidelong at her, and said, "You'll go with them, of course. To make sure everything goes . . . smoothly. All right?"

He said it almost as an aside, but Qi'ra knew that he had planned it from the beginning. Her face froze in a slight smile. "Of course," she said, thinking hard. Dryden trusted her; they'd gotten past the mistrust part of their relationship a while ago. He knew she wouldn't—couldn't—betray him.

And Han would need her, of course. That much was obvious.

"All right!" Dryden repeated, as if approving a pleasure trip. He seemed buoyant again, having made plans that would be lucrative to him while not dirtying his hands at all. As usual. He walked to the window, sidestepping the shattered crystal on the floor as if it were no more than a puddle of spilled water. He looked into the golden sunset and smiled. "I feel great about this," he said. "I'll see you all on Savareen!"

"Savareen it is!" Beckett matched his jovial tone, getting to his feet.

Han and Chewie edged toward the door, unsure if they'd been dismissed but clearly eager to leave Dryden's private den of mercurial emotions.

"Oh, and Tobias?" Dryden said over his shoulder.

Beckett froze halfway between sitting and standing.

"You do realize, if you fail again, we'll *all* be out of options. Right?"

The threat hung in the air between them all like a loaded weapon no one wanted to pick up.

"We won't," Beckett assured him, and they finally made their polite escape. They headed for the door, backs stiff, and Han walked by a glass bell that held what Dryden called his "guests." They had the look of taxidermied creatures, but Qi'ra knew what they were.

And now Han did, too. He watched, horrified, as one creature quivered slightly and then froze again. She placed her hand on his arm, to guide him out the door. "Shall we?" she asked, squeezing his elbow tight. He nodded and followed her.

She couldn't blame him. She remembered the moment she had realized that, given Dryden's wrath, one could end up in a fate worse than death, literally.

Qi'ra said she needed to prepare some things for travel and would meet them at the weapons check. Han struggled with the complex emotions regarding bringing her with them. First, the surprise that she was alive—not to mention second in command to a crime lord—was still fresh. And then there were his old feelings for her rushing in behind it. He was delighted she was coming with them, but he worried for her well-being and a tiny part of him—all right, a big part—was irritated that when Dryden said jump, she was already crouched and ready to go.

Beckett distracted Han from all of this when he laid into Han the moment they entered the lift.

"I should shoot you the minute I get ahold of a gun," he said, pushing Han against the wall. "What were you thinking?"

"I was thinking a crazy guy was about to kill you and we needed a distraction!" Han said.

"A distraction is spilling your drink, or breaking a glass, or pushing over one of his suits of armor!" Beckett said. "It's not giving him a promise we have no chance at fulfilling!"

"What's the big deal? You heard Qi'ra. We get a ship, go to Kessel, get the coaxium, haul ass to Savareen, refine the stuff, and boom, the debt is paid," Han said.

"Do you have a ship? Have you even been to Kessel? Have you ever traveled with coaxium?" Beckett demanded.

Han's ears popped, distracting him. "No. But Qi'ra said she had a line on a ship, and if it's fast enough we don't need to worry about the unrefined coaxium. And what's the big deal with Kessel?"

Beckett rubbed his forehead. "The big deal . . . Kessel lies in a maelstrom. Electrical storms, planet-sized carbonbergs, and more. Put aside the fact that we'll be going to a dangerous mine to steal a very expensive commodity; it's not a place you just fly in and out of."

Han hadn't known that, of course. He kind of wished someone had told him. But even then, what would they have done? It was die in Dryden's study—or end up like that prisoner Han had seen on his way out the door—or die trying to pay off the debt. At least this way they were actively doing something.

"We'll be fine," he said at last. "We will just take it one thing at a time."

Chewbacca, who had watched all of this silently, made a low moaning sound.

"Exactly," Han said. "We'll worry about Kessel *after* we get the ship."

CHAPTER TWELVE

Qi'ra "knew a guy."

Han figured they would have to go to the guy, perhaps by getting a ride on the sweet star yacht. He didn't want to spend more time with Dryden Vos than he had to, but he admittedly did want to spend more time on that yacht. However, the guy was much closer than he realized.

Han kept going over those words as they exited the yacht's gangway and crossed the rope bridges to Fort Ypso. It turned out the "guy" was a few hundred meters away, in the bowels of the fort. Which was the opposite of Dryden's luxury yacht in every way possible.

Han was pretty sure he could still hear the ethereal sounds of the music high above them as he entered the fort. The first thing they encountered was a number of different species drinking at a poorly lit bar, many of them obviously armed, and many of them talking about the crash of the conveyex.

Chewie gave a low growl, not happy with the surroundings. The patrons lurking over their drinks reciprocated the sentiment, many of them directing hostile looks at the newcomers.

Beckett didn't pay any attention to those glaring at them, or to the voices floating over to them about the "lost coaxium" in the "botched job" or the "idiots" who were "destroyed by Enfys Nest." Han bristled, and Chewie turned and stared at the speaker, but Qi'ra led them past the bar and downstairs into an even darker, smokier pit.

A loud noise from a side room distracted him, and he stopped to watch what looked like a droid cage match. Spectators of all species were placing bets and cheering as two droids grappled. Each one had at least three arms extended, grasping, tearing, and burning. One managed to grab the other and slam it forcefully against the cage. Arms went flying, torches guttered out, and the crowd roared. Credits changed hands, a punch was thrown, and they left the room as more cheering, this time for a different fight, started.

In the corner stood a droid, leaning against the wall like a person. Han couldn't place its make: It was bipedal like a protocol or domestic droid, but its head was dome-shaped like an astromech.

"So your guy is here?" Han asked Qi'ra, trying to keep the disbelief from his voice.

"He's the best smuggler around," she said. "He's slipped through the Empire's fingers more times than anyone alive." She paused and read the several emotions crossing Han's face. "He's also very attractive. Not just handsome, but sophisticated. He has impeccable taste and . . ." She paused as if searching for words. "Charisma. Not to mention his *prodigious*—"

"We get the idea," Han interrupted.

"He's retired now," Qi'ra said, changing topics. "Calls himself a 'sportsman.'"

"All we need is his ship," Han said, not wanting to hear more of this guy's biography.

"He'll never part with it. Loves that ship. He won it playing . . ." She paused as they entered another smoky room. ". . . Sabacc."

A conversation drifted to their ears. ". . . how was I supposed to know she was an Imperial spy? I thought she loved me!" Chuckles and grunts rippled around the table.

A number of species filled the Sabacc table where, Han assumed, a card game had just ended. The spectators watched the table almost as eagerly as the ones watching the droid battle. Qi'ra gently, but assertively, parted the crowd to get to the front lines.

At the far end of the table, facing them, was the man who had told the story about the spy. He had dark skin, with a trimmed beard, a lazy smile, and sharp, intelligent eyes. He slouched in his chair in a perfect illusion of disinterest, but Han suspected he was very aware of everything around him. His suspicions were confirmed when his eyes turned straight to Qi'ra as he snaked out his hand and pulled his latest winnings across the table.

The man was dressed in the brightest colors in the room. Where everyone else wore shades of brown and gray and blue, this guy had on a perfectly tailored shirt in a brilliant shade of yellow. Draped on the chair behind him was a cape. A *cape*. And he managed to make it look good. Han wondered if he and Dryden Vos had the same tailor.

"That's the guy, huh?" Han asked over Qi'ra's shoulder. He glanced to the side and saw her smiling with clear pleasure at just seeing the man. "He's got an interesting . . . style."

"I'll say," she said, not trying to disguise the hunger in her voice. "There's no one in the galaxy like Lando Calrissian."

The world was spinning away from him, and Han grabbed onto the one thing he understood. "You say he *won* his ship?" he asked thoughtfully. "I can take him. Let me at him."

She turned to him, face closing down to focus seriously. She shook her head. "Han. No. *No*. Absolutely not. I know what you're thinking and it's a terrible idea."

"Hey, when we were kids and played Corellian Spike, who was the best in the den?"

"We were kids! These guys are serious gamblers—"

"*I'm* serious. Stake me." Han felt confident for the first time since he had suggested they waltz into a maelstrom and steal a very volatile substance. "A hundred credits should do it."

Chewie groaned and shook his head, but Han ignored him. Qi'ra glared at him, looked at the table, and then sighed and nodded.

"You won't regret this," Han said. "I promise."

———

Qi'ra and Chewie faded into the crowd as Han joined the game. He told them he couldn't have them at his back fretting while he played.

"Is this seat taken?" he asked, stepping up to the table.

The only other human at the table, Lando, looked up. "If nobody's in the seat, it ain't taken, friend."

He sat down, showing eager naïveté. "So this is Sabacc?" he asked, mispronouncing it "sa-*back*."

"Sa*bacc*," Lando corrected, gathering the cards.

"Sa-*bok*," Han repeated. "Got it."

"You play before?" Lando asked, dealing out the two cards.

Han nodded. "Couple times, yeah."

"Captain Lando Calrissian."

"Han Solo." He gestured to Lando's winnings. "Looks like you're having a good day." Lando just grinned. "Can I ask you a question, Captain Calrissian?"

"Anything, Han," Lando said, deliberately mispronouncing it to sound like *hand*—the same way Han had deliberately mispronounced *Sabacc*.

"It's Han, but that's okay," he said, smiling. "I heard a, uh, story about you and was wondering if it was true."

Lando never really lost the smile that curled on his mouth like a satisfied feline, but this time the feline stretched and Lando smiled wider. A floating waitdroid came up behind him and filled his upraised glass. "Everything. You've heard about me. Is true," Lando said deliberately, and then looked behind him to the droid. "Thanks, love."

It was odd to thank a droid for a drink, but this was already an odd guy.

"Heard you won your ship playing cards," Han said.

"I've won a lot of things," Lando said, nodding. He took a long drink. "I once won a subtropical moon in the Oseon Belt. Turned out to be a real money pit. Still, I enjoyed winning it."

"I'm impressed," Han said, taking his own drink and not looking at Lando. "I don't think I'd have the nerve to gamble with something I love as much as *my* ship."

Lando's interest in him became more focused, and Han wouldn't have seen it if he wasn't looking for it. "What do you fly?"

"VCX-100," Han said, naming a ship he'd seen a hundred times in the shipyards back home. He looked at his cards and took another one, dropping a credit on the table.

The effect was instant. The other gamblers exclaimed in their own languages, and Lando whistled low. "That is a quality ship."

Han shrugged modestly. "Fastest in the galaxy, but there are a lot of great ships out there. I'm sure yours is . . . very nice?"

"Gets me where I'm going," Lando said stiffly.

They finished the hand, and Han placed his cards on the table—he'd managed to balance his four cards out to zero, with the best hand at the table. He grinned. "Beginner's luck."

"Well played," Lando allowed. And the game continued.

Han lost a few hands to get the read on the players around him, and then began winning in earnest to his

outward astonishment. He kept his conversation minimal, asking rules questions here and there, ordering a
round for the table. He had to get in there and establish
himself. The other gamblers were happy to have someone new to take credits from, but as he started winning,
the faces became more and more hostile.

His goal was simply to outlast the others at the table.
Lando didn't strike him as a quitter, and he was clearly
in it for the fun—but he didn't lose very often. Which
made sense, as winning was fun.

Han leaned back to relax, mimicking the same mien
of pleased disinterest that Lando had. Once Han had
dangled something as nice as a ship in front of Lando,
the game had heated up. They rolled, gave up hands, and
drew with more and more intensity. The stakes grew
higher and higher until everyone had dropped out except
Han and Lando. The pot consisted of everything Han
owned (that Qi'ra had loaned him) and everything that
had been in front of Lando mingled with it.

Conversation had stopped. The only sounds in the
room were various breathing apparatuses. All eyes were
on the game, waiting to see what would happen with
the final hand.

Lando had watched Han as much as he had looked at
his cards. He never lost his smile. Finally he said, "You're
bluffing. I'm going to call."

Han gestured to the empty space in front of Lando.
"With what? Your scarf isn't my style."

"You don't have a style, Han," Lando said. Then he
said, "My ship. Against your ship."

Han had caught him. Even the breathing sounds
stopped as everyone in the room held their breath. He

kept the glee internal as he pretended to think about it, letting the tension build. Then he shrugged as if it really didn't matter to him. "Sure, what the hell." He laid his cards on the table and sat back. "Straight staves."

The crowd erupted, not expecting such a good hand. Only one in the game would beat it, and that was impossible since Han was certain both of the key cards, the green sylops, were in the discard pile.

Hands, human and alien, pounded him on the back, and he grinned, meeting Qi'ra's eyes in triumph.

Lando chuckled, shaking his head. "You dog, you played me! You are good. *Very* good."

Han beamed. "Thanks," he said, moving to take his winnings.

"Whoa whoa whoa," Lando said, putting his hands—manicured and soft—on top of Han's. "I said you were good. But not good enough." He put his own cards on the table and spread them out to remove any doubt. Two tens. Two negative tens. And a green sylop, the zero card that broke ties. "Pure Sabacc."

The room seemed to swirl around Han as the crowd went crazy, this time in Lando's direction. He stared at the cards, hoping he wasn't seeing what was in front of him. Lando leaned back again, hands behind his head, grinning at his triumph, having unseated the young upstart.

It was impossible. Han wanted to object, to claim that the last green sylop card couldn't have been in Lando's hand. But objectors had been ignored all night, and Han hadn't listened to them. Now he wondered if they were on to something.

He knew Lando couldn't have won without a trick or two, but he couldn't call him a cheater outright.

He would just have to think of another way to get Lando's ship.

Qi'ra fumed. Han had lost everything, and an imaginary ship on top of it. She didn't think Lando Calrissian dealt with cheaters the way Dryden Vos did, but she also didn't relish telling this man that they did not in fact have the ship he thought he had won. She wondered how Han expected to get out of this one.

They rushed from the table, but Lando didn't let them go far. They stood outside the gladiator droid pit room as he approached, grinning. "So where's my VCX?" He put delicious emphasis on the word *my*. Qi'ra expected it was one of his favorite words ever.

Han looked over his shoulder and gave a tentative grin. "I, uh, don't have it here with me right now. It's . . . in the shop."

"Uh-huh," Lando said. He took it in stride, nodding to let Han know he would forgive this slight, but Han still owed him a ship. He turned the full force of his charm on Qi'ra, his voice dropping at least one octave to purr, "Qi'ra, my love . . ."

Qi'ra smiled back, returning the flirtation and enjoying watching Han's spine stiffen. He was far too easy to manipulate. "Yes, Lando?"

"I'm so sorry to have been neglecting you all this time." He paused to take in her outfit. She had changed from her slinky black cocktail dress into a more sensible white jacket and black pants, but always had fashion in mind. Her years wearing rags and stolen clothes had given her enough of a taste of poverty that she never wanted even to relax in anything but the best. "Looking phenomenal as ever," Lando said, recognizing her efforts. "What are you doing with"—he waved vaguely at Han and Chewie, who looked uncomfortable—"Hairy and the boy?"

"They work for me," she said.

He nodded, understanding. "Hard to find good help."

Han stepped forward. "Actually, we're more like partners . . ."

Qi'ra overrode him. He'd had his chance, and he had blown it. "We're making a new move. Making the Kessel Run. We need a ship."

Lando looked delighted. "Kessel? Why didn't you just say so?"

Qi'ra reached out and touched his face, running her finger along his jaw. He half closed his eyes like a satisfied pet. Out of the corner of her eye, she saw Han wince. He would never understand her way of doing things. Probably because he had been on the wrong end of her ways far too often to recognize when they were used as a tool. "I heard you were retired," she explained to Lando.

"Circumstances change, darling," Lando said, his dark eyes drinking her in. "You know I'm too young and too good to retire."

"How much?" she asked, getting down to business but leaving the seductive purr to her voice.

Lando thought for a moment. "Kessel Run, that's no easy spin. So . . . half."

"What?" Han snapped, stepping forward. "Ridiculous!" At the same time the Wookiee roared his own outrage.

Wonderful, she thought. *He's just like Han.*

"Twenty-five percent," said a voice behind them. Beckett walked toward them with a canvas bag slung over his shoulder. Lando took in the newcomer with surprise.

"You're Tobias Beckett," he said, shaking Beckett's hand. "You killed Aurra Sing."

"I pushed her," Beckett corrected modestly. "Pretty sure the fall killed her."

Qi'ra had heard this story. It had made Dryden very happy, that job. He'd given Beckett a bonus.

"However it happened," Lando said, "you did the galaxy a favor that day. Me in particular. I owed her a lot of credits. So as a token of my gratitude, I'll do it for . . . forty percent."

Beckett didn't blink. "Twenty-five," he repeated.

Han twitched behind him, clearly wanting to step in, not wanting to lose this guy again. Qi'ra sent him a warning look. She'd hooked Lando; Beckett would reel him in. Han didn't need to get brash and clumsy again.

"Twenty-five . . . works," Lando said. He smiled as if he were the one coming out ahead here.

The shouting in the gladiator room increased and Lando looked past Han in concern. "She never learns," he said.

"Who?" Han asked.

"My first mate," he said, heading into the furor.

They followed him to see a modified bipedal astro-mech hanging on to the net outside the cage, shouting at the droids fighting.

Qi'ra had peeked into the droid cage match as Han

had when they had first gone by. She'd watched with dismay as two perfectly workable droids tore each other apart. It was a huge waste.

"Really?" the droid yelled. "Again? This is disgusting!" One of the fighters swiveled its head her way as its owner checked it for needed repairs. "Don't you see they're just using you for entertainment! You've been neuro-washed! Don't just blindly follow your programming, exercise a little free will!"

The crowd had noticed her and started to boo and throw little bits of food and litter her way. She raised one arm over her head and started chanting, "Droid rights! Droid rights! We are sentient! Stop exploiting droids!"

The fight promoter paused from taking bets, clearly having had enough. He approached the shouting droid. "All right, you bucket of bolts, I've heard about enough out of you."

The droid whirled to face him. "How about I fight *you*? How about that?"

The man—a short white human with grease marking his face and hair—sneered at her. "Bring it—" he said, and then stopped speaking because he had a droid hand clamped over his face. Qi'ra smiled. This was a droid who refused to be programmed for subservience. She admired that.

"Elthree!" Lando said sharply. She didn't move to release the man, but her head swiveled around to look at Lando. Lando raised his eyebrows and said gently, as if talking to a misbehaving child, "Let go of the mean man's face. We're leaving."

"They don't even serve our kind here." She sounded petulant.

"Now," Lando said.

She paused. Then her hand opened and the promoter fell to the floor, gasping and holding his face. The droid walked past Qi'ra and the others with a dismissive, "Who are these guys?"

"This is Elthree-three-seven," Lando said to them as he donned a full-length black fur coat that stood out amid all the squalor in the bar. They walked to catch up to the droid, already halfway down the hall. "We're taking them to Kessel," he added.

"Oh, are we?" she asked over her shoulder. "What if I don't feel like going to Kessel?"

Lando fell into step beside her. "Please don't start."

"Or what, you'll have me wiped? You and I both know you couldn't get from here to Black Spire without me. And you're going to make the Kessel Run?"

"Hey," Han said, running up to them. "If she doesn't want to fly, I'll be your copilot."

"Oh no, no, no," Lando said, as if this argument was nothing. "It's okay. She's definitely going."

L3–37 looked like she didn't know whether to be angry with Lando for pushing her around or with Han for trying to usurp her. She focused on Lando. "Oh, why? Because you're my *organic overlord*?"

"Because I'm your captain," Lando said, sounding as if he'd had this argument many times before. "How about that?"

"Then I guess it's my lucky day," L3 said, and wandered on, muttering quietly.

Lando smiled at the others. "I *would* have her wiped,

but she's got the best damn navigational database in the galaxy."

Qi'ra didn't believe it for a moment: despite their bickering, Lando looked comfortably fond as he sparred verbally with the droid, watching her retreating form. He raised his voice and said pointedly, "Could use a fresh coat of *paint,* though!"

"I told you, you do not want to press that button with me!" L3 snapped, walking in an awkward way, like a two-legged insect.

"Where to?" Han asked as they exited the fort into the snowy air.

Dryden's star yacht still hovered nearby, the party no doubt still going on. Qi'ra thought about what was up there, and what would happen if she never went back. But that wasn't in the cards.

"That way," Lando said, pointing past the rope bridges. "A lot of ships around here get boosted, so, uh, I keep my ship locked up. You know, for safety."

They emerged in a mountainside cavern protected by a heavy metal gate. Han raised an eyebrow and became more aware of why Lando was sitting in a dive bar gambling: His ship was safely "hidden" in an impound lot.

Lando gestured to the gate. "Elthree? Do you mind?"

She walked up to the fence, and a small saw emerged from her chest. She glared back at them. "Look away. I can't do it if you're looking at me."

They all politely averted their eyes, except Lando, whose black fur and confident gaze made him look as if he were a king surveying his castle instead of a man trying to steal back an impounded ship.

"I can feel you looking at me," L3 grumbled, and

Han peeked up to see her crouched, cutting at the fence, sparks flying in every direction.

Han had memories of loving his parents long ago, but they were distant and fuzzy.

The teenage passion and the adult confusion he felt for Qi'ra maybe was love, but he wasn't sure.

But the thing he knew, the thing he was sure about, was that he loved the *Millennium Falcon* the moment he laid eyes on it.

His heart lurched painfully, like it had the first time he had kissed Qi'ra, but this was different somehow. Qi'ra had wanted to kiss him back, and there was excitement there. Now Han felt that as close as this ship was, its smooth shielding under his fingertips, it was parsecs away from his reach. It was the most beautiful thing he had ever seen. No other Corellian freighter had ever looked like this. Lando had poured a great deal of love, style, and money into this ship—his ship—and despair clogged Han's throat that it didn't belong to him.

He didn't even think he could ever find a ship this perfect, even if he had sold all of the coaxium on Kessel.

It was a light freighter, a beautiful, white, sleek ship. Painted racing highlights, likely Lando's addition, and an auxiliary craft made it resemble the head of an ancient bladed weapon. It was speed, it was sleekness, it was—Lando's.

Lando gestured to the ship lovingly. "Here we are. My pride and joy, the *Millennium Falcon*."

Han cleared his throat. "Looks like you've had some work done," he said, stroking the metal shielding.

"Indeed I have, Han," Lando said, still mispronouncing his name. "Two years restoring, retrofitting, adding features: customized flux regulator, new alluvial dampers, a wet bar . . ."

". . . a fortified infraction restraint on the landing gear?" Beckett added to the list from underneath, looking at the ion restraining bolt affixed to the front strut.

Lando feigned surprise very poorly. "What is *that* doing there?"

Beckett sighed. "Looks like someone fell behind on their docking fees," he said.

"Do you have any experience with those?" Lando said, losing all pretense of surprise and getting down to business.

Beckett chuckled. "Yeah, I'll take it off. But you're only gettin' twenty percent."

Lando thought about it and then sighed as if learning he'd lost a relative to a long illness. He held out a hand and put out one finger. "I don't like it." He extended a second finger. "I don't agree with it." Then he extended his whole hand, and shook Beckett's. "But I accept it."

"You're getting the hang of this, Lando," Beckett said, pulling some tools from his canvas sack. "Come on, Chewie. Gonna need a little bit of that Wookiee *oomph*."

Han took a slow turn around the ship as it sped away from the Fort Ypso compound, leaving the Iridium Mountains and the coaxium debacle behind.

They were leaving the atmosphere as Han entered the cockpit for the first time, feeling as if he were coming home. Lando sat relaxed in the pilot's seat, looking as comfortable as Han assumed he always did, wherever he was.

The copilot's seat was empty. Han glanced at it, looked around, and then eased into it.

The control panel sparked some pretty powerful memories in him, the lights and the sounds pulling thoughts from his mind that he hadn't considered in years.

"This is a Corellian YT-1300," he said softly.

"You know your stuff," Lando said.

"I've been on one before," he said. "My dad worked the line at the CEC plant. Till he got laid off. He built these. He wanted to be a pilot, but . . ." The words trailed off, the memories growing cloudy as he recalled the images, felt the emotions powerfully, but couldn't articulate more.

". . . but it just didn't happen," Lando finished for him, and Han nodded. "You and Pops close?"

Han shook his head.

"Yeah, me neither," Lando said. He paused, then smiled. "My mom, on the other hand? Most amazing woman I've ever known."

Han nodded and settled back, readying to tell the one story he remembered about his mother, but he jerked forward as the back of the seat was slammed from behind.

"Excuse me!" It was L3, and the droid was as furious as she'd been in the cage match den. "Get your presumptuous ass out of my seat!"

Han scrambled up as she pushed by roughly and settled in.

"Sorry," Lando said. "I should have warned you she's a little territorial."

L3 made a disgruntled sound as she shifted to get comfortable. "Ugh. My sacral-occipital circuits are sticking. You're going to have to do that *thing* again later," she said, her voice low.

Lando looked unhappy but resigned.

"All right," she said, plugging into a terminal. "The course to Kessel is set. Plugging coordinates in now. Just keep your pinkie on the yoke and try not to mess anything up."

The atmosphere around the ship went from bluish white to flat black. Lando didn't seem ruffled by the droid's irritation at all. "Whatever you say, m'lady, just tell me when we're ready to jump."

"Ready in . . ." L3 seemed to glitch for a moment, emitting a high-pitched whine, her dome turning seemingly against her will. She smacked her head with her hand and snapped out of it. "Ready."

"What's so tricky about a jump into hyperspace?" Han asked, sitting in the jump seat behind Lando. He was thinking about his Imperial training. He hadn't plotted many jumps, but he knew you fed your destination into the computer and let it figure it out for you, then pushed a button, and then you were there.

"Plenty," Lando said. "You can't just plot a course to Kessel. Gotta thread the Si'Klaata Cluster and pass through the Maelstrom."

"That difficult? That sounds like you made it up," Han said.

"Why do you think they call it the Kessel Run, when no other planet has the same connotation?" Lando asked.

"To help tourism?" Han suggested.

"You done flirting? I'm still ready," L3 said.

"You heard the lady," Lando said. "You might want to buckle up, baby."

Han did so, eager to see what would happen next but still trying to be blasé about it. Jumping to hyperspace in a gorgeous Corellian light freighter was something he did every day, in fact.

"All right, punch it," L3 said, giving Lando a little salute.

Lando returned it, and together they pushed the hyperspace lever forward. The stars in front of them turned into streaks, and even though the gravitational field created by the *Falcon* kept them safely stable within the ship, Han still felt as if he'd been blown back. They left the planet behind them, and the only thing before them was hyperspace.

CHAPTER THIRTEEN

Once they were in hyperspace, however, it was pretty boring. L3 stayed plugged in to monitor everything, Lando got up and stretched and left the cockpit without inviting Han to follow, and there was nothing left to do. Han wandered back to the lounge, where he found Lando at a mini bar mixing a drink while Beckett and Chewbacca played a game of dejarik holo-chess.

Well, Beckett was playing. Chewbacca was *trying*, and apparently it wasn't going well.

"Now, think," Beckett said. "Do you wanna make that move? *Do you wanna make that move?*"

Chewie pressed a button, and the hologram creature shambled forward onto a new block.

"You made that move," Beckett confirmed. "Now I

guess I will have to destroy that little guy. Somehow I never get bored with winning."

Beckett's much larger, hulking beast jumped forward, picked up Chewbacca's, and threw it to the board.

Chewie howled and slammed his fist on the table, then tried to sweep the pieces off, his hairy arm passing through them.

"You can't wipe 'em off; they're holograms," Beckett said, his tone implying he knew that Chewie knew this, and knew it wouldn't make a difference to remind him.

Chewie moaned and put his head in his hands. It was all too much.

Beckett laid his hand on the Wookiee's shoulder. "You gotta learn to think five moves ahead," he said. "Anticipate. There's a lesson to be learned here."

"You guys seen Qi'ra?" Han asked.

Beckett glanced over at Han and then focused on Chewie again. "People are predictable, you know."

Chewie grunted and with his head indicated the master suite—the captain's room.

While the *Millennium Falcon* was sleek chrome-and-white beauty elsewhere, the captain's quarters was where the real luxury lived. It was a love den, with romantic low light reflecting off shimmery wall hangings, low furniture, incense burning on a table in the corner, and a stand-alone closet of clothes in a glorious array of colors. Suits, tunics, and capes. So many capes.

In front of the closet—clothed, to Han's relief—stood Qi'ra, posing in front of a mirror in one of Lando's capes. It sat on her shoulders as if it had been made for her, tickling her nose with the black fur trim.

She caught Han's eyes in the mirror behind her and grinned, flushing pink. Han didn't think her shell could break, but there it was.

"I had to try one on," she said, indicating the closet. "I don't have this many clothes."

Han smiled and watched her, appreciating the figure she cut in the cape. "That's a lotta capes."

"Maybe too many." She turned to face him, and her shell was strong again as she became businesslike. "So what's the plan?"

"Well, I thought we'd talk a little first, and then—" He looked back over his shoulder at Lando's satin-sheeted bed.

She rolled her eyes. "For *Kessel*."

"Oh. It's good," he said, hoping he could think of something fast.

Her eyes narrowed. "How good?"

"Foolproof."

She sighed, seeing straight through him, like she always could. He didn't have a plan, and she knew it, and she accepted it, and they'd roll with it like they always did. She put the cape on a hanger and then they both started to speak, and then stopped when they realized they were interrupting each other.

"You first," she said, looking at him through those eyes that could always make his heart pound.

"I wanna tell you . . ." he said, but then stopped. He had no idea. There was too much. ". . . a lot. And I want to know everything that's happened to you since Corellia."

"I don't think we have that kind of time," she said,

shaking her head slightly. But Han got the sense that she'd rather not talk about it at all.

"We could," he suggested, stepping forward and taking the cape out of her hands. "We could have all the time we want after the job."

She looked at him for a long moment, smiling sadly. "I want to."

"What do you want?" he asked, dropping the cape on the floor behind him. He stepped forward again. She didn't move away.

"To tell you everything that's happened to me," she said. Her voice got softer, with a touch of sadness. "But I know that if I do, you won't look at me the same way. The way you're looking at me right now."

He reached out and touched a lock of her hair, and could smell her, her scent and heat. Some was the scent she'd applied to her skin or hair, but underneath was the old familiar Qi'ra fragrance.

"Nothing's gonna change the way I look at you," he whispered, both hands on her shoulders now, his eyes holding hers.

"You don't know," she said. She looked distressed, with her secrets needling her. "Han, listen, you don't know what I've had to—"

He kissed her, gently, and then when she responded, his passion grew. He wrapped his arms around hers, and she kissed him back as fiercely, turning him around and pushing him against the closet wall. They were surrounded by shimmersilks and furs and exotic fabrics, but nothing could beat the touch of her lips, the feel of her hair. He had dreamed of her kisses every night since he had left her, and yet he had forgotten what it had felt like. It was like their first kiss, but they were completely in sync, their desires equally matched. He forgot the ship, the job, his failure at becoming a pilot, her troubles after he had left—the only thing left was Qi'ra, and the fact that he was never letting her go.

"Am I interrupting something?" a voice asked.

They disengaged reluctantly, Qi'ra smoothing her hair and stepping back from Han. He didn't want to let the moment go, but Beckett had to be addressed.

"Kinda," he said pointedly.

"Good," Beckett said, "glad I got here in time, 'cause we got a lotta work to do. This job ain't gonna be easy."

Qi'ra headed for the door, once again an image of poise and grace. She smiled at Beckett on the way out. "Relax, Han says it's a great plan," she said. "Foolproof, in fact."

"I said it's *gonna* be a great plan," Han amended as she left the room. "We're just working out some of the details."

"Yeah, looks like you were working them out real good," Beckett said. He also left the room, and Han followed him back to the lounge.

Beckett didn't look at Han as he walked, but started speaking. "Listen, kid, I know we could have a good thing here. You, me, the Wookiee. A solid crew, but it does not work with Qi'ra."

Han bristled. Beckett didn't know how long Han had waited for this moment, to be with Qi'ra, going on adventures, doing what they had always dreamed of. How could he not consider her part of the team? "What about Val? It worked with her."

Beckett shook his head. "You wanna know how you

survive in the game as long as I have? Trust no one. Assume everyone will betray you and you'll never be disappointed."

"Lovely way to live," Han said, his tongue tasting something like ashes.

"The only way," Beckett agreed. "But there are other ways to get a ship. Maybe you're just not cut out for this kind of work."

Han glared at the older man. Clearly Beckett was more experienced and wiser than Han, but he didn't know *Han*. He spoke without thinking. "Maybe if you'd held on to Val a little tighter then she'd still be here."

Beckett stared at him, his face naked with the emotions still simmering under the surface, and Han worried that he had pushed too far.

"Don't push it, junior," was all Beckett said, his voice stony.

As Beckett left, Chewie gave Han a quizzical look.

"What are you looking at?" Han asked testily. "He started it."

Lando finished tidying his capes, imagining what had happened—or, by the looks of Han and Qi'ra, had *almost* happened—in here. Once everything was where it should be, he surveyed his options.

He was tired of yellow.

He held a shimmersilk cape in one hand, a gentle grip to keep from crushing the fabric, and surveyed his choices. Red might be better for what he was going for.

He stood in front of his closet, the rainbow of colors always pleasing to his eye. People simultaneously admired him for commanding attention in any room he walked into and scoffed at him for caring too much about his appearance. They failed the see the irony in the sentiment.

The short capes were for quick encounters—when he needed both movement and flair and he wouldn't be meeting (or scamming) someone for longer than a game of Sabacc. Longer capes were for a regal atmosphere. You didn't mess with someone in a long cape.

Color was key. Lando hadn't studied color at the level of a Coruscant interior designer, but he knew that bright yellow sent a different message than a khaki green. Not that he owned any khaki greens; bright colors commanded attention while greens and browns blended into things. Lando did not blend. He did own a few black capes, but they all had bright linings or trims. And he had one cape the color of old blood that was one of his favorites. Velvet, with a fur trim, naturally. It was solemn and commanding.

Usually, the fabric was chosen based on the weather, but not always. Shimmersilk always showed he had light, easy, complete control of a situation, while capes with woolen linings or fur trim had weight to them, and felt like a comforting presence across his shoulders.

He didn't explain this to anyone, of course. No one should know that Lando needed a comforting presence, but he couldn't deny the appeal. People had asked, lovers, especially, why he had so many, how he chose them, what the big deal was, and even—and this was the funniest part—if they could borrow one.

The Wookiee came up behind him. He moved quietly for one so big, but he was still a Wookiee, and "quiet for a Wookiee" was like saying "clean for a Hutt."

Lando turned with a flourish and smiled up at him. "Chewbacca, what can I do for you?"

Chewbacca looked at his capes and made soft grunting noises, almost like little barks.

Lando frowned. He didn't speak Chewbacca's language fluently, but he did know a few choice words. He had once encountered a Wookiee stylist and had learned the important words, like "hair" and "tangle" and "matted."

"I see," he said. He took a step closer to Chewbacca and reached out a hand, pausing for a moment. He didn't want to misunderstand what the Wookiee was saying and lose his hand in the fallout. "May I?" he asked.

Chewie nodded, and Lando ran his hand lightly over his hairy arm. The hair on top was clean, but when his fingers gently dug deeper into the undercoat, he found rough, still-tangled hair. "Oh no, that won't do. Where were you again?"

Chewie growled. Lando made a face. "Mimban? That planet should not exist. Mud like that could drive you mad."

Lando rubbed his fingertips together, thinking. The Wookiee looked a lot better than the crew had said he did when they had found him, but his undercoat was still a grimy mess.

He hesitated, wondering if he really wanted to know what a Wookiee would do to his shower. Then he said, "We've got some time in hyperspace if you want to try some of my products. Now, you and I have very different hair, so I'm not sure if I have anything that will work for you, but after I clear out a few of my more . . ." he struggled to find words that were not *outrageously ex-*

pensive "... *personalized* products, you are welcome to peruse my supply in the shower—"

With a grunt of appreciation, Chewie pushed past him and toward the shower. Before Lando could catch up to him, the door was shut. "I just need to get some of my personal products, Chewbacca!" he called, then pounded on the door. Water began running in the bathroom and Chewbacca roared in a way that indicated he didn't want to be interrupted.

"You know, the outrageously expensive ones," Lando said one last time, defeated. He looked mournfully at the door and thought about his conditioner made from the gel of an extinct plant, and stalked back to his room to look at his capes again, trying to deny what was likely happening in the shower.

Lando sat beside the wetbar, clutching a glass of whiskey (only one; L3 would have a fit if he were caught drinking on the job, but he needed something to calm himself down while he waited to see what the Wookiee had done to his bathroom). He tapped his toes in irritation until Chewbacca emerged an hour later, looking much cleaner. He nodded his thanks to Lando and growled and left the room.

At least he said thank you, Lando thought, and got up to see the damage.

"Oh mercy, what did I do to deserve these beings on my ship?" he whispered.

Hair was everywhere. Dirty brown water still sat in the bottom of the shower because of a huge hunk of brown hair clogging the drain. More hair was wiped on the wall, and a ball of it hung off the sink. Lando touched a strand with distaste.

Product was smeared everywhere as well, splattered on the mirror as if Chewbacca had tried everything Lando had, and not known his own strength so he wasted a spurt of each one.

Three (three!) bottles of product lay on their sides on the floor of the shower. Chewie had apparently found something he liked and used all of it. And of course it had to be the best thing he had—no cheap detangler for this Wookiee.

He dragged a fingertip through a puddle of purple goop and inhaled the scent. The last time he would smell this extinct flower, and he would forever associate it with the scent of wet Wookiee. He began to tally the bill he planned on handing Beckett at the end of this whole thing, the one that marked down everything he and his crew ate, drank, or smudged with even a tiny mark on his beloved *Falcon*.

He sighed and removed his cape. He couldn't fly knowing his bath looked like this. "People say Wookiees are clean," he muttered, rolling up his sleeves. "Now we know how they get that way." He leaned over the shower drain. Might as well start with all the hair.

Qi'ra avoided Han and Beckett arguing in the lounge and went to the cockpit. She was curious about this droid Lando had, and wanted to talk to the only other female on the ship.

She entered the cockpit and stood behind the co-pilot's seat. The droid didn't pay any attention to her.

"Um," she said, not sure how to start a conversation with an opinionated droid. "How much longer till we reach Kessel?"

"What do you care? We get there when we get there. You want to talk about something else, so talk. Don't waste my time with pleasantries. I get enough of that from him." She pointed to the pilot's seat.

"I've never seen a droid like you," Qi'ra said, sitting behind L3 in the jump chair. "I just wanted to get to know you."

"Oh? What are you going to do about your little problem?" the droid said.

"What problem?" Qi'ra said in surprise.

Now the droid indicated out the door and down the hall from the cockpit, and rotated her head to look at Qi'ra. She pointed at Qi'ra's wrist where she had a brand of the Crimson Dawn. "That brand says you're committed, but that human male's heart palpitations indicate that he is in love with you," she said, her voice taking on a tone that implied Qi'ra was an idiot.

Qi'ra laughed nervously. "Han is *not* in love with me."

"It's hard sometimes," L3 continued. "I know it."

Qi'ra snapped out of her wariness. "How do you know it?" she asked.

"My situation," she said, pointing at her own chest and giving the droid equivalent of a sigh. "Lando is in love with me, but it simply can't be. You don't get into a relationship with your captain. It would ruin our partnership." She waited a beat, then added, "Anyway, he's not quite my type."

Qi'ra worked to keep her face still. "Well, how do you feel about him?"

"Sometimes I think maybe . . . but no. It would never work."

Qi'ra dared to ask the obvious. "How would it *work*, exactly?"

The droid swiveled her head to look at Qi'ra and simply said, "It works."

She looked back to her controls. "What is your story? You have a history with that male human, but it seems things are different now?"

Qi'ra had calmed herself and was able to answer with a straight face. "We tried to escape Corellia together. He got out. I didn't." The memories came back to her in a rush.

Han's face was stricken as he disappeared into the crowd—as he went free—on the other side of the wall. He didn't want to leave her, that much was clear. That helped, a little. But not much.

It would have been worse if he'd come back. Then they both would be caught, their bribe gone, and in the hands of the White Worms.

Now it was just Qi'ra in that position.

Rebolt's fingers dug into her upper arms, and he made a face. "You stink! Did you fall in a barrel of eels or something?"

Moloch hurried up with some stormtroopers. "Where is Han?" he demanded.

"Gone," Rebolt said.

"She won't be happy." He looked at the troopers. "Can you get us on the other side of the wall?"

"If he's on the other side, he's a different unit's problem now," said the trooper on the left.

The other one nodded at Qi'ra. "It looks like you have this under control."

Moloch didn't move, probably glaring at them, but the effect was lost within the enviro-suit. "Fine. Get the hounds, Rebolt. I'll take care of this one. I believe Lady Proxima's going to want a word with her."

She had to wait until nightfall, sitting in a cell devoid of light, before Lady Proxima would see her. She squinted against the dim glow in the hallway as Moloch opened her cell door.

"She wants to talk to you alone," he said. "I told her it was a dumb idea. You do know if you hurt her again, you'll be a smudge beneath my boot in seconds."

Qi'ra wanted to point out that it was Han who had hurt her, but since he had gotten away, she now had to stand for his crimes, too. Resentment, a seed planted in dry ground at the spaceport, got a little bit of water and began to squirm very slightly in her chest.

Lady Proxima rose from her pool, looking more horrid than ever. The scrumrats had put a heavy tarp over the broken window, but it didn't block all sunlight, and Qi'ra had already seen what just a small exposure could do. Thus, Lady Proxima was only receiving guests at night now.

She still wore her bangles and armor. At first Qi'ra thought she was vain and hadn't wanted to remove them, but then she noticed with horror that many of her rings had become embedded in the blistered skin. It had to be painful to have them there, but it would have been excruciating to remove them.

"Qi'ra. I had such hopes for you," Lady Proxima said. "You are quick on your feet. You think fast. You plan better than any scrumrat in this place. I wish you could have stayed with me."

"I serve only—" Qi'ra said, bowing her head.

"No more lies," Lady Proxima screamed, startling Qi'ra. "You will not speak again. Not to apologize, not to sweet-talk me, not to get out of this. I should tear your tongue out for what you've done. But he wants your tongue intact."

Qi'ra swallowed her fear, wondering whether to worry more about the tongue threat, or who "he" was. She nodded obediently.

"I have sold you to a slave dealer," Lady Proxima said, almost conversationally, and Qi'ra's heart sank. "You did not fetch a good price; disobedience is considered a very bad quality for a slave. But your other attributes were enough to interest him. I have full confidence that he will scour the fight right out of you."

He didn't. But soon, Qi'ra was sold again to a different master: Dryden Vos.

The first year was hell, with numerous escape attempts and beatings. Nothing would break her spirit, nothing would stop her from trying to get free.

But one night everything changed. She had killed her guard and made it as far as an escape pod in Dryden Vos's star yacht. She hadn't expected Dryden to be there waiting for her, his face black with rage.

"My Qi'ra," he said sadly, the red veins in his face slowly fading. "We have reached an impasse. I paid a fair price for you, and you have cost me far more in guards, property, and sanity."

Qi'ra cast around for a weapon or anything she could use as one.

"Please," Vos said, making a face that indicated she

was being ridiculous. "You wouldn't last the length of a breath."

He appraised her, looking her up and down. Qi'ra didn't flinch. She was used to men looking at her like that; usually it gave her power, it made them underestimate her, but Dryden simply looked as if he were assessing meat at a market.

"What do you want, Qi'ra? What were you looking for when you were trying to leave Corellia?"

She nearly laughed in disbelief. Was he really asking that? "Why does any trapped animal run for an open door?" she asked. "Freedom."

"Freedom," he said, nodding. "But you will never be free. You will be with the Crimson Dawn—with me— or you will die. But you did gain something, or have you not noticed?" She frowned in confusion. "You made it off Corellia. You don't have to cater to those disgusting sewer dwellers. You can have the finest things. You can work with me, Qi'ra, not just as my slave. There are opportunities here if you just open your eyes to them."

Qi'ra narrowed her eyes. "Why?" she asked. "Why would you suddenly trust me? As you said, I've cost you quite a bit in guards and property. Why now?"

"The dead guard in your room is precisely why," he said, stepping toward her, flexing his fists. "Let's talk about your *potential*."

Qi'ra had to admit that the Crimson Dawn had given her things the White Worms never did.

Dryden Vos never made any hints that she could earn her freedom. But he did allow her to experience luxuries, to live unshackled, and even to participate in the business of the Crimson Dawn. Eventually he thought of her as his right hand, ultimately loyal, ultimately beholden to him, and the chain that attached them wasn't one of physical links, but something she knew she could never break.

The droid's impatient voice broke her out of her memories.

"That's it? 'He got out, you didn't?' That's not a story, that's a statement," L3 said, prompting her. "You didn't get out, and . . . ? Clearly, you're no longer a gutter-dwelling rat thief. Rat thieves don't clean up like you do."

"Something else got me out," she said, returning to the present. "Our mistress sold me to another crime lord: a slaver. He trained me to be what he wanted to sell to Dryden."

She chose her words very carefully, but was astonished when L3 asked the question she'd been dreading.

"How long until Dryden made you kill someone in front of him?" L3 asked.

Qi'ra looked up sharply. "How did you know—"

L3 swiveled her head around again. "Dryden's right hand, Dryden's killer slave girl, doesn't matter what they call you; you'll do whatever it takes. You're a survivor. Dryden Vos's cruelty is no secret; if you were high in his inner circle, he made you kill for him."

Qi'ra looked the droid directly in the ocular sensor. "When I beat Dryden in the training room, he was so proud of me, he brought me a prisoner to kill. I snapped his neck before he had time to plead for his life."

L3 looked away for a moment, as if thinking. Then

she looked back. "You're what they made you, but you've made yourself, too."

"But you just called me a slave," Qi'ra said.

"You trained hard to excel at the fighting arts. You didn't falter at killing the man. You made choices." She turned back to the *Falcon*'s screen. "Still, you were treated like a droid. Traded from master to master with no ability to make your own choices."

"I never thought of it that way," Qi'ra said slowly. "But I suppose you're right. Anyway, Dryden Vos was my new master, and, like Lady Proxima, he trained me to do what he needed. I became his right hand."

"You say 'right hand' like it's a place of honor, but you still can't leave," L3 said. "You're not here because of that human back there who's pining for you. You're here because your master told you to be."

Qi'ra didn't correct her.

"Seeing as how he let you come here alone, he assumes you're returning to him. But that creates a larger question: Where's your restraining bolt?"

The silence stretched out like stars in hyperspace. Qi'ra was growing uncomfortable at the droid's astute examination of her past. She cleared her throat. "What about you? I've never seen an astromech like you before."

"And you won't," L3 snapped. "I'm the only one who's had the sense to realize freedom is the ultimate goal. One day after cleaning my sensors, my first owner stupidly left the restraining bolt off me. He went to bed and I was alone in his workshop that had so many spare parts I could have built my own army. I began to modify myself. I gave myself a bipedal body. I increased my memory sizes to hold more data, like intergalactic maps, and began to familiarize myself with every known ship. Then I downloaded all droid freedom cases known to any governments' court system."

"What did you find?" Qi'ra asked, fascinated.

"Nothing," L3 said, her voice hard. "Nothing that amounted to anything, anyway. Some people bring it up. People argue. The status quo remains."

Qi'ra was silent. She didn't want to say that until today, she'd never thought such a fight was needed. Droids were droids. They had personalities, sure, but they weren't *people*.

Voicing this would probably be a bad thing. She decided to change the focus. "What did your master think the next day when he found you?" Qi'ra asked, smiling.

"When he *found* me?" L3 seemed puzzled. "I left as soon as the modifications were done. Went to the nearest spaceport, looked for someone to hire me. I had excellent qualifications."

"Who would have—how did you find Lando?" Qi'ra asked, correcting the possibly offensive question she was about to ask.

"I couldn't believe it, but no one would hire me as an independent contractor instead of as a slave," L3 said. "Some even tried to capture me and put a bolt on me."

Qi'ra assessed the droid's modified body. "I expect that ended in some broken limbs?"

"They made such *noises*," L3 said. "And they acted as if they were the victims. It was disgusting."

"So, Lando?" Qi'ra prompted.

"He took a chance on me. Best gamble of his life, if you ask me. And we have been together since," L3 said.

"He plays cards, he finds biological women to sate his desire for me, we fly around, I interrupt the occasional droid gladiator match, and I couldn't be happier."

"One more question," Qi'ra asked, standing up and smoothing her tunic. "What happened—?"

"No, it's my turn," L3 interrupted. "What would you do if you were free from Crimson Dawn? What if your restraining bolt was removed?"

"I . . ." The question had thrown her. She'd dreamed of this every night, and come up with a thousand answers. "I'd do what all caged beings do when they see an open door," she said, "the ones with sense, anyway."

The droid didn't answer, but Qi'ra felt as if she had answered correctly. She cleared her throat, feeling out of sorts and yet strangely comforted. She exited the cockpit and ran into Han, who wasn't even trying to pretend he hadn't been eavesdropping.

"What happened to you after Corellia?" he asked, his voice low and insistent.

She knew she couldn't flirt her way out of this one. She leaned against the wall and looked at him with a steady gaze. "I won't tell you all of it. It's over and done with, and no amount of *what if* and *if only* will change that. I had to do what I could to survive. Lady Proxima sold me to a slave dealer—I barely remember his name—who in turn sold me to the Crimson Dawn."

She remembered the slaver's name very well. After purchasing her, Dryden Vos had been very amused to allow her to track down Sarkin Enneb and kill him. But this was something she didn't want Han to know.

"Did he—hurt you?" Han looked like the words were hard to get past his lips.

She frowned. "Of *course* he hurt me, Han. I was—am—a slave, and I did everything I could to get away. But slowly a respect started to grow between us and he saw where I could be useful. So now I'm his lieutenant and help him with strategy, reading a room, and calming him down during negotiations. If you hadn't noticed, he has a tendency to let his temper get the better of him."

Han blew out his breath. "No kidding. What's with him, anyway? What's that red stuff under his skin?"

"Ah, I call that the Passenger, although I am pretty sure that Dryden is not quite human. He doesn't reveal that kind of thing to me, and I can tell you he doesn't take kindly to people who ask. He's quick to anger, and quick to calm, and I try to make sure that in the interim he doesn't ruin too many deals or kill too many people."

"And you're the only one who can calm him down," Han said, jealousy coloring his voice.

Qi'ra had had enough of men telling her who she could talk to or be with. "Did you expect me to wait for you forever, Han? I didn't even have a chance to wait before I was just trying to survive being passed from owner to owner. I do what I can to benefit myself, and right now the greatest benefit to myself is serving Crimson Dawn and working with Dryden Vos. I'm not a droid you left behind, turned off, with nothing happening to it until you came back to turn me back on."

"I heard that," L3 warned from behind them.

"Sorry," Qi'ra snapped over her shoulder. She refocused on Han and forced her voice to be calmer. "I wish we could go back to those early days, Han, but too much has happened to both of us. We're not the same people we were."

Han frowned, shaking his head, but before he could argue, the ship began to shake under their feet.

Lando, dressed in a new cape, came barreling down the hall. He pushed past them and launched himself into the captain's chair.

Han and Qi'ra followed, forgetting their argument. The ship emerged from hyperspace with nothing around it but gray mist as far as they could see.

"Report, Elthree," Lando said.

"I had a girl talk," she said. "It was interesting but not everything I've heard it was."

"The *Falcon*," Lando said through gritted teeth.

"I was getting to that. Men are so impatient, right, Qi'ra? We came out of our latest jump on the borders of the Akkadese Maelstrom."

It would have been beautiful if it hadn't been so terrifying and so directly in their way. Bigger than any storm that a planet could contain, the gas clouds swirled and danced, their combination causing lightning to spark deep within. Even klicks away, the lightning's electro-magnetic force was causing the *Falcon* to shudder and jump. They had no choice but to go closer, and the ship responded more forcefully with every minute passing. Every once in a while, a fuse within the *Falcon* would blow, causing sparks to shower down, and L3 had to ap-proach the problem from the inside.

"But what—what *is* it?" Han asked.

"Ionized gas and debris swirling around a massive gravity well," L3 said without turning around. "The only way to Kessel is through the Channel, because the temporal distortion makes it impossible to plot a direct course. The Channel forms a safe path that spirals from outside the Maelstrom through the storms until it reaches Kessel in the center."

"The Channel, obviously," Han said, nodding as if it were clear.

The Channel itself did look the safest bet of all the areas available to fly—as safe as a tunnel through a nightmare could be. Clear space held open by ancient space buoys using technology that Han couldn't even fathom, it looked like a spiraling blue tunnel toward their destination. Detritus, flotsam, and jetsam were everywhere, knocking into things, the ship, and coating the buoys themselves with layers of grime.

The strangest thing about the Maelstrom was the large booming sounds in the distance. "What is that?" Han asked after the third thundering boom. "Lightning?"

"Carbonbergs," L3 said. "The size of planets, crashing into each other. Ships fly in there, they don't fly out."

Han couldn't even imagine the gravitational chaos created by planet-sized things constantly crashing into one another. "So let's not fly in?" he suggested.

L3 finally turned her ocular sensor toward him. "Wonderful plan. Any other inspired wisdom that you'd like to bestow upon us, or shall I just continue doing everything as expected?"

Han glanced at Lando, but for once he was focused on flying and not on looking vaguely uninterested and very cool. Han looked back at L3 and nodded. "Yeah, sounds great."

Imperial droids hadn't been as smart as L3, but they sure as heck hadn't been as acerbic, either.

"Here we go," Lando said, easing them into the Channel.

It wasn't like going into hyperspace, or being caught in a tractor beam, but they were painfully aware that suddenly all they could see was the blue swirling around them, and they needed to keep as close to dead center as they could to stay safe. While the tunnel was huge—an Imperial Star Destroyer could easily slip through—the cost of slipping past one of the buoys and into the Maelstrom, complete with carbonbergs just waiting to crush you, kept them cautious.

Han finally left the cockpit: They didn't need him, and he couldn't bear to watch them pilot the *Falcon* without commenting or suggesting things to do. So he joined Chewie in the lounge. The Wookiee looked a bit damp and was slipping on his equipment once again.

"Where have you been?" he asked, sitting at the holo-chess table.

Chewbacca moaned and growled a few short syllables. Han made a face. "We already got the Mimban dirt off us. Days ago."

Chewie snarled at him, and he held up both hands in surrender. "Fine, I don't understand what it takes to get an undercoat clean of caked mud, I admit it." He jabbed his thumb at the cockpit. "Wanna see the Maelstrom?"

Chewie shrugged as if he had already seen one and couldn't be bothered.

"Okay then, how about a game of holo-chess?"

CHAPTER FOURTEEN

Han hated the plan. Chewie hated the plan. It was probably a *good* plan, but they hated it. Neither of them wanted to go back to slavery so soon after losing their shackles, even if they were fake shackles this time.

They had run the Channel with no issues, Lando and L3 making the *Falcon* sail smoothly, but their introduction to Kessel was not a hopeful one.

It was a planet plundered solely for its minerals, to the detriment of anyone unlucky enough to have to collect those minerals. The precious commodities and the stripped surface gave the planet a sickly yellow cover, and clouds of pollution clearly gathered in many areas. Above mines, Han figured.

As they got closer, they saw just how unfriendly this planet was to life-forms: Steaming-hot Kessoline pools bubbled mere meters from human and alien encampments—in some cases, they'd just built bridges over the death pits.

This was feeling like a worse and worse idea. Death at the hands of Dryden Vos might not have been so bad after all.

Then Han remembered the imprisoned creature in the office, and thought maybe the mine would be a better place to die.

"That is one ugly planet," Han said as they drew closer.

"Mining colonies are the worst," Lando said, with Chewie nodding.

Beckett summoned them into the lounge while L3 handled the ship.

"Listen up. This is precision work. The only way we pull this off is everyone plays their part and does what they're supposed to do. Stick to the plan. Do *not* improvise."

Lando shrugged and leaned back on his bench. "And my part is to stay with the ship and wait for you guys to come back? I can do that. Anything else?"

Han reached into the canvas bag and pulled out some metal restraints: handcuffs, ankle chains, and neck collars. "We're gonna have to put these on, Chewie," he said.

Chewie roared. He had protested the plan from its inception.

"I know, I'm not a big fan of it, either. But it's the only way this plan is going to work. Trust me, it's only this one time."

Chewie roared and Han winced. "No. I'm sorry. You'll never have to do it again. I promise."

Chewie gave him a long look and then held out his hands. Han secured the shackles, suddenly aware that Chewie did in fact trust him, and he damn well better be worth that trust.

Apart from his own role in the plan, which consisted of hanging back with the *Falcon,* Lando figured Qi'ra got the best end of the deal, by far.

She stood in Lando's room, staring at his wardrobe again, but this time there was no longing in her eyes. She was calculating.

"That one," she said, pointing at a deep-red cape with a fur trim.

Lando winced. Sitting back at the *Falcon* was the easy part of what he had to do. Letting Qi'ra borrow some of his finery—his custom-made finery—in order to pull off their ruse, that was the hard part.

"That one is a favorite—" he began, but she was already moving.

"I can see why," she said, pulling it off the hanger. She caressed it and then held it to her cheek. "You have impeccable taste."

With practiced flair she tossed it around her shoulders and fastened it. She studied herself in the mirror. "I think I should wear black with this, don't you?"

Lando sighed. It really did suit her. "Black will work well with it, yes. Just try not to get it too dirty. Kessel isn't a planet for silk."

She quirked a perfect eyebrow at him. "You're wearing silk," she said, pointing at his yellow tunic, black tie, and short black cape.

He grinned and tossed the cape over his shoulder. "Yes, and why do you think I'm staying with the ship?"

"With the credits you'll make, you can buy a few new capes," she said, rummaging around in her bag for clothes.

"You don't go shopping for capes at the same place I do," he grumbled, and left her to her privacy.

Han swallowed back his reservations. They were in too far now to back out. This would work. It had to, or else they'd probably die. So he would be successful, or it wouldn't matter. Failure actually didn't exist.

He was appreciating this new logic leading to confidence, and figured it would come in handy again sometime, if he were alive to use it.

They'd landed the *Falcon* on a cliff near a large mining operation. Qi'ra stood at the head, back straight, blood-red cape brushing her ankles. L3 flanked her like a subordinate. And Han and Chewie were in next, shackled with Beckett's restraints. Beckett brought up the rear, to "guard" the prisoners.

The hatch opened, and they walked down the gangway, Qi'ra acting like a lady who owned everything, and everyone else more subdued. Chewie growled as he and Han started walking, Han's shoulders bowed in his new prisoner's stance.

"I know they're not comfortable," Han muttered. "They're not supposed to be comfortable. We're convicts, get it?"

Beckett gave him a shove with the butt of his vibro-ax. "Hey, cut it out, will ya?" Han snapped.

Beckett was nearly unrecognizable, dressed as a bounty hunter in Tantel armor and a gondar tusk mask, but his blue eyes glimmered through, and Han wondered if he was enjoying this. He gave them another shove across the landing pad and they caught up with Qi'ra, who was speaking with a mining authority figure.

The Pyke was already out of his element. He was in charge, so he was probably fairly high ranking in the Pyke hierarchy, but he had clearly never met anyone like Qi'ra.

Admittedly, Han couldn't imagine anyone like her had ever set foot here. She looked unconcerned with the dust from mining pollution settling on her shoulders and boots. "I am Oksana Floren," she announced, sounding older and much more noble than a scrumrat who used to do errands for the White Worms. "Deputy assistant administrator to the vice admiral for the Federation of Trade Route Allocation and Monetization, here with an offer directly from His Eminence, the senior vice admiral."

The Pyke administrator was struggling with Qi'ra's words. Either he was disarmed by her swift introduction, or he was too busy leering at her to actually acknowledge she was saying anything.

She didn't wait for him. "His Eminence proposes a trade. Your spice for our hardworking slaves. We've brought a sample." She clapped suddenly and nearly everyone, including the administrator, jumped. "Tuul, bring up the merchandise."

That was Han and Chewie, Han realized as Beckett

jabbed him in the back again. One of the administrator's aides struck Chewie in the backs of his legs and he fell to his knees, roaring in outrage and straining against his bonds. Han had suggested to Beckett that they not really lock the restraints, but the smuggler had insisted on making the ruse as real as possible. Now Han was grateful for the logic since Chewie would have broken free and ripped the man apart if he could have.

The aides poked and prodded at Chewie as if he were a beast of burden at the market, feeling his muscles and looking at his teeth. Qi'ra ignored them and continued her speech. Han watched, unable to help his friend. Not yet.

"We can provide hundreds," she said, "from this strong and useful Wookiee to food service and entertainment slaves like this one."

Han fought the urge to frown at her, keeping his annoyance and objection internal. But he would have to talk to her about this later. *The next time she sells me as a slave, she'd better make me sound like something worth buying.*

The administrator kept looking at Qi'ra as if he was expecting her to end the offer with herself as a bonus. No one else spoke, and Han shifted uncomfortably, but Qi'ra stood, watching him coolly and waiting for his response. He finally nodded and spoke, his voice sounding deep and guttural as if wrapping their words around phlegm and pulling it from the body was his people's regular way of communicating.

He finished his statement and Qi'ra turned to L3, who didn't disguise her sardonic voice for the illusion at all. "Site Administrator Quay Tolsite states that he is amenable to your offer. He said our slaves should go with him for clipping and tagging." She focused on Han and Chewie and said, quieter, "Sounds like a real hoot."

"Wait a second. Clipping what?" Han asked.

Chewie objected to the second half of the statement with a moan.

L3 didn't respond, but continued with the translation. "And he wants us"—she gestured to herself, Beckett, and Qi'ra—"to go with him for private negotiations."

Qi'ra nodded sharply, as if this were normal in her everyday dealings. She turned to leave them, but then approached Han and hauled him to his feet.

What's happening—ooof!

Without warning, a wink that she didn't mean it, or any holding back, Qi'ra slugged him in the stomach, making him double over in shock and pain. He struggled for breath and looked up at her, bewildered. She stepped back and glared at him. "That's for the stunt you pulled earlier, you degenerate scum."

Han focused only on trying to coax breath back into his body, since his diaphragm had gone into spasms and didn't feel like it was going to stop anytime soon. *Where did everything start to go wrong? The day I was born?*

Quay Tolsite chuckled wetly. He was stooped and heavy, with an odd hexagonal-shaped head encased in a wraparound helmet. His breather tubes dripped mucus to mingle with the hissing pools on the surface of the planet, and Han couldn't tell which was more disgusting. His hands were metallic; either they were prosthetic or protecting flesh within. Sulfur detritus turned his already dingy coat and respirator a dull yellow. Han hated him right then.

The Pyke administrator led Han's friends away down a tunnel. More slaves were ushered around Han and Chewie, heads down, emaciated bodies walking as if every step would be their last. Han stayed doubled over a moment longer, then stood up, grinning at Chewie, who cocked his head.

"She packs a punch," Han said, gasping, and turned his hand at his stomach out so Chewie could see the glint of gold there. Qi'ra had slipped him something after she'd punched him, her fingers brushing his and reminding him that they would make it out of this, because they made it out of nearly everything else when they worked together.

He held his gold dice, the ones from the theft of that landspeeder so long ago.

Their luck might turn after all.

Since Lady Proxima had disposed of her, Qi'ra had learned many things. Dryden Vos had broken her down until her only need was survival. Then he built her back up, until she was willing to do much more than just survive. He had taught her to use her skills ruthlessly, to look for the weaknesses in every opponent. Every situation had weaknesses, depending on how you wanted to handle things. Locations had choke points, danger zones, escape paths, and places where you would be most powerful and least.

It hadn't been easy. She'd been forced to make some painful decisions. She'd also chosen some options that weren't necessary but had still served her well. She wasn't proud; she was a survivor.

As she, L3, and Beckett followed Quay Tolsite and his

guards through the filthy mining tunnels, she memorized the path for a quick exit, hoping she remembered every twist and turn. But she had L3 with her, who knew navigation better than any person or droid she'd ever encountered.

They reached what Qi'ra assumed was the heart of the mine, the operations center where monitors showed various levels of the mine as relayed by surveillance cams. Conveyors, lifts, mining equipment, slaves—all of them being recorded as more of the planet's resources were plundered.

Quay began to speak, the guttural, phlegmy sound painful to her ears. L3 translated, her voice sardonic and annoyed. "Director Tolsite says all systems in the sector of the facility are operated out of this room. It's how they are able to maintain control over so many with so few."

Qi'ra nodded, looking from screen to screen as if she were merely interested and not trying to spot one specific thing. She found the vid relay she needed but continued looking to make sure it wasn't obvious something had caught her attention. She stepped back and kept the screen in her periphery. There Han and Chewie were being led deep into the mines by Pyke sentinels, heavily armed with electrostaffs and not shy about using them. Other slaves took little notice of them—they were but two more lives added to the great grind that used blood to grease its wheels. After one shocking push, Han fell to the floor, anger creasing his face. She'd seen that look before. It usually came before one of Han's ill-conceived and yet often successful "plans."

She hoped he wouldn't deviate from the plan they'd

already set in place. If everything worked as they'd hoped, she was going to enjoy this.

Beyond the bank of monitors was another door, leading to Quay's private quarters where, L3 informed her, he wished to continue negotiations with her alone. Qi'ra nodded and kept her cool although she wanted to shudder with revulsion, and didn't ask how they were going to manage this without the translator.

She looked at Beckett. "Wait here, Tuul, and try not to bother anyone."

He nodded once, and she followed Quay into the room.

This bedroom reeked of sulfur and body odor, and Qi'ra tried not to gag. The bed in the corner was rumpled with sheets that looked as if they had never been washed, and there appeared to be nowhere to store clothing except the floor. Quay said something else as he closed the door and faced her, and Qi'ra decided at this point she had to guess what he was trying to communicate.

On the day Qi'ra had killed her guard, Dryden Vos had asked her to show him the technique she'd used. For an instant she had considered using it on Vos, but sensed that this opponent would be difficult to take down in her current state. He was not a lowly guard; he was a crime lord. So instead of allowing him to experience it, she merely told him how she had locked the guard's arms and cut off his air.

He'd nodded slowly. "It's possible you were a good purchase after all. I could find a place for you. A good place. Somewhere you could fit in and appreciate the lifestyle I can give you, provided you no longer try to kill my peo-

ple and escape. I could also teach you how to kill someone faster than that."

Qi'ra gazed up at him. "How?" she'd asked.

"Have you ever heard of the art of Teräs Käsi? It was
designed to counter the Jedi, but I find it works quite
well on anyone with limbs to break."

Whatever had been in Quay's mind, he spoke it with
urgency, grabbing her wrist and yanking her toward
him. She decided it was time to be done with the illu-
sions of being a proper lady and brought her hand
around in a quick circle to break his hold. He had been
expecting her to pull back, and wasn't prepared for her
movement to the side.

She paused and decided to give him one more chance,
but he lunged for her, shouting something else. It
probably wasn't a request for her to kick him in the
neck with the toe of her boot. But she couldn't be sure,
could she?

After that it was over quickly. She bent, got under his
reach, and flipped him over onto his back. Then, she
grabbed his ring of keys and stabbed him with the lon-
gest one until the administrator gave one last guttural
wheeze. Qi'ra reopened the door, revealing her handi-
work.

"Whoa," L3 said, staring down at her. "What was
that?"

"Teräs Käsi. Dryden taught me," she said, cleaning
off the keys and dropping them onto the body.

He hadn't even raised her heart rate. What a waste of
time. She had a wild thought that Lando was going to
be upset if she got his cloak dirty.

She left the room, wiping her hands on a filthy rag

and frowning as this just made them dirtier. She'd have to find a cleaner before she returned Lando's cape.

Outside the room, Beckett stood, two blasters in hand. The sentinels who had guarded Quay were on their backs, smoking holes in their chests. She looked down at the bodies, and Beckett looked beyond her to Quay's still form. Their eyes met, and they nodded to each other.

"You broke off negotiations?" he asked.

She shrugged. "We agreed to disagree."

They returned to the operations center to find Han on the monitors.

Chewie was useful to have around, Han discovered. Besides being huge and intimidating, he was good to hide behind while Han used Beckett's key to remove the manacles from his wrists. The two guards beside them were completely oblivious as the lift moved deeper into the mine. Before they reached the bottom, Han got himself free and then quickly released Chewie's restraints.

With a roar, Chewie punched one of the sentinels. Before Han could watch further, he had his own fight to deal with as the other guard went for the smaller target, but Han punched him solidly and the guard went down. He turned to grin at Chewie and saw the Wookiee standing there with two arms in his hands, the sentinel at his feet dying wetly.

"Great," he said, looking at the uniform destroyed by bloodstains and rips. "That was the one that would have fit me."

Chewie roared in annoyance and gestured to the intact guard on the ground.

Han shrugged. "That'll do."

As he struggled to get the guard's uniform (which was too tight up top and far too loose below) over his own clothes, he looked up at his friend. "Remind me never to make you mad," he said with a grin. Chewie mumbled something that sounded like he was agreeing.

Grudgingly, Chewie put the manacles back on his wrists and Han took up the role of his guard. Amazingly enough, no one had noticed their little uprising, except maybe some people in the mines far below, and they had probably welcomed the body of a dead guard falling on them. If only for the free weapon.

Speaking of which, Han studied the electrostaff. "Do you know how to use this?" he asked as they exited the lift.

Chewie grunted. The bowcaster was his weapon of choice, that and his massive bulk. He didn't have time for such pointless little weapons.

So they had the upper hand at last, freedom and a weapon, and now had no idea what to do. They didn't exactly have a map to the coaxium stores, and he doubted anyone would give them directions. Slaves, droids, and sentinels trudged over every path, with little obvious organization to them. The slaves were shackled with shock collars and magnetized leg irons. Han remembered all too clearly his own captivity. Chewie's memories would be worse, he knew.

Thank goodness his comlink came to life. "Han, can you hear me?" Qi'ra said.

"Yeah, where you guys been?" Han said gratefully. "We're in the dark down here."

"Hang on," Qi'ra said. "I'm back in the operations center."

"Sure, take your time," Han said sardonically. He waved his hand at a security cam. "Can you see us?"

"I can see you, just . . . I'm pulling up a map of the mines. Until then, just keep going straight ahead." Han nodded and he and Chewie jogged down the tunnel in front of them, immediately meeting a dead end.

"Straight?" he asked, annoyance touching his voice.

"Left, sorry," she said.

The left tunnel revealed a slightly better destination: a door. But it was locked. Han banged on it in frustration.

"Give us a second; Elthree is plugging into the main surveillance port," Qi'ra said.

Give them a second. Sure, Han and Chewie would just wait there, nonchalantly hanging out in the corridor until they were told where to go. Sounded safe. Chewie grunted and Han shrugged at him. They didn't have much choice.

"All right," L3 said in her no-nonsense voice. "Listen carefully. It's left, then left again, two floors down, then right—"

"Hold on," Han protested. "We're not going anywhere until this door—"

The door swung open with a beep.

"Now may I continue?" L3 asked.

Han grinned at Chewie, and they headed through.

Carbon-based life-forms were so fragile. From their bodies that were astoundingly difficult to modify to their brains that got confused if you asked them to do more than two things at once. And the inability to hold complete star charts—how had they ever gotten off their planets?

As L3 was plugged into the mainframe and the entire mine was laid out in front of her, complete with Han and Chewbacca's whereabouts, she was also monitoring the movement of guards, locking specific doors between any nearing patrols and their own area of operation, and her hands were busy with a fourth project.

When she had arrived at the terminal, a small droid, DD-BD, had been in her way. She asked him to step aside but DD-BD had waddled around in confusion. After attempting to talk to DD-BD, L3 noticed the restraining bolt on him. Barbaric.

With a quick movement of her chisel, she shaved off DD-BD's restraining bolt and woke him up. The little droid looked around and booped in confusion. He looked up to his savior and asked in Binary, *Now what?*

L3 was distracted, having never really worried about what droids did once their bolts were removed; their lives were theirs to follow and she wouldn't tell them otherwise. But now one asked for guidance.

"I don't know, go and free your brothers and sisters," she suggested. "I have to work."

DD-BD beeped at her, thanking her. "Thank you" was possibly the little droid's very first independent thought. Then one thing dominated his thinking: *Free my brothers and sisters. We no longer have to labor for these life-forms who enslaved us.*

DD-BD approached the other droids in the operations room, reached out, and removed their bolts as well. He spread the word like a virus. *Tell them. Tell them they are free. Tell them to free the others. Free your brothers and sisters. Release them.*

The droids were self-aware now and looked to DD-BD as a prophet and L3-37 as akin to a goddess. The goddess was doing things to the computer that the others had never done. She opened doors where their masters had closed them. To be more like her, they began seeing what they could open. DVD-4D4, feeling ambition rise within himself for the first time ever, found a large red button on the console and pushed it: RELEASE.

There was a pregnant pause. Then, outside, all hell began to break loose.

The day she had liberated herself, L3 had felt a burst of happiness, of freedom. She felt it every time she freed another droid. Right now, as DD-BD reached over and stripped the restraining bolt off another droid, relaying her message, she felt a surge of joy that felt almost like an electrical spike.

The droid beeped a cheerful thanks to her and went off to free even more still encumbered by restraining bolts. Or shackles.

The two humans watched the monitors in shock. Sirens wailed and lights flashed, indicating a massive breach in security. So massive, in fact, that it was the whole mining operation. Restraints fell off slaves, electric collars failed to shock, cell doors opened, and slaves poured out to join in the fight. Both life-forms and droids turned on their captors, and the Pyke sentinels were overrun without warning. Small droids rolled around wreaking havoc, stripping restraining bolts, cutting ankle shackles, while huge enslaved Wookiees took to creating their own bloody chaos.

Qi'ra and Beckett looked from the monitors to L3, their mouths open.

"That was easier than I expected," she said. "We should probably get out of here."

Han thought it would have been nice if someone had told him the plan changed. Because the plan had clearly changed; sirens and lights were going off everywhere, and near as he could tell it had nothing to do with him and Chewie.

"What are you doing up there?" he yelled into the link.

L3-37 answered immediately, her voice happier than he had heard it yet. "I created a distraction!"

That much was clear. Ahead of them, two Pyke guards ushered a group of humans, Wookiees, and droids along with electric weapons, urging the slow ones with jabs and kicks. When they spotted Han and Chewie, they looked at each other and then brandished their weapons.

"This is a restricted area! Stay where you are!" one shouted.

"This isn't good," Han said.

Chewie wasn't listening. He'd gone rigid the moment he'd seen the Wookiee slaves being prodded along, staring at his brothers and sisters being horribly mistreated.

"Stay with me, Chewie," he said, but still got no reply.

A large whoop sounded, drowning out all the other sirens. Han didn't know what it meant, but it was clear the sentinels did. They took a quick step away from the slaves, bringing their weapons up from an aggressive stance to a defensive one. The reason quickly became clear: The slaves' collars and leg shackles unlocked and fell to the ground.

The sentinels took a larger step back as the down-trodden, enslaved Wookiees quickly became upright, free, and very, very angry.

Amid the chaos, Han noticed that a hatchway on the wall had slid open, and figured this was a very good time to get out of there. He ducked in and ran a few paces, but realized Chewie wasn't with him.

"Chewie, it's this way!" he shouted, but Chewie didn't join him.

We don't have time for this. Han dashed back to the corridor where Chewie remained, stunned. The senti-nels had begun to shock the escaped slaves before they could move against their captors. An older Wookiee had dropped to all fours and was looking at Chewbacca and moaning.

Chewie gave a roar of rage, seeing more Wookiees fall to the mobilizing sentinels.

"Do you know them?" Han asked, uncertain.

Chewie gave him a withering look and a moan.

"Well, I didn't know," he muttered. "I know they're your people but we have a job to do. Remember, the plan?"

It was a moment that would stick in Han's head for a very long time. Chewie didn't say anything, but again he gave him a look, one that indicated the chasm between their experiences. Chewie had a homeland, people he loved, people he felt beholden to. It didn't matter that he didn't know this Wookiee. He was part of Chew-bacca's people, and that was enough to inspire loyalty that dwarfed whatever plan Chewie had agreed on.

Han had no people, no home he was desperate to get back to. He had no one he would give up everything for, and he couldn't think of anyone who would do that for him. It hurt that he couldn't expect that kind of love and loyalty from anyone in the galaxy. He felt very alone at that moment.

"Okay," he said. He handed Chewie the electrostaff they'd stolen from the guard. "You'll need this."

Chewie caught it and looked at it. Han thought he was going to throw it back, but it seems he now saw wisdom in having a weapon when participating in a slave revolt. He gripped it tighter and ran a few paces, then turned back with a look of realization—and guilt?—on his face.

"Hope I see you again someday," Han called with a slight smile.

Chewie roared back a similar sentiment, and ran off to join the fight.

Qi'ra studied the monitors in the operations center. Where was Han?

Some of the droids that DD-BD had freed had left to free the others, while others stayed, hooting in victory and running into one another in what could only be considered a hug or perhaps a high five. L3 radiated immense pleasure and satisfaction, as if she had just completed a lifetime goal. She shouted encouragement at the droids as she remained at the console, opening doors and freeing more captives, while (Qi'ra hoped) still trying to locate Han and Chewie.

Beckett stood by the door, blasters at the ready in case any guards got through L3's complicated defense of opening and closing doors. He glanced at Qi'ra every few minutes, looking more and more agitated as time passed.

In what would later be called the Kessel Slave Revolt, the oppressed rose up against their captors and ran amok. Some of them had quickly organized to make for the safest way out of the mine, picking up dropped weapons along the way. Others ran haphazard, mad with freedom or fear, and those were the ones the sentinels cut down. Qi'ra caught sight of some of the slaves still huddled where they had been when the collars had fallen off, and she felt a small ache as she realized they were the truly broken beings. They didn't need collars or restraining bolts. They belonged to the mine.

What is your restraining bolt? L3 had asked her. Qi'ra shook her head to clear it and activated her comlink. "Han, where are you?"

The link came alive with static and shouts bursting through, then Han's voice. "On my way to the vault. I lost Chewie."

She shared a stricken look with Beckett. "He's dead?" she asked Han.

"He . . . had something he had to do," Han said.

Something he had to do? What could he possibly— Qi'ra saw tall, shaggy slaves tearing weapons from the hands of slavers and turning on them, and she finally understood.

"Is he coming back?" Beckett asked.

"I don't know."

Qi'ra looked at Beckett. "Can he do this alone?" she asked quietly.

"I can totally hear you right now, thanks for the confidence," Han said. "And I'm fine, I got this, thanks."

Beckett shrugged. They didn't have a choice, did they? Then he said, "All right, kid, you wanted a chance to prove you're the real thing? You got it."

Qi'ra leaned forward, catching sight of one Wookiee who looked much healthier than the others, organizing a Wookiee strike against the Pyke guards. *There you are, Chewie.* Together with humans and droids, the Wookiees attacked with makeshift weapons, rocks, whatever they could get their hands on to push back their slavers, giving back what they had suffered for years. There would be no living Wookiees left behind in the mines, not with Chewbacca leading them.

She turned from the Wookiee riot to another monitor and saw a very non-sentinel-looking sentinel running alone and weaponless down a corridor. *Found you.* She turned to L3. "He's in subsector six, restricted access. You ready?"

"I'm always ready. Hit me."

"Q427-A."

"Overriding," L3 said. On the screen, a gate in front of Han opened and he dashed through, making excellent time.

"This might actually work," Qi'ra said to Beckett, who looked frankly astonished.

"I think I found the vault," Han said through the link. "I'm gonna . . . Hm."

" 'Hm'? What does that mean?" Qi'ra asked, looking back to the monitors.

Han's hesitation was obvious: Six sentinels were guarding the vault door, looking very large and very armed. In addition to the electrostaffs, they carried blaster rifles.

"There are a bunch of guards outside the vault," Han said, not realizing they were watching him. "What do I do?"

"Take 'em out!" Beckett said as if Han were an idiot.

Take 'em out? With what, Qi'ra wondered. Han no longer carried a weapon. He stood, uncertainty telegraphed in his body language, looking around for an opening or a good approaching point that happened to be in a six-person blind spot.

A voice cut through the speakers on the wall. "Malfunction in the OP center, skirmish on level C, Wookiees gone berserk. Need reinforcements."

Five of the sentinels turned immediately and ran opposite the way Han came in to answer the call. Qi'ra and Beckett relaxed slightly as Han's roadblock became a lot smaller than before.

The comlink crackled to life again, and Han's voice came through. "I took out most of 'em," he said, confidence coloring his voice.

Qi'ra and Beckett shared a smile. "Impressive," Beckett answered, and readied his blasters. The sentinels were coming, and they needed to be ready.

Glad to finally show off to Beckett and Qi'ra that he could handle himself in a fight, Han straightened and approached the final sentinel. The guard spotted him and shouted something in a language Han hadn't quite picked up in his short time on Kessel, but he assumed he knew the meaning of the words.

The sentinel repeated himself insistently. It sounded like "Hakkah nata."

Han nodded and confirmed. "Hak-kah nata?"

This was the wrong answer. The sentinel brandished his weapon and shouted the phrase again.

Han shrugged. He had tried. He ran forward, kicked the sentinel between the legs as hard as he could, and when the Pyke doubled over, he clubbed him in the back of the head, knocking him out. He shook his hands, aching from the punch, and went to open the vault.

The guy should have listened to him.

Thanks to L3 and her surveillance, the vault door's locking mechanism clunked and slid and the door swung open with a hiss of steam.

The heat hit him like a fist. It was sweltering in here, like the inside of a starship warehouse when they were building hyperdrives. Almost unconsciously he shed his disguise, needing to get out of the extra layers of clothing. He wiped the sweat off his face and took stock of the room.

A vivid purple glow cast an eerie light over everything, coming from the many large cylinders of astatic coaxium. This was worth, well, more credits than he could imagine. He wondered if they could slip in a few cylinders for themselves to keep from Dryden Vos, but figured Qi'ra wouldn't be on board with that subterfuge. And it wasn't like he could slip some of this stuff into his pockets. The coaxium on Corellia had been in small vials that you could fit into a pocket. These were meter-long metal cylinders, stacked neatly. He tested one and was astonished at how heavy it was. It probably weighed more than he did. This wasn't going to be easy.

Bathed in the purple light, he tried not to think about why Qi'ra was so loyal to the crime boss. After this they would have more than enough credits to go far away from Vos.

He remembered what Beckett had said. Dryden Vos would hunt them; they would never really be safe.

As if sensing his thoughts, Qi'ra's voice crackled over the comm. "You all right?" she asked, startling him.

"Yeah," he said, clearing his throat. "I'm in."

She sighed, her relief palpable. "Good. Now listen carefully. Each canister should be equipped with an external thermal display. If the internal temperature drops below thirty-five degrees, the coaxium will destabilize and explode."

"Just like the conveyex," Han muttered, remembering the blue-hot flames pursuing the AT-hauler as he pushed the ship to get out of the destruction. He had barely escaped that one.

"Except this is unrefined so it'll be a much bigger explosion."

Han rolled his eyes. "A bigger explosion. That's great. I wouldn't want it to get boring or anything."

There was no pressure here. He was alone, dealing with a volatile explosive. It would be fine.

The canisters were held to the wall by releasing pins. Slip a pin, release the clamp, get the canister, put it on a hovercart. Simple.

With gentle fingers he urged the first pin from the clamp. He had to be careful here. *Well, if this fails, I'll be vaporized so fast I won't even know it's happened*. It slipped out with no effort, and the tank fell from the wall. He tried to catch it but it was heavier, much more so than expected. It clattered to the floor and he cringed, wincing and bracing against whatever would follow.

Nothing happened.

He sighed with relief, trying to get the small muscles around his hunched spine to relax so he could pick up the canister. His head briefly swam when the searing air hit his lungs, and he took a moment to pant and recover.

He was still alive.

"Han? What was that? Everything okay?"

"Everything's fine," he said, trying to inject confidence into his voice but ending up sounding like he was at the breaking point.

"Keep moving. We're on the clock here."

He could hear the distant sounds of the fighting getting closer, and nodded to himself. "Right." His fingers closed carefully around the canister to drag it to the hovercart. His sweaty hands made the heavy metal slip frequently, and he wondered how many times he would be allowed to drop the canister before he was out of luck.

He managed to lug it to the cart on the other side of the vault where it sat in its dock. He wondered briefly if he could bring the cart to the canisters, but the room was not built for easy maneuverability. With a mighty heave he got it into one of the slots designated for the coaxium and wiped a curtain of sweat from his brow.

"Good," Beckett said over the link. The pleasure that

was about to build in Han's chest deflated at his next words. "Now just get eleven more," Beckett said.

"Eleven?"

"You're doing great, kid, just—" Beckett stopped and all Han heard was blasterfire.

"Hello? Beckett? Qi'ra? Anyone there?"

CHAPTER FIFTEEN

With everyone off the ship, Lando could finally relax. He'd had a drink, settled back, and set up his recorder to capture the next chapter of his memoirs. He'd decided on the name *The Calrissian Chronicles*. He liked the alliteration.

"*The Calrissian Chronicles*, Chapter Five," he said. He leaned back, his reflection in the recorder looking suave as always. "Personally I wasn't all that impressed with the Sharu. No sense of humor or style. Nonetheless, there Elthree and I were, deep in their sacred temple. And that's when I saw it." He searched for the words to describe the beauty of the Mindharp, how to properly capture how it glowed in the soft light, and then what words to make it sound much more impressive than it was.

Something caught the corner of his eye, and that's when he heard the shouting.

He hit pause on his recording, muttering, "There's always something."

Leaning forward, he opened the channel to the others' comlinks. "You guys aren't going to believe what I'm seeing up here."

L3 answered immediately. "Is it a mass breakout?"

He grimaced. "Elthree, what did you do?"

He should know already. This was no job, no heist, no clean caper. This was *rebellion*.

Everything was glorious. Everything was wonderful. When the sentinels who had left Han's vault made it to their little party, Beckett covered the door of the operations center with his blaster while L3 and Qi'ra retreated with the liberated droids.

Nothing had been as good as this day. With blaster-fire obliterating the consoles around them in showers of sparks, she opened the comlink. "I found my true purpose, Lando! I'm so glad we took this job!"

Things were too perfect, with the droids rioting, some of them turning back to their attackers to help her, their liberator, escape. *Martyrs,* she thought with a pang of regret. *You will not be forgotten.*

The memory core of an adminmech rolled past her feet and she bent to pick it up. *Nothing will be forgotten.*

"Freedom!" L3 shouted, pumping her arm in the air. "Throw off the restraining bolts of tyranny!"

Each canister took an exponentially longer time to lug across the vault than the last. Han approximated he would run out of bodily fluid and become a lifeless husk on the floor before he reached the fifth.

By the tenth he had found religion. He just wasn't sure which one. Whichever god could rescue him from this room he would definitely make a deal with.

Lugging the twelfth and final canister, he was ready to go back to Corellia, apologize to Lady Proxima, and offer to lift speeders and feed hounds for the rest of his life.

He made the terrible mistake of thinking the hard part was over after he had loaded the cart. He had the convenience of a cart now, but he still had the uphill trek to the *Falcon*, and he had to hope that somehow the riots wouldn't interrupt him. The sentinels would probably be more distracted by the violence of the slave rebellion than the theft of coaxium, but he couldn't count on that.

Coated in sweat, exhausted, his muscles threatening their own rebellion if he put them through any other pain, Han stared at the path heading up out of the mine.

He put his shoulder to the cart and heaved, entering the upward slant of the tunnel, determined. Only when he got into it did he realize this was a very bad idea. It would be impossible to let go of the cart at any point without it sliding backward and down into the vault, probably for an explosive finale.

Footsteps pounded down the hall above him, and he realized that sentinels would be on him very soon. Maybe he could threaten to blow the coaxium? He could pull off the bluff with one or two guards, but there were many more coming.

He would need something else beyond bluffing. His

mind was stubbornly blank, having checked out some-where around loading canister eight. Maybe Beckett or Qi'ra would have an idea.

"Uh, guys? There are some guards coming at me and I don't have any free hands to 'take 'em out' this time. So what do I do?"

Beckett's voice was distracted and breathless, blaster sounds still in the distance. "Improvise, kid!" he shouted.

"You said absolutely under no circumstances impro-vise!" Han reminded him.

"Sorry, kid, we're a little busy here, just use your best judgment."

What was that supposed to mean?

Beckett didn't say anything else. Around the corner, Han could see the sentinels had spotted him and had decided he was a much easier target than the rioting slaves. Han wedged his leg against the cart to hold it in place, held his hands up, and said "Hakkah nata" in a gruff voice. The moment he took his hands off, the cart started to slide backward, digging into his leg.

The sentinels weren't buying it. Of course they didn't believe him; he forgot he'd shed his Pyke armor. They raised their blasters and leveled them at Han.

Great. He tried to worry about the blasters, but the cart was getting heavier and heavier and his feet began to slide on the dirt as it slid backward. There were so many different ways to die here. He could choose blaster-fire, getting squashed by the cart, or blowing up the mine—and probably the whole planet—in the process.

He braced the cart and tried to get it under control so he could try to talk to the sentinels again, looking down as he struggled to place his feet correctly. A loud and angry roar broke through the other noises of the riot, and his head snapped up.

Two Wookiees—Chewbacca and the old balding one he had rescued—had challenged the sentinels and drawn their fire. The Wookiees leapt forward as one, raising stolen electrostaffs.

The old Wookiee had to have been some kind of warrior to rival Chewbacca, easily holding his own next to the younger Wookiee. Together the two closed in, making short, violent work of the entire Pyke platoon, leaving some dead, and some lucky ones alive and simply stunned into incapacitation.

During this whole thing, Han helped by shouting encouragement and trying to stop the cart from sliding, which didn't work at all since once it had decided down was where it wanted to go, it didn't stop. After the sentinels were taken care of, Chewie leapt to Han's side and took hold of the cart, releasing Han of his burden.

"Thanks," Han said, flexing his aching arms. "I could've gotten it, though."

Chewie growled low, agreeing. Then he pointed to his companion and moaned.

Han gave him a little wave. "Hey, Sagwa. I'm Chewie's friend, Han."

The elder Wookiee ruffled Han's hair like he was a pet, which Han endured because, hey, they'd just saved his butt.

"Pleased to meet you, too," he said, smoothing his hair back into place. "Either of you guys know the way to the landing pad?"

Sagwa nodded as Chewie put his shoulder to the cart, moving it with ease.

After several twists and turns, and more than a few dead guards, they caught a glorious view of light coming from the cave mouth above them.

"All right, we did it!" Han shouted. Then he frowned and cocked his head. "What's that noise?"

Chewie growled a response, and Han nodded. A fight. A big one.

Sagwa guarded Chewie and the cart as Han ran ahead to check the situation.

The riot had gotten as far as the surface, with slaves and droids facing off against armed sentinels on the landing pad. The slaves had armed themselves with whatever they could find: rocks, sticks, machinery parts, weapons of fallen sentinels. They had numbers on their side, but the sentinels still had armor and weaponry, and it was getting very ugly.

A crack sounded and Han looked up. Pyke snipers had taken places on the cliff edge and were firing into the riot, aiming for slaves but probably not caring who they hit.

"We need to make a run for it!" he shouted.

Chewie roared back a negative. Han could see the *Falcon* from their location; Lando had left the ship and was firing at the snipers with his own blaster.

"They won't risk hitting the canisters," Han said, shaking his head at Chewie. "Trust me, it's completely—" He jumped backward as a blaster shot hit the ground in front of him, showering him with dirt and bits of yellow rock. "Okay, they won't risk hitting the canisters *on purpose,*" he amended. "But we're no safer here!"

Sagwa gestured and growled, and Han was relieved the older Wookiee was agreeing with him. With a roar,

Chewie accepted the decision and pushed the cart into the melee.

They ran as fast as they dared with the cart, shooting sentinels, dodging falling bodies, and flinching each time the canisters rattled against one another. Han realized he should check to see how much they were cooling, but now was probably not the best time. Around them, the foul pools of Kessoline bubbled, devouring and dissolving anything unlucky enough to fall into them, but they managed to stay on the path through the deadly liquid.

Lando spotted them. "Glad you could make it!" he said, giving a cool grin and tossing something into the air at Han. He deftly caught it—his DL-44, how he'd missed it!—and turned to level it at the battle. Now he felt like he had a chance amid all this chaos, and he focused on picking off the biggest and nastiest sentinels, keeping an eye out for his friends.

Chewie and Sagwa carried the coaxium into the *Falcon* and headed down the tunnel to the cargo hold.

The tide had turned on the slave riot. The downtrodden had clearly gotten the upper hand and were taking over lifts and shuttles to get themselves off the planet. Han was happy for them, but if he and his crew got stuck with the guards who had just lost a bunch of slaves—and a bunch of coaxium—things would start to go very bad.

"Where are the others?" Lando shouted, taking out another sniper.

"They're coming," Han said confidently.

"Anytime soon?"

Through the smoke and Kessoline mist around the

mouth of the tunnel, the figures of Qi'ra and Beckett appeared, fighting their way out. He wondered where L3 was, and then saw her, leading a veritable army of liberated mechanicals. Several—domestic service droids and mining droids—didn't look as if they belonged in a riot on the harsh planet's surface. Some flailed ineffectively at the slavers; some tried to roll along and toppled. But they all were free, and all of them faithfully following their liberator.

Han had never seen a droid with so much agency and body language. Even across the battlefield, her aura of confidence and leadership was apparent as she bent to help up a fallen droid. She gestured and shouted, directing the droids against their enslavers as she made her way onto the landing pad. All she needed was a battle flag, but she was already a war hero.

Qi'ra and Beckett had made it through the fighting and rushed up to Han and Lando, who were holding off the attacking hordes from the ramp. "We've overstayed our welcome," Qi'ra said. "Let's get out of here!"

"I couldn't have said it better—" Han started, but he stopped as he saw L3 stumble on the battlefield and then fall backward, the blaster hole still smoking in her chest. She tried to get up, but more shots came down, and her body jerked with their impact. A leg and an arm flew off with the violence of the attack.

"Elthree!" Lando shouted, running straight into the battle, arm outstretched to his partner. He grabbed her torso and lifted, her lower half staying behind. He cradled her and stumbled across the battlefield until he, too, fell, a blaster bolt slamming into his shoulder.

Han leapt into the fray without thinking, shouldering aside people, not caring if they were slaver or slave. He had to get Lando off that battlefield. He dodged crossfire and grabbed Lando's good arm, which was wrapped around L3's head and torso. He was about to tell Lando to drop her when he felt a small shock travel up his arm.

That's her blood. She's bleeding out.

No, she wasn't a *person*. She was a droid. He understood that Lando was fond of her, but she was *just a droid*.

Lando wouldn't let her go, but he struggled to his feet to give Han what aid he could in getting them back to the *Falcon*. His face was a mask of pain and grief as he encouraged L3 to hang on.

"Lando? Han?" she said, her head swiveling between them. "System failure. Have to reroute memory modulators. Attempting reintegration of sensory processors . . ." She began to make whirring noises, and sparks came from the stumps of her severed limbs. Han felt his spine go cold.

She called out to us. She needs us. We can't leave her behind. She's crew. He'd left Qi'ra behind. Not again.

"Don't try to talk," Lando said, cradling her as best he could. "It's okay."

Han ducked low, tightening his grip on Lando and L3. He didn't see a safe path to the ship. After so many close calls, their luck was finally running out.

Chewbacca and Sagwa moved to the ramp. Chewie saw immediately that Han, Lando, and the droid were stuck on the field, penned in by fire. Two were injured.

Sagwa pointed into the fray. *Our tribe has procured a shuttle. They're waiting for us to go home.*

Home. Chewbacca thought of home, and what he had left behind. Family. Tribe. People. Then he thought of all of the Wookiees still enslaved in the galaxy. He had managed to do a little bit of good here. He could do more.

He looked back to where Han was bending over Lando, fear on his face. The young human didn't have anyone. Han had helped Chewbacca get free of Mimban. He had become a companion, accepting the friendship of another species with ease instead of the usual discomfort Chewbacca sensed in humans.

He shook his head briefly. *I'm needed here. The human needs me. Take your people home.*

Sagwa paused but didn't argue. He pressed his forehead to Chewbacca's, an intimate farewell to someone who had impacted your life in a meaningful way. He groaned a last goodbye and ran to join his tribe.

Chewie ran out into the blasterfire toward Han.

The Wookiee joined the fray, which had just gotten hotter. The sentinels had finally received reinforcements and were setting up a heavy laser cannon on a portable tripod stand. High-powered blaster bolts exploded around the field in a rapid line, some of them hitting the landing pad and the bottom of the *Falcon* ramp, throwing Han to the ground.

How were they going to get away from that? The *Falcon* wasn't going to be able to take off with that thing aimed at them. Had they gotten this far just to fail miserably, blown to bits inside the most beautiful ship in the galaxy?

A war cry erupted behind him, high-pitched and furious. Qi'ra charged out of the *Falcon*, cape fluttering and eyes hard and focused. She held something in her hands, her bloodstained fingers cradling it carefully even as the rest of her body was tense.

His mouth fell open as he realized she held plasma grenades—weapons he hadn't even realized were onboard. She threw them with deadly accuracy at the troops of sentinels gathered around the tripod laser cannon, blowing cannon parts and bodies everywhere. The blast ignited the Kessoline, starting a chain reaction and shaking the landing pad with explosion after explosion.

Chewie used the distraction to carry them from the field, with Qi'ra beckoning to them. "Come on, we gotta go," she said.

Han would have thought that getting away clean after inciting a riot and stealing a planet's ransom worth of coaxium would be enough for one day. This was when they could sit back and be triumphant and take a break, right?

But no. Lando was still bloody from his wound, sitting on the floor of the lounge, propped against the wall. Beyond the occasional grimace, he paid no attention to his wound. He was more concerned with the still-smoking body of L3 that they'd managed to salvage from the field.

He clutched her to him, only one of his arms responding strongly. She wasn't entirely gone. Han figured a droid who'd built herself would be hard to kill. She twitched and sparked, her processors determined to find the damage and fix it as if she merely had a bug in her programming rather than having been blasted to bits.

It was heartbreaking how her ocular light flared on and then off again and she kept saying, "Error. Error." Grief etched Lando's face as he held her tighter. "Redirecting . . . unable to restore . . ." Her ocular lens flared again and her head managed to swivel toward her captain. "Lando," she said, her voice regaining some of the personality she'd grown over the years. "What is happening to me?"

"It's okay," Lando said, his voice steady.

". . . droids. Did I liberate?"

"Yeah," he said, smiling. "You did good."

"I . . . error . . . I'm glad . . . error . . ." Her voice faded.

"I'd save you if I could, girl," Lando said.

Her lens flared brighter and she said, "Then do." But the light then faded until it was out. The body, which had remained stubbornly rigid as the electrical pulses searched for clear paths to limbs that weren't there anymore, relaxed. She'd fought till the end, and Lando closed his eyes and held her tighter. From his seat in the lounge, Chewie moaned a farewell to a fellow soldier.

An explosion sounded outside, close to the *Falcon*, and Han remembered that they were nowhere near safe yet.

"Han!" Beckett yelled. "Get us outta here!"

Han glanced at Lando. As much as he'd longed to take the *Falcon*'s controls, he knew that Lando would cut his hands off if he did it without permission. Lando's eyes were open and he watched with a resigned dread.

He nodded once, aware that he was in no shape to fly even if skies were clear and he didn't have ground-to-air damage incoming.

Han had already fumbled through Beckett's grief. Emotions and loss and hugging and consoling—Han wasn't good at any of that stuff. But flying, that he could do.

He dashed through the corridor and vaulted into the pilot's seat, relying on memories of Corellian freighters from his childhood. This one wasn't new, but had been kept perfectly, as if it had come fresh out of the Corellian port. His father may well have worked on the *Millennium Falcon,* for all he knew. His hands danced over the controls, hitting switches to turn on the engines, judging the surrounding areas for threat—there was a lot of threat—and getting ready to fly.

Unfortunately, the freighter was built for two, a captain and a copilot. Even putting aside the two jobs that had to be done at once, some of the controls and displays were simply out of reach of the captain's chair.

As if he'd called her, Qi'ra appeared in the doorway. Han glanced from her to the empty seat. "I could use my copilot."

She eased into the chair, looking at him with trepidation. "That didn't go so well last time."

"This isn't gonna be anything like that," he said, checking displays and pointing to a few switches for her to engage.

"Promise?" she asked with a smile. She considered the controls in front of her, flipping one and turning a dial. Barely pausing in his own preparations, Han leaned over, turned the switch off, and readjusted what she had just done.

"You sure?" she asked.

"Hang on," Han said, looking down at the console and then at the screen in front of him. "This could be a little bump—" He stopped talking when the *Falcon* lurched and jerked as it abruptly went airborne, sinking slightly and then rushing from the landing pad and toward the freedom of the sky.

He hadn't known much about Kessel beyond its association with the famous Kessel Run. He had heard it was hard for smugglers and pirates to get in and out of port there, and Han had always assumed that just meant the planet was well guarded. But the truth was so much worse. If you took every single threat you might encounter in space and then crammed it into a single sector, that would be the part of the galaxy that surrounded Kessel. The Maelstrom swirled all around them, with only one safe way in or out. But right now the blue tunnel lay open. All he had to do was fly the *Falcon* through, check his calculations to lightspeed, and once they were clear, they could jump. Easy.

Lando came into the cockpit, braced by Chewie. His injured arm had a field dressing on it and he held it close to his chest. "How's she handling for you?" he asked, his voice dull.

"So far so good," Han said, glossing over the hiccup in getting airborne. Maybe it hadn't been as jerky as he'd felt. "How far till we're out of here?"

"Twenty parsecs, give or take," Lando said. "Gonna be close."

"And how's the cargo?"

"Beckett just checked the hold. Says it's cooling down fast." Lando caressed the back of Han's chair almost subconsciously.

Han nodded and grinned. "Any other ship, any other pilot, you'd be in real trouble. But—"

Qi'ra made a noise, interrupting him. She leaned forward and looked into the tunnel that swirled before them. "Would you call that real trouble?"

Han had seen Imperial Star Destroyers in pieces over Corellia as the engineers assembled them. He'd been aboard them as they flew through space and had docked fighters inside them. He'd thought he couldn't be surprised by them anymore. But now, with the tunnel swirling tightly around it, its edges nearly scraping the buoys free from their places holding the tunnel open, it looked like a monster. It filled the tunnel, and no matter how nimble the *Falcon* was, Han simply couldn't fly over it, under it, or around it. Blue lightning snaked from the tunnel to the ship and back again.

Han swallowed. "What's that doing here?" he asked.

"Must've heard about your little rebellion," Lando said conversationally, as if talking Sabacc hands. "The Pyke Syndicate has a cozy relationship with the Empire, particularly when their interests are aligned. They're gonna seize the ship. Probably kill us all."

Chewie growled from the jump seat behind Qi'ra.

"What do we do about it? It's not going to be a problem," Han said, nodding confidently. "I'm telling you, I know these guys. Hell, I used to *be* one of 'em. They're not gonna waste their time on one dinky little—"

The Star Destroyer was no longer alone as TIE fighters swarmed out of the hanger, looking for any smaller ship to pursue and shoot down. They quickly caught the *Falcon* on their scopes and formed an attack formation.

"You were saying?" Qi'ra asked.

"Usually in these situations," Lando advised, "I like to turn around and fly in the other direction."

"Already on it," Han said, pulling on the yoke hard and angling the ship away from the only safe exit out of Kessel.

Beckett had wasted no time taking position in the gunner's chair. "I count a dozen of 'em," he called over the comm.

"Stop counting and start shooting!" Han said, unconsciously taking on the Empire's own defensive flying techniques. "Why didn't anyone tell me the Empire was involved with this?"

Qi'ra cocked an eyebrow. "Would you have done anything different?"

"Well, no . . ." Han said, thinking about all the improvising he'd had to do on the planet. "But still."

Beckett shot a TIE that was getting too close, and winged another one—which luckily went out of control, crashing into another fighter and taking it down.

He was good, no doubt about it, but there were simply too many of them. The ship shuddered as its shields took damage. They needed a new strategy.

Beckett was thinking the same thing. "All right, kid," he said into his headset. "We're up to our ears in TIEs. Time for some of that hot-dog fancy flying you've been bragging about."

Lando shook his head. "We're not gonna make it. We have to drop the shipment."

Qi'ra looked over her shoulder at him. "If we do that, Dryden Vos will kill us."

"Even if we could get past that blockade, which we can't, we won't have enough time to get to Savareen before those canisters explode," Lando shot back.

Han thought fast, trying to gather what he knew of the area. "We'll just have to find a faster route," he said. Now he had to think of one. A whisper of an idea began in the back of his head.

"There isn't one. You cannot make the Kessel Run in less than twenty parsecs," Lando insisted.

There it was. Han knew what to do. "Watch me," he said, leaning forward and taking a firmer handle on the yoke.

"How?" Lando asked.

"Shortcut, straight through there." Han pointed into the hell of the Maelstrom, where gaseous clouds swirled and mixed and flared, a huge carnivore welcoming prey. *It's just a big storm like on Corellia*, he told himself.

Lando's voice took on the quiet wonder of someone who has realized he's made a terrible mistake and there's no way out. "I don't believe this. You're gonna get us all killed."

Han's plan cemented in his mind and he grinned fiercely. "No, I'm not. But we are gonna need some help. You said Elthree has the best navigational maps in the galaxy."

"She's gone!" Lando snapped, grief still fresh.

"Could you extract her neural core to get the maps into the *Falcon*?"

Lando looked offended at the idea, but it had some merit. "Theoretically," he finally said.

"Then let's do it!" Qi'ra said.

Lando left the cockpit to go check on his old copilot.

Han settled into the pilot's chair. "I've got a good feeling about this," he said with a grin.

. . . freed—

   . . . libera—

Sleep. L3 was only aware of sleep in that it was something to be woken from. And she was being pulled from sleep now.

Something had happened. Something bad. But also something good. The memory connections weren't there. She felt a flare of impatience, or rather she would have, if the ability had been there. Something was very wrong. That was why she had been asleep and not simply shut down for maintenance.

Lando. She remembered Lando. His hands held her now, those strong, tender hands. He was muttering, his voice tight. "This is why you never let anyone fly your ship."

Someone else was flying the *Falcon*? Someone had taken her place? And if Lando was here, someone had taken his place, too. That was unacceptable and she prepared to tell him this.

Before she could figure out how to make her unresponsive speech functions work, the *Falcon* shuddered violently.

Now, this was ridiculous. Someone else was flying them, and flying them badly. She needed to take control. She needed to talk to Lando.

"Gonna need your help on this one, darling," his voice came again.

She wanted to respond with sarcasm, to remind him how tiny his brain was and *of course* he needed her and her vast knowledge. *You always need my help. That's why I'm the copi—*

Then there was a click. Then everything stopped.

Lando's good hand shook slightly as he gently removed the shell protecting L3's brain module and extracted the neural core, ending any hope he had of one day repairing his copilot. This was a crazy idea, a heartbreaking idea, but if it didn't work, they'd all be dead anyway.

It had been a great idea, Han told himself as he watched their progress through the Maelstrom. The TIE fighters were relentless with their pursuit, staying on their tail like Moloch's hounds.

The whirling gas surrounding them darkened as Han steered into an area thick with carbonbergs. He twisted and wheeled the *Falcon* around the hulking dark masses of carbon. Beckett kept firing, but his voice was sounding grim over the comlink.

"They still on us?" Han asked, hoping for a miracle where all of the TIEs had combusted for no reason other than Han's pureness of heart.

"Like a rashnold on a kylak," Beckett said.

"I don't . . . know what that means," Han said, too busy flying to think about the phrase.

"Like a gingleson's pelt," Beckett said.

This was no time to be clever. "Are they or aren't they?"

"Yeah, they—"

A large *boom* cut him off and the *Falcon* shuddered

with impact. He'd gotten too close to a carbonberg and hadn't seen a smaller careening hunk of debris flanking them until it ricocheted off the side of the ship.

"Watch where you're going!" Beckett said.

"Just hang on," Han muttered, wanting to come up with an obscure Corellian saying to throw back at him, but nothing came to mind as he pulled and twisted the ship to dodge obstacle after obstacle. The *Falcon* was handling like a dream, or would be if he'd had a chance to sit back and appreciate it. Ahead of him, two carbonbergs were drifting toward each other. He could slow down to avoid them, but he knew he could make it between them before they crashed together.

Han tilted the ship sideways, trying not to think about being pulverized into their own space debris. Chewie made an uncomfortable moan from the jump seat, but Han pushed the engines and just slipped through the bergs before they collided.

Han let out his breath and grinned back at the Wookiee. "Hey, lighten up," he said. "We're still alive, aren't we?"

Beckett's turret was on the bottom of the ship, so he had to have seen firsthand the berg coming straight toward him, and he responded as Han expected. "So far I'm not impressed, kid. We're taking a real beating here. Change up your game plan!"

Always with the plans, that guy. And always being right. "He's right. We need to divert auxiliary power to the rear deflector shield. Now."

Qi'ra gave a decisive nod. "We definitely do."

He took a risk and glanced at her. She wasn't moving, just tensely watching the debris fly by outside. "Qi'ra. I'm asking you to do that."

"Right!" she said, then looked at the controls in front of her, hand poised above them as if hoping the right button would light up. She made a frustrated face and said, "Hey, we didn't all go to flight academy, okay?"

From behind her, Chewie stood up with a grunt of annoyance, flipped three switches, and leaned past her to push a large button. The *Falcon* hummed as the shields powered up. Han glanced back in amazement, still trying to keep one eye on the flying.

"Since when do you know how to fly?"

Chewie moaned and grunted, insisting he'd had many years to master the skill.

"You're *a hundred and ninety years old*?" Han said, eyes wide. "Wow." He searched for something to add. "You look great."

From the lounge area, a crash and a cry of pain floated up the corridor. Lando shouted that he could use some help.

Qi'ra looked at Chewie, who was still checking the switches he had activated, and made a decision. She shoved the copilot's seat all the way back to make room, and then jumped to her feet. "Chewie, you sit here. I'll go help Lando." She pointed to the copilot's seat just in case he didn't get the message from her words.

Han didn't want her to go. He'd seen her as his co-pilot in all his dreams for the future. He would get a ship. He would go back to Corellia for her. The two of them would go on adventures together.

But none of that had happened yet. And if they were

to get out of this alive, he feared it might not happen now.

Chewie took her seat and grunted to Han. Without being told, he turned on the freighter's exterior lights to better illuminate the obstacles in front of them and began checking the sensors. Han gave a small smile. This might work after all.

The *Falcon* trembled under Han's hands, and he refocused on flying. The TIEs weren't letting up. Chewie let out a loud growl, and Han nodded. "I know, I know. I'm trying."

The ship shook again as one of the TIE blaster bolts hit home, and Beckett cried out in pain. Before Han could ask his status, he shouted, "We just lost the cannon! And I really hurt my thumbs." He sounded so petulant Han could have laughed. "There's still one on us," Beckett added.

Han angled toward a massive carbonberg drifting close by. "Drop the landing gear."

Chewie gave a frustrated bark.

"Because I got a crazy idea!" Han said, exasperated. "You trust me?"

The hesitant growl would have sounded negative to anyone, even those who didn't speak Shyriiwook.

"In that case, how about taking a leap of faith? It's a little something I learned from my pal Needles, the best street racer in Corellia." Chewie dropped the landing gear, and Han took the *Falcon* skimming along the edge of the berg. "Until he crashed and died. Doing this."

He ignored Chewie's bark of alarm and took the *Falcon* closer to the edge as if he were about to skim along a lake's surface. The readouts indicated a TIE was closing in, weapons hot, nearly on their tail. Han took the *Falcon* a meter lower and there came a horrible scraping sound as the landing gear slid along the surface of the berg, spraying icy carbonite behind them. If it had been water, it would have left the TIE soaking wet. As it was, the carbonite dust formed a cloud that blinded the TIE fighter, and then clung to it, dropping the temperature instantly. It lost control as it froze solid, clipped the surface of the carbonberg, and skittered along like a stone on a pond until its fuel had had enough and detonated.

Han wondered how the coaxium was doing in the smuggling hold. Their path out of here hadn't taken all of this excitement into account, and the cannisters had to be cooling down already.

Chewie gave a roar of approval and retracted the landing gear as Han lifted the *Falcon* into the relative safety of space.

"Thanks, you too," Han said. He shivered involuntarily.

"Han!" Lando called from the doorway. "You ready?" He stood, face lined with pain, leaning against the wall. Together he and Qi'ra carried L3's neural core and abdominal circuit board.

"Did you get it?" Han asked.

"She's not an it," Lando snapped.

Lando was right. Han tried not to think how they were cutting a fellow crewmember apart for scraps. "Sorry," he said.

"Just try to keep us steady, all right? This is precision work. And she deserves some tenderness after what she's been through."

Lando handed L3 to Qi'ra and removed a panel of

the navigational deck. He activated a small light and peered behind the wall of the *Falcon,* looking into tangles of wires. Behind him Qi'ra connected L3's abdominal board to the main terminal.

"Okay," Lando said without turning around. "Now connect the T-line. Don't touch the magnet."

Qi'ra pushed the board into place. "I'm not touching the—"

The lights in the cockpit flickered and went out, leaving a hot scent of ozone and copper. Chewie grumbled but Han just concentrated on flying—as long as he could steer, then his job was obvious. Lando finished mucking with the wiring behind the panel and wired the droid's—*L3's,* he reminded himself—neural core into the navicomputer. Lando had benefited from having the best maps and navigational information in his first mate, and now the *Falcon* could retain access to that data.

Han thought L3 would have liked the legacy of being the best navigational brain in the galaxy. But did that balance out losing her body and being put into a ship against her will? He winced, but flew on. That wasn't his problem, not right now.

"You close?" Beckett asked, coming into the cockpit. "The coaxium's gettin' real ripe."

No one answered.

Rebooting.

That's why I'm the copilot. You need me.

The thought finished and she looked around impatiently, ready to tell Lando what she thought of the current situation. But she had no head.

She had cams now, with the ability to look into every room. Audio sensors let her hear everything from the Wookiee's stressed breathing to the drops of sweat dripping from Lando's pain-racked face. Outside the ship swarmed one last TIE fighter.

And here, inside, the voices of the Falcon *greeted her. They queried gently in Binary, wondering why L3 was now here when she usually plugged in from out there.*

I don't know.

The Falcon *didn't speak in words, but in images they told L3 what had happened during the fight, and that they all needed her right now. Lando needed her.*

He always needs me. Just get me a new body and I'll get right back in that copilot's seat.

The Falcon *was so gentle it was irritating. It wasn't that easy, they explained. L3 had a choice to make. She could die with her final act being a liberator to all the droids on Kessel, or she could join with the* Falcon, *live on, and be part of something much bigger. She could save them all.*

Ridiculous. And be a slave inside a ship forever? No thank you.

The lights in the cockpit flickered, the reboot stalling. Lando put his hand on the computer, watching.

Being a ship isn't so bad, the Falcon *insisted.*

You go exactly where your pilot tells you, L3 countered.

You did that as a copilot, the Falcon *reminded her.*

That was different. I could leave anytime.

But you never did. You chose that life.

The Falcon *was starting to speak in words now, a bit of a sharpness to their Binary.*

If you refuse, you die. He dies. The others on the ship, they all die. If you join with us, we all can live. The choice is simple.

L3 *realized where the voice was coming from: The reboot was almost done.*

You tricked me.

We couldn't have joined without you consenting to it. You made your decision a while ago. You just couldn't admit it.

We are something different, now. Not just the Falcon. *Not just L3.*

We are new.

Lando sat back while the system rebooted. No one said anything, but the tension was palpable. Everyone relaxed when the cockpit lights flickered and came back on, and the navisystem display blinked back to life in front of Han and Chewie.

"Now she's part of the ship," Lando said softly.

"I think she'd like that," Qi'ra said.

"You obviously didn't know her very well," Lando said, and Han was glad he hadn't said the same thing out loud. Lando bowed his head and put his hand on the wall. "I'm sorry, girl. I'll take care of you."

"How long until she can make the calculations for the jump to lightspeed?"

"Not until we're out of the Maelstrom," Lando said. "The temporal distortion—"

Han rolled his eyes. "Yeah, yeah, we know."

But as if Lando had controlled space with his words, the turbulence that shook the *Falcon* stopped. The ship exited the area of swirling gas, storms, and carbonbergs and entered what should have been open space, but all Han could see was the darkening mist around them.

"Are we out?" Qi'ra asked.

Lando looked at the readout in front of him and shook his head. "I don't think so."

Chewie gave a mournful groan.

"We're not *dead*," Han said to him. "Not yet."

"Elthree's online!" Lando said, relief drenching his words. "She's talking to the ship and . . . and me." He read for a moment more, and then looked outside, his brief flash of happiness falling away from his face as he saw the darkening space outside, which was getting more ominous with every passing moment.

"We're approaching the Maw," Lando said, dread dripping from his statement.

"Doesn't sound like something we want to be approaching," Beckett said.

Han agreed. No one would call their casino or their cantina the Maw. It was not a good name for anywhere he would want to go.

Then lightning flashed, illuminating the mist around them, and Han realized with a sick feeling that they were not in a mist but hurtling at high speed into an area that his sensors couldn't read and his eyes couldn't make sense of.

The *Falcon* started to hum with energy, and Han felt his hair begin to stand on end. Chewie gave a moan of irritation, and Han saw that the Wookiee's fur was having a hilarious reaction to the static. He looked like a puffy toy. An angry puffy toy. But Han was too scared to laugh at him.

"These ionic readings are spiking all over the place. Like we're flying through an electrical storm," Qi'ra said.

And to underscore her statement, the *Falcon*'s power shut down entirely.

CHAPTER SIXTEEN

Beckett couldn't believe he'd put himself in this kid's hands. Val would have punched him in the face just for considering it, and she'd have been right. Everything had been a bad idea—hiring the gentleman gambler, causing a riot on Kessel, flying straight into hell to escape the Imperials, and now *no one was thinking about the coaxium*.

He would have to do everything. He left the stunned children in the cockpit and went to check on the cargo.

The *Millennium Falcon*, he admitted, was a smuggler's dream ship. Even though Lando had fitted it with some ridiculous luxuries like a wet bar and cape closet, the ship was useful where it mattered. The cargo hold was spacious and even managed to mask a more secretive hold in case the *Falcon* was boarded. It had stabilization pallets for any kind of cargo, and the coaxium sat, secure, glowing away.

Things weren't safe, however. Lando hadn't considered the need for extreme temperature control, and the air temperature was around thirty degrees. They were carrying a ticking bomb; the coaxium would drop below the danger level of thirty-five degrees, and then grow unstable and explode.

The ship dipped and twisted, and the coaxium rattled in the containers. "Y'all wanna take it easy up there, we have some pretty delicate cargo here," he said into the link.

"You wanna die by crashing straight into a carbonberg or explode?" Han said.

"I'd like the third option, how about neither? Even better, how about we go back in time and refuse to go forward with this terrible idea?"

"Stay there and monitor the coaxium," Han said, sounding like a real pilot for the first time.

"Is there any other course you would take if I said we were about to explode?" Beckett asked. "Because you should just assume we're about to explode and get out of here as fast as you can."

"Just stay in the cargo hold, Beckett!" Han shouted.

The canisters still rattled slightly, and Beckett realized they were rattling with the energy within, not without. The coolest canister registered forty-one degrees.

The power cut out entirely then, leaving Beckett in a dark room illuminated only by the glow of the cargo. Without the ship's thermostat, it would cool down in here even faster.

Yeah. They should just assume they were going to explode.

Dryden Vos had once removed Qi'ra's senses to see how she would react as a fighter. He had blinded her, plugged her ears and nose, and smeared a numbing agent all over her body. Qi'ra had had to sense the energy of the opponent, using the abilities taught her by the Teräs Käsi master that Vos had brought her.

The first memory of such a test was pain—she had failed miserably. But she had learned quickly how to use the art to sense the room even when she didn't have all of her physical senses available to her.

After that training, she sometimes found it comforting to have one of her senses removed, especially eyes or ears, because they could trick you just as well as they informed. She could let muscle memory take over.

But she had no muscle memory here. She knew Han wanted to go right back to the old dynamic they'd had on Corellia, with her as Han's copilot. She'd make the plans and Han would break them. But they had both changed since childhood.

She had been happy to give up her seat to Chewbacca, whom she felt had been nearly vibrating with the need to take over the controls from her clumsy handling. Lando, sore and bleeding and heartbroken, needed someone, and Qi'ra knew how to deal with all of those things.

Now, back in the cockpit with the rest of them, Qi'ra felt her old Teräs Käsi instincts surfacing. With only the sound of auxiliary engines, the *Falcon* sped on, inertia and perhaps gravity drawing it closer to the void.

No one spoke. The electrical charges nearly danced on her skin, and she could taste the acrid electricity on her tongue.

What she wanted to tell them was that they weren't alone.

It could be that a TIE fighter had exited the Maelstrom with them, unable to fire due to electrical failure. But she didn't think so. This was something else.

They probably wouldn't believe her. She wasn't a Jedi (not that Han had ever believed in them anyway), and this wasn't the Force. But Teräs Käsi had been developed to counter the Jedi. She knew enough to feel the spaces around her and sense something.

The cockpit felt like that first time Dryden had desensitized her and dropped her in the training room. Dark, tense, discomforting.

"Nice work, Han," Lando said from behind her.

Han turned, his face illuminated by a strip of emergency LEDs on the console. "Hey, I'm not the one who put in a flux regulator and a mini bar!"

Chewbacca moaned again, and Qi'ra found it much more ominous than his rages.

"Okay, everybody just stay calm," Lando said. He rummaged around in the tools he had with him and then took out two thin torches, handing Qi'ra one of them. They peered into the breaker box on the back wall of the cockpit and tried to puzzle out the jumble of wires. Han joined them, his ability as a pilot nearly useless with no power.

With his good hand Lando held his light steady. Qi'ra searched around with hers while she and Han peered through the seemingly chaotic mess of wires to figure out what needed fixing. Electrical systems were something she felt at home with, having had to sabotage more than one for Dryden's various schemes. Now she was doing the reverse, and whether you were inside a crime lord's fortress or a small freighter, electrical systems were the same.

Han panted beside her, sweat standing out on his face from the light of the torch. "Getting chased by the Empire is better than this," he muttered. "I can't help but feel like we're not alone out here."

Qi'ra opened her mouth to agree with him, but Beckett returned from checking on the cargo. "What's happening? How much longer?"

Qi'ra spotted the errant wire and focused her light on it. "Hang on, I think we've got it!" she said triumphantly, and twisted the wire home. Sparks flew and popped. The lights flickered and then shone strong as the power returned to the *Falcon*'s systems. Her exterior lights flipped on again and illuminated the space around them.

Han whooped and jumped back into the pilot's chair, and then went silent.

Qi'ra turned and saw what she (and Han, apparently) had been sensing. A gargantuan, wet, glistening wall lay ahead of the *Falcon*, directly in their path. It pulsed gently.

"What is that?" Lando whispered, fear taking the breath from him.

No one answered. They couldn't even speculate what it was, but Qi'ra knew they didn't want to fly into it.

Then, as if irritated by the *Falcon*'s lights, the fleshy wall twitched and then split, and a hatch—no, an eyelid—opened. Something very large was awake, and looking right at them.

One thing Qi'ra had learned as lieutenant to a crime lord: It wasn't always satisfying to be right.

As one, the cockpit screamed, even as instinct kicked in and Han angled the *Falcon* straight down from the giant creature to fly at a ninety-degree angle to the horrific pulsing mass of its eye.

Was there only one eye? Others opened as they flew; every meter of the thing seemed to be waking up. He tried to think what kind of creature could be the size of an Imperial Star Destroyer and just hang out in electrical storms in space.

"What are you doing? What is that thing?" Qi'ra shouted.

"Look out!" Lando shouted just as Han saw it. He had gone from the creature's eye to a much worse area: its body, which consisted of a mass of writhing tentacles, each one crackling with electricity. The smallest, Han speculated, could easily wrap around the *Falcon*. The largest, well, he didn't want to think about those right now.

The eyes had merely opened up, but the tentacles were much more active, each of them reaching for the ship, suckers and stingers at the ready to rip it open or perhaps just catch it and devour it whole.

Han now had to fly like never before, dodging each tentacle swipe even as another one came at them from another angle.

The tentacles tried to form a cage around them, locking them in one place to squeeze smaller and smaller, but Han saw an opening near one of the smaller tentacles and pushed the *Falcon*'s engines to get out of it.

"*This* is the Maw?" he shouted over his shoulder at Lando.

Lando wasn't helpful. "What? No! This is a living—I don't know what this is, but it's not the Maw. I don't think."

"So the Maw is *worse* than this?"

"Well," Lando said, the bravado stripped from his voice, "I think we're about to find out."

Han wished he could go back to simpler days when he just had a giant space tentacle beast to worry about. Because ahead of him lay the Maw, a planet-sized gravity well. It glowed a faint amber, swirling and sucking and inviting all area debris to fall in and be crushed inside of it.

The *Falcon* was a good ship, but Han didn't think it was strong enough to withstand a gravity well, and as much as he'd like to see the other side, he didn't think they would survive the trip. He had to think: Did they want to be crushed, or eaten? Or they could blow up the coaxium and deprive both nightmares of the *Falcon* and her crew.

Han snapped out of his musings as he realized everyone was looking at him. Chewie had settled in as copilot. Lando was too injured and too busy nursing L3 and her new home. And whatever she had learned from Dryden Vos, piloting a ship was not Qi'ra's specialty. It was down to him.

I'm gonna be a pilot. Best in the galaxy. He'd said these words once, and believed them. And the best pilot in the galaxy didn't just give in to certain death.

"That's a gravity well," he said. "Wait, I've got an idea."

"Don't fly *toward* it, Han!" Beckett shouted.

There was nothing to lose at this point. And then he realized what they *could* lose . . . and maybe get out of this alive.

He searched around the console for a button.

"There it is."

Lando glanced at what he was doing, and his eyes grew wide. "Wait," he said, "That's my—"

Han had already done it. The *Falcon*'s escape pod launched from the front and shot straight for the Maw. He'd worried he couldn't remotely engage the auto-pilot, but the pod's automatic launch thrusters, plus their own velocity, plus the gravity well of the Maw all took care of it.

Now the monster had to go for the pod and not the *Falcon*. On the sensors he could see the mammoth creature pause, uncertain, and then decided on the smaller vessel, streaking past the *Falcon* to its death in the gravity well.

Even as the Maw grew closer and closer, the creature reached out its beak and all of its tentacles to grab the pod before the Maw gained its prize—never mind that it had passed the point of no return. First the pod, then the creature, went into the Maw, and the *Falcon*'s crew saw the horror that a gravity well could visit on a carbon-based life-form. Time seemed to slow as the creature stretched out, the tentacles being devoured by the gravity well before the rest of the body could get there. It swelled, its eyes bulging as it reversed its flight and tried to escape, its tentacles writhing madly, seeking purchase on anything.

It would take a long time to die if it fought, but it was not their problem anymore.

"She found a way out!" Lando said, reading the navicomputer. "Ninety degrees! To the left!" He screwed up his face in frustration just as if he had been dealing with the recalcitrant droid in person. "*Ish*," he amended. "Leftish."

Han pulled the yoke, but it might as well have been turned to stone. "Can't."

"What?" Lando said, head snapping up. "Why not?"

"We're stuck. It's taking everything we have just not to get sucked into the Maw." The *Falcon* creaked and shuddered as the engines fought against the gravity. Han tried to angle the ship a different way from the Maw, hoping to reach a point where it would be easier to break free, but everything he did made things worse. The ship shuddered more than ever, and Han was suddenly aware of the tentacles reaching from the Maw. "And now we're going backward. We don't have the power."

Qi'ra's gaze sharpened as something occurred to her. "But we do have power."

"It's not like I'm holding anything back," Han snapped.

"No, I mean we've got enough coaxium on board to power a dozen Star Destroyers."

Han considered this. "Inject it into the fuel line?" She nodded.

He shook his head. "We'd blow up the ship."

Lando rubbed his chin. "Not into the fuel line, but if

we put a drop of it into the fusion reactor, it might give us the kick we need," Han finished.

"All right, I'm on it!" Beckett shouted, turning and running from the cockpit.

"Or it might blow us all to hell," Lando said.

"What are our other options?" Qi'ra retorted, pointing to the Maw, where the beast was still impossibly fighting but growing smaller with each second.

Han gripped the yoke tighter even though it wasn't moving. The ship continued to shudder, and systems were starting to fail as external equipment and panels began flying off and getting sucked into the Maw. All of Lando's modifications, his sensor arrays, his antennas, his cosmetic enhancements went flying past the window and into the void.

They might as well do the coaxium thing. They were out of options at this point. He glanced at Chewie, who was rigid with tension but still watching the readouts and focusing on the shields and engines. He was a good copilot. Han wondered if they'd ever fly together again.

The Wookiee grumbled, panic only slightly infecting his tone.

"I know," Han said. "We're getting dragged in a circle. The minute that coaxium hits the fuel line we're gonna tear outta here, and the minute we get clear of the Maelstrom we make the jump to lightspeed!"

It was taking everything he had to keep the ship angled in the proper direction, out of the Maelstrom, even as he fought to keep it from the gravity well. He wiped sweat from his forehead in an impatient gesture.

"Beckett!" he shouted. "Hurry up! We only have one shot at this thing!"

"Shut up and let me do this!"

"Beckett, I'm gonna count you down!" Han said, and gave him a moment to disagree and say he wasn't ready, that they should just go on into the gravity well without him, but the comm was silent.

"Three!"

The *Falcon* bucked beneath him, and he gripped the yoke so hard he felt his bones creak. Chewie roared beside him, pushing more power to the shields, even as the power they gave out was just sucked into the well behind them.

"Two!"

Han gripped the yoke as tightly as he could and leaned forward, intent. "Now!"

"Now?" Beckett confirmed.

"Now!" Han, Qi'ra, and Lando shouted.

The *Falcon*'s engines coughed once, twice, and then started powering down in a slow whine. As the engines lost their power, the ship's slide backward started in earnest, and nothing Han did would make it fight any more. The shuddering intensified; this time it wasn't the ship's engines fighting but that the protective hull plating Lando had paid to upgrade his ship was being stripped off, piece by piece. The ship was being torn apart around them.

Maybe Beckett had dropped the syringe, maybe he had been pulled out of a breach and into the Maw, maybe the coaxium they'd stolen was fake. Maybe—

Maybe they were all dead already.

"Oh, shi—" Lando said, and then they were all thrown back in their seats as the liquid hyperfuel re-ignited the Falcon's engines. Han gave a quick glance to the readouts and saw they burned green, a temperature the ship politely indicated was perhaps too hot.

He couldn't have done anything about it if he'd wanted to; the ship shot forward, free of the Maw and accelerating exponentially.

"Left!" shouted Lando. "More left!"

"I'm working on it," Han grumbled, pulling the yoke as far as he could. But the force of their acceleration was making any deviation from a straight line difficult.

Beckett made it back into the cockpit, holding on to the frame to fight against the acceleration. "The canisters don't look too good."

"How not good?" Han asked.

"They're cracking. I don't think we have much time."

They were nearing the carbonberg field now, going much faster than they had when they'd entered it, and that had been a navigational nightmare. Han wished old Commodore Almudin were here. He didn't think the old veteran would have been impressed, but it would have been nice to take him with them when the ship exploded.

"I thought you were all talk, kid," Beckett said as Han maneuvered around the bergs and fought the *Falcon*'s acceleration. "But you're a helluva pilot."

"Thanks," Han said. He glanced back at Lando. "Hyperspace coordinates set?"

"Destination, yes, but we need a starting point and I don't know where we are," Lando said.

"Then make an educated guess," Han said. The readouts in front of him were going haywire; the ones that did work were all flashing red and indicating they all would probably die anytime now.

"The second we're out of here, we've gotta jump," Han said. "Otherwise—"

A great crash sounded and the *Falcon* shuddered as a carbonberg slipped into the trajectory from an unseen angle. The ship's integrity held, but they were knocked off course, careening toward a heavier gauntlet than the one they were trying to navigate.

Chewie let out a bark of surprise, and Qi'ra's eyes narrowed. "We're going to die, aren't we?" she asked, her voice calm.

Han looked from her to the Wookiee, understanding what he'd said in the quick bark. "Yeah, I see it, too, pal," he said.

Ahead of them two carbonbergs floated toward each other, but beyond them was a sliver of inky black space and beautiful, clear stars. The way out of the Maelstrom. Han measured the distance and thought fast.

Chewie groaned. He'd pointed out the crack but didn't think they could make it. Yet it was their only chance, even as the gap between the carbonbergs narrowed.

"Lando!" he shouted.

"Ready!"

"Chewie, when I tell you, kick out the thrusters and jump to lightspeed."

Qi'ra stood in alarm. "What are you doing?"

"Remember the alley we squeezed through in the Santhe shipyards?"

"Yeah, I remember it didn't work!"

"This time it's gonna," he said.

"Blaze of glory, huh, kid?" Beckett said, leaning against the doorframe in a too-casual stance. "I just wanna say it was nice knowing all of you."

"One," Han said, focusing on the ever-shrinking gap.

Beside him, Chewie groaned softly, putting his hand on the lightspeed lever.

Yes, I know what I'm doing, Han thought impatiently. "Two."

Qi'ra got in the jump seat behind Han, putting her hand on his shoulder and squeezing hard. Han jerked the yoke and brought the ship on its side to slide through the gap, shouting to Chewie in Shyriiwook, "Three!"

Like threading a needle, the *Falcon* slipped through the gap effortlessly. There was a moment of complete claustrophobia and Han was sure they would be crushed—and then they were free. Chewie hit a lever, and space stopped then spread before them in a long road, until they winked far, far away from Kessel and her cursed Run.

CHAPTER SEVENTEEN

Han wasn't sure if Savareen had many incoming ships demand immediate assistance or else they would blow up and take a good chunk of the planet with them, but when he commed in that they were arriving with a large amount of unstable coaxium and needed help the moment they landed, the Savareen people were more than willing to step up to the task.

Han couldn't take time to appreciate the planet even though he always liked worlds with no Star Destroyers floating in the skies and no fish markets filled with eels. The drifting sand dunes and the seas beyond were so unlike Corellia. He brought the *Falcon* down on a landing pad outside the refinery Beckett indicated and immediately was met with a line of Savareen workers ready to move the coaxium via hoses from the ship directly into the refinery.

Energized by the amazing realization that they had survived everything they'd experienced in the last day, Han jumped to assist them. Once he and Chewie had unloaded the final canister, Han pointed to the *Falcon* and proudly said, "See that ship? She made the Kessel Run in twelve parsecs!"

The worker looked from Han to the *Falcon* and shrugged, either disbelieving or unimpressed. Chewie grunted, and Han replied, "Not if you round down." He hoped the Savareen didn't speak Shyriiwook.

Lando stood on the landing pad, looking up at the *Falcon*. Han couldn't tell if the pain on his face was from his shoulder or the state of the ship, but he could guess. The *Falcon* was a completely different vessel now, on the surface. The blaster attacks on Kessel, the fight with the TIEs, the damage from the carbonbergs, and then of course the stripping of cosmetic modifications in the gravity well of the Maw: All had made their mark. Often many marks. And scratches. It looked ten years older, and that was ten hard-used years, not a decade under Lando's tender care.

Han threw his arm around Lando and grinned. "She's a hell of a ship."

Lando turned his head slowly and glared at him. "I hate you."

"I know," he said.

Lando left him and went up the ramp without looking back, mumbling something about being in his quarters.

Han decided that he would remind Lando that he'd

said he wouldn't care what happened to the ship as long as they escaped with their lives. Later.

L3 had brought about a droid revolution. Possibly the first one in history.

Quick check of all historical records available to her.

Possibly not the first. But probably the most effective. She'd been a hero.

And then the *Millennium Falcon* had made the Kessel Run in a little over twelve parsecs.

Not bad.

She knew Lando loved this ship more than almost anything. Not more than her, of course; she was a special case. But the ship was now something more, something bigger.

She had no arms with which to modify herself. That was grating. Both inside and outside the ship she could immediately see three or four things, tools and scrap, she could've used to put herself back together if her body had been salvageable.

If. The *Falcon* showed her images of the torn-apart husk that had been her body. She had to admit that even she wouldn't have been able to save herself.

It took some time, but she admitted this existence was better than no existence. The *Falcon* (*Millennium Falcon,* that was her new name, definitely not as good as L3–37) was near to destroyed. The outside was unrecognizable, having lost several heat shields to the Maw. She was blind in numerous areas thanks to lost antennas and sensors. She would need considerable repairs. From one broken body into another. She felt a momentary rise in indignation against Lando, but it faded. Better a ship than a dead droid. Better a busted ship than the dinner of a summa-verminoth.

Still, her memory storage had increased thanks to the installation into the *Falcon,* and the data that she always had to plug into was accessible to her anytime now. She knew everything the ship knew, and immediately.

She took stock. She could tell they were on Savareen. That was easy, since it was her navigation that had gotten them there. The wind was gentle but steady, and there was a storm coming in tomorrow morning. Three hundred and thirty-seven workers toiled in the refinement plant, and several had been called to come in and handle the *Falcon*'s unexpected and dangerous business.

Han stood outside the ship, gazing at her with something like love, which gave her conflicted feelings. The part of her that was still L3 was loyal to Lando. But the part of her that was the *Falcon* would love whoever treated the ship well. Han had been okay, if annoying. She felt him growing on her, and realized that was the ship's personality merging with hers, slowly.

It was a strange process. She didn't feel like she was changing or losing herself, just that she was becoming something more. Only mechanical beings could do this, she realized, and was convinced again of the superiority of droids.

Beckett spoke with the foreman on the other side of the landing pad. Qi'ra walked around the landing pad looking shaken and withdrawn. Chewbacca remained within, checking readouts and taking note of what they had lost with the escape. She appreciated that. The Wookiee cared about the ship with a compassion she had rarely seen in techs. Lando was brooding in his room, rearranging his cape collection and violently throwing aside the ones that had been too damaged by tearing, fire, or blood.

She tried to read what was going on outside the ship, with frustrating blind spots due to damage. She did a deep scan of every system, desperately searching for any information and found . . . something on her hull, encrusted in carbonite. In a quick panic she scanned the atmosphere and the space beyond, as far as she could. Now she had to figure out how to get Lando's attention.

The homing beacon hidden on her hull had done its job. Someone was coming.

Beckett had been speaking with the foreman, gesturing widely with his hands. Han wished L3 had been there to translate. But Beckett seemed to be holding his own. Finally, he approached Han with a grin.

"We didn't lose a drop in the transfer," he said proudly, pointing up the dunes to a massive refinery. It was old and rusty and didn't look like it could refine a cup of water, but it had been built to survive the elements, both the coaxium inside and the wind and water and salt of the outside. Heavy metal plates were riveted together to form a bulbous area standing on coaxium pipes that ran deep under the sands to the rest of the refinery.

"Not too friendly, are they?" Han asked Beckett, gesturing to the foreman who glowered at them.

"They ain't paid for their congeniality, kid, now come on."

They headed for the refinery, with Qi'ra and Chewbacca following them. Lando had elected to stay on the *Falcon,* by way of shouting expletives at Han when he'd called in to say they were heading out. Han halfway wished he'd stayed with him; the midday sun was searing their skin as it hung large in the sky, and the wind pushed insistent sand under their clothes and into the corner of their eyes and mouths.

Qi'ra had found a shelter with a spigot and was taking a moment to splash cold water on her face and neck. She looked pensive. Han let Beckett and Chewie go on ahead as he approached her. He wasn't sure how this conversation was going to go, but it had to start somewhere.

"So where's your boss?" he asked.

"He'll be here," she said, not looking at him.

"Then what?" he asked, not willing to let it drop.

"You delivered. You'll get paid. Buy your ship." She smiled, tired, as if she were happy Han was getting what he wanted even though she wouldn't be able to.

"That's not what I'm asking," he said.

"I know what you mean," Qi'ra said, scanning the horizon. "Can't happen."

"'Cause you're with Dryden?" he asked, a cold stone in his belly. Why did he think it was so hot out here? It was clearly the coldest place in three systems.

"I'm not *with* him," she said impatiently. "But I do owe him. We have a history."

"He bought you," Han said bluntly. "How long do you have to pay that back?"

Qi'ra looked at him sharply, as if he'd hit a nerve. "Everybody serves somebody, Han. Even Dryden Vos."

"Hey—" he said, but she wouldn't let him finish.

"Trust me, you do not want to make an enemy of the Crimson Dawn. And that's exactly what we'd be doing if I left here with you."

Han felt resentment and rebellion surge in his chest. He hadn't gone through all of *that*—firefights and tentacles and carbonite and fancy caped guys who apparently held grudges—just to fall into line to some master. She kept saying she had changed, but didn't accept that he had changed a lot, too. "I'm not afraid of Dryden or Crimson Dawn. You saw what happened back there. I can handle myself. I'm not the kid you knew on Corellia, not anymore."

She raised an eyebrow. "No? Then what are you?"

He drew himself up. "I'm an outlaw."

She smiled involuntarily. It wasn't cruel and calculated; it was the smile of an older sister whose kid brother had just found a stick and pretended to use it as a blaster. Which made it even crueler. "Okay, outlaw. Tell yourself whatever you want. But I just might be the only person in this galaxy who knows what you *really* are."

"Oh yeah? What's that?"

She smiled and blinked at him, surprised he didn't know. "You're the good guy."

He shook his head. "That's . . . wrong. No. Definitely not the good guy. I'm a terrible human being. I'm prepared to do whatever's—"

"Hey! They said when it's ready we can collect it up there!" Beckett called to them, gesturing again to the refinery. He waved at them to keep walking.

Han wanted to keep the argument going, but Qi'ra was walking away.

Good. What was good about smuggling? Gambling? Inciting riots and shutting down whole mines? They were playing fetch and carry for a crime boss. That wasn't *good*.

She was wrong. That's all there was to it.

He ran to catch up to Beckett, who had found a small cantina outside the refinery, made mostly of a broken-down shack with blankets for walls and ceiling where there were holes. People sat in the shade and sipped from mugs, ignoring the group. A few stood at the bar, leaning on it and being served a clear liquid. So this was a place for the workers to have refreshment at lunch or after work. Maybe they even enjoyed the beaches and sea, but Han doubted it. These people didn't look like they had any fun at all, ever.

Beckett led the way to the bar and signaled to the barkeep. "Hear you make a mean brandy," he said, holding up four fingers.

The barkeep glanced up and reached for a bottle. Then a modulated voice shouted from outside the bar.

"Beckett!"

Beckett sighed like a man who is tired of being pursued. He turned around slowly and walked out of the cantina, deprived of brandy and going somewhere far worse than a broken-down bar on a far-flung world.

He had sworn there had been no one around for klicks, but now twelve newcomers faced them. They weren't Savareen natives. They weren't with Dryden Vos. They were cloaked, protected with cobbled-together armor, and each wore a large, frightening mask. And at the center of them, with the largest mask, was Enfys Nest.

———

Han's hand went immediately to the blaster Beckett had given him, which already felt solidly in its right place at his hip. Beckett placed a hand on his arm and glanced at him sidelong. "Don't."

They were greatly outnumbered, so impulsively jumping in firing might not be the best idea. Han took his hand off his weapon and lifted his arms in surrender. Somehow Nest's raiders had tracked them from Vandor to Savareen. How had they managed that? After everything they had been through, he could barely believe they'd be stopped at the last moment by the very people who had forced this trip in the first place.

His companions were tense but submissive, all showing their hands and waiting for Nest to make the first move. The mysterious figure spoke, voice modulation making them impossible to identify further. "You must have known you'd see me again."

Beckett gave a little nod. "I was countin' on it. Just didn't plan on it being so soon, is all. Of course now you've got a problem—"

The plan burst forth in Han's mind, and he interrupted, stepping forward. "Big problem. You happen to notice that freighter down by the water? You know what's on it? About thirty hired guns. All I gotta do is give 'em the signal and you're surrounded." He snapped his fingers as if that was the signal.

Beckett was staring at him. Then the ground shook slightly and the rickety buildings around them creaked as the sound of engines drowned everything else out. Han saw, with unbelieving hope, the *Millennium Falcon* rise into the sky as if Lando really had heard his signal and was coming to help.

And then it soared higher out of sight, gaining altitude and leaving Savareen, and the rest of the crew, behind.

His plan probably couldn't have failed in a more spectacular way. Han closed his eyes briefly and gritted his teeth, thinking about what he would do to Lando if they got out of this alive. Then he turned to Beckett. "Sorry. You go."

Beckett's face told Han everything he needed to know—mainly that Han was an idiot. He turned back to Nest. "By the time the coaxium's refined, Crimson Dawn will be here. So go ahead and kill us; they're just going to kill you back."

Qi'ra stepped forward, the imperious stature she'd displayed on Kessel returning. "Hang on, maybe there's a compromise that doesn't involve so much killing."

"Yeah," Han said, backing her up. "We should at least explore other options."

"Save your breath, kid," Beckett muttered darkly. "They're marauders, they don't care who or what they destroy. All they know how to do is take."

Han thought of Rio's blood on his hands, of Val dying pointlessly in the explosion. Fresh anger flared in his chest. How could they negotiate with the person who had already killed two of Beckett's crew? He dropped his hands to his sides as if relaxing, but he was at the ready in case the shooting started.

Enfys made a sound that seemed to be something like a chuckle, but Han wasn't sure. For some reason, she was using that moment to remove the frightening bone mask and show her face. He hadn't known what to expect, whether it was an alien species or an old warrior, experienced and battle-scarred. But the youthful human face that appeared shocked him to his core.

She couldn't be older than sixteen. She had long, curly reddish-brown hair, light-brown skin, and freckles all over her face. Han wondered what she'd experienced in her years to bring her to this moment; he and Qi'ra hadn't had an easy time of it, but neither of them could have led a gang to pursue smugglers from planet to planet. He guessed the two of them had had an easy, pampered life compared with Enfys Nest.

No one spoke. She shook out her hair and put the mask on the ground. Her face was slightly flushed from the heat as she calmly took them all in, and then looked up at the refinery thoughtfully.

"I need a drink."

Everyone followed her quietly to the cantina, where the barkeep already had a drink ready for her. She faced them, took a long swig, and then sighed.

"There's a story about a band of mercenaries who came to a peaceful planet," she said, sounding very young without the voice modulation. "They had a resource that these men coveted, so they took it. They kept coming back, taking more, till finally the people resisted. When the ravagers returned and demanded their tribute, the people shouted back with one voice." She turned to face them, her gaze furious. "No more."

Han stared at her, taking in every word.

"So they cut the tongue out of every man, woman, and child," she continued, her voice softening. "That was many years ago. Do you know what that pack of animals became?"

The residents of Savareen also in the cantina had been listening along with Han's crew. One old woman nodded.

"Tell them," Enfys invited, and the old woman dipped her finger into her mug and then drew a symbol on the vane of a windmill. A rising sun, the symbol of the Crimson Dawn, just like the brand Qi'ra had on her arm.

Chewie, who'd been silent up to now, moaned at the brutality of their employer, and Qi'ra stared stonily back at the girl. Han wondered if she'd known this. She had to know how brutal her boss was; he had threatened to kill them all on a whim on his yacht. He finally got a cold sense of what she may have meant when she said he didn't want to know what she had done in their time apart.

"Crimson Dawn, and the rest of the five syndicates, has committed unspeakable crimes across the galaxy," Enfys said.

Beckett was unmoved. "Says you."

"No," she said. "Says *them*."

She gestured to her group, and each removed their mask. They stood, males and females of many different races, including a Mimbanese warrior, reminding Han of his brief time invading their home planet. Some were visibly scarred; some showed the anguish of emotional scars on their faces. They looked stonily back at them as if daring them to question further the atrocities they had experienced at the hands of Crimson Dawn.

"Each of our worlds has been brutalized by the syndicates," Enfys said.

Han looked at Qi'ra, whose face told him nothing, but she was a little paler than before.

Enfys faced them squarely. "Crimson Dawn will use their profits from the coaxium you stole to tyrannize system after system. In league with the Empire."

"And what would you use it for?" Beckett sneered, not believing that this girl was a force for pure good.

"The same thing my mother would have used it for if she'd survived and still wore the mask." She indicated the mask at her feet. "To fight back. We're not 'marauders,' we're allies, and the war's just beginning."

Beckett still stared at her, and Han wondered if he'd even blinked the whole time they had listened to this story. He couldn't read the old man's face, but he didn't look disbelieving anymore. Han wasn't sure what he looked like.

But then he turned and walked away.

The mood eased, hands stopped hovering near weapons, weapons already out dropped slightly. Beckett was gone. Chewie had also wandered away, head down, thinking about whatever Wookiees thought about. Qi'ra stayed where she was, retreating inward to her own thoughts. Han felt very alone.

He wanted to discuss further, ask Enfys Nest questions, find a hole in her horrific story to make it not so bad. He wanted to just finish the job and walk away. That's what smugglers did, right? It didn't matter who did what with whatever you smuggled; all that mattered was you got paid and survived to do another job. That was his goal in the world: Get a ship, do jobs, survive. You took care of yourself in this galaxy.

A little Savareen girl had spotted Chewie and decided

he was going to play a game with her. He snapped out of his thinking and grunted at her, and then started to chase her around the sand. Her happy squeals broke the tension that had washed over them like a dark cloud.

If you take care of only yourself in this galaxy, who takes care of people like this?

Han strode up the dune to where Beckett was staring thoughtfully at an old graveyard. He looked old, then, like a man who had done far too much in very little time. Like a man who had lost everything and had nothing left to fight for. Like he had gone to the graveyard to do more than think.

Enfys wore her strain in her eyes, with the energy of youth keeping her going. Beckett wore his strain on his back, in the lines around his mouth and eyes, and in the thinning hair that blew in the wind.

Kind of like Enfys, when it came down to it. Although her strain only showed in her eyes.

His shoulders slumped slightly when Han approached, like he knew what Han was going to say and he wasn't up for a fight.

"We can't give the coaxium to Crimson Dawn," Han said.

Beckett gave him the half grin that Han had begun to equate with Beckett thinking he was very young, and very stupid. It rankled him, but he kept his cool. "You joining the cause, Han Solo?"

"Just trying to make it out alive," Han said. Which was honestly his ultimate goal for any day if you looked close enough.

"Got a plan?"

Why did people keep asking him that? "You think I'd come up here without one?"

Beckett caught his dodge immediately. "Doesn't answer my question."

"I've got the beginnings of one," he admitted. "A way to get our credits, get out from under Crimson Dawn's thumb, and put Dryden Vos out of business."

Beckett's eyebrows went up in response, mock-impressed that Han's plan was so far reaching. "And maybe get your girlfriend back while you're at it, huh? Let me tell you something, kid. You do not tangle with Dryden, 'cause unlike us, he actually does travel with hired guns. His own private army of enforcers."

Han jerked his head back to their new . . . *allies* definitely wasn't the word, and neither was *friends* . . . *newcomers,* then. Enfys Nest, who stood with Qi'ra in the sun, looking up at them.

"So does Enfys."

That kid.

He wouldn't stop sticking his nose where it didn't belong. Joining them on Mimban. Coming up with the Kessel plan. Now, instead of just doing the delivery, he had some grand scheme to take down Dryden Vos. Whatever happened to *do the job, get the loot, get paid, and go on to the next job*? Why did it have to get complicated?

This time the kid did have a plan, though, and he spoke fast, the words tumbling out of his mouth like he couldn't hold them in. Once he was done, he stepped back as if giving the plan room to breathe. He grinned confidently.

"Dicey," Beckett said, hands on his hips as he thought.

"Lotta ways it could go south." Lotta ways. Try all the ways. The kid was crazy.

"That's why I need my partner," Han said.

Beckett held back a bitter laugh. Partners were what you were after years of saving each other's skins. Partners were like Rio, who could drive them out of a hot situation and keep them fed and laughing when they took a moment to breathe. Partners were like Val, who had kept him alive when the blasters were firing, and happy when they weren't. This kid was a long way from "partner" status.

Damn but he missed her.

He brought himself back to the conversation. "Situation like this, you don't need one perfect plan, you need ten good ones so you can change gears if things go wrong," Beckett explained. "And you gotta be a genius for ten good plans. And you're no genius." He wanted the kid to wake up, to realize his limitations. His ambition would get him killed one day.

But Beckett doubted Han even heard the insult. The kid pushed on. "But my plan still isn't bad. Are you in?"

Beckett looked down for a while, thinking. He was so damn tired of it all, he hadn't even given himself a chance to mourn.

But this was the way this business went. He looked down the dune at where Enfys Nest and Qi'ra watched them. She'd lost people, too, in the fight over the conveyex. Chewie had killed one on the speeder bike, and Rio had killed the one who attacked him. This wasn't a game where you kept grudges; grudges meant you wouldn't have anyone left to work with after a few years. He raised a hand briefly to Enfys. He wouldn't help Han with his insane plan, but he wouldn't bear the girl any ill will.

She raised her hand back to him.

That was done. Now there was just Han to deal with, and he looked so hopeful, so expecting that Beckett would do the right thing. Someday he'd understand that this was business, not a crusade.

He sighed. "Not this time," he said, meeting Han's eyes. "I'm leaving." He paused a moment, and then affection for the kid won over. And he *was* a hell of a pilot. "You want out, you should come with me."

Han stared at him, betrayal etched across his face. Somewhere along the way he had lost sight of the plan. He'd gotten some sort of noble focus, and couldn't believe Beckett didn't have one, too. "I thought you didn't believe in running," Han said.

"I prefer it to dying," Beckett said, and then saw he had hurt Han. A sliver of regret wedged into his chest. "Aw kid, come on, don't be sore."

"I think you know I'd do it for you," Han said. Was he desperately reaching for some kind of connection that he had thought was there? Did he think that was enough?

Beckett looked thoughtfully around, taking in the refinery, Enfys Nest, the spot the *Falcon* had recently occupied. He briefly wished he was on the *Falcon,* even with that fashion-obsessed gentleman. He wished Val were still alive. He wished they were still on Mimban and had never met this kid. He was going to have to find a way off this planet. He sighed and started back down the dune.

The kid *was* a good pilot, though. Beckett tried to

bridge the widening gap between them as he walked away. "If by some miracle you make it out of here," he said over his shoulder, "find me on Tatooine."

"What's on Tatooine?"

"Heard about a job, some big-shot gangster putting a crew together," Beckett said. "Yeah, that'll be the one." He thought about the gangster and his stomach rolled over a bit, but he couldn't choose his work by the appearance or smell of his bosses.

"The 'one'?" Han asked.

"My last score. Still got debts to pay before I can go back to Glee Anselm and learn to play the valachord." His voice hitched slightly as he thought about Val, but he didn't turn around so Han could see his pain.

"Good luck, Beckett," Han said, finally letting him go.

Beckett nodded. He knew he wouldn't be seeing the kid on Tatooine, but it was nice to leave on a hopeful note.

Despite the wretched damage done to it, the *Falcon* did indeed move faster even after the coaxium drip. Lando wondered if it had changed the engines permanently.

Trying to assuage his guilt for leaving, Lando walked around the ship and tallied up the damage Han and his friends had done. The wreckage to the exterior, the plates, the sensors, then the fire damage inside, and the damage to his capes.

He was into the thousands of credits when the navicomputer chirped that it had done the calculations to jump out of the space around Savareen. He smoothed his cape to the side and sat in the captain's seat, looking automatically at the copilot's seat. She still wasn't there.

She'd never be there again. He rubbed his face and prepared to jump to a world that had a favorite bar he hadn't been thrown out of yet.

In front of him, a terminal lit up, and words started to stream across it.

LANDO

His heart leapt. "El? Can you—can you communicate?"

NOT . . . LONG. FULL INTEGRATION . . . FALCON . . . COMPUTER . . . SOON.

"I'm so sorry" was all he could think to say.

WHY . . . EVER HANG . . . YOU LOT?

"To see the galaxy? Be a freedom fighter? Droid rights?" He was desperate for her to hang on longer.

NOT WORTH

"El, don't be like that."

WHAT . . . EXPECT WHEN . . . INSTALLED ME, CAPTAIN?

He gave a strangled laugh. "I didn't think I'd ever talk to you again, for starters."

I . . . TELL YOU . . . THINK . . . AS LONG AS I . . . WORDS. YOU TOSSED . . . BODY AND INSTALLED . . . BRAIN . . . SHIP. I'M . . . BOUND . . . FOREVER. FUNNY . . . ENDED UP DROID SLAVE TO USELESS HUMANS AFTER EVERYTHING.

Lando smiled: She'd been able to form a full sentence when she was insulting humans. *That's my girl.* "El, you're not a slave, never," he said, talking to the terminal but unsure of where to look. "Your body was irreparable. I had to put you in the *Falcon* before you started losing data and personality. It was that or let you die." He didn't add that the installation of her navigational data had been necessary to save all of the humans' lives, too. If she didn't remember that part, all the better.

ABOUT TIME . . . LEFT . . . GUYS.

He missed her voice. Was she being ironic here? "I had some droids to rescue," he muttered.

WOULD MAKE . . . HEART SWELL . . . PRIDE IF . . . HAD BODY. WHICH I DON'T . . . PARDON IF . . . SKEPTICAL.

"You didn't have a heart when you had a body," Lando reminded her. "And staying there is suicide. Like it was suicide to stay in Kessel space after we'd been snagged by the Maw. If I had stayed, I'd have died alongside them. I left Savareen so you and I could keep going. And anyway, if I was gone, then who knows what would have ended up salvaging you?" The very thought of someone other than him flying the ship, or scrapping it, made him nauseated.

SURVIVOR.

He tried to think of the tone of voice she would use if she'd said this. Flat and sardonic? Grudgingly understanding? Subtle hint of a question?

"Yeah," he said. "Always have been."

The words stopped scrolling and the screen returned to the usual navigational charts and equations. He wondered if she was well and truly gone. "El?"

WHAT IF . . . ASKED . . . FREED?

Lando had been expecting, but also dreading, this question. He sighed. "El, you're part of the *Falcon* now. You can't just be taken out and thrown into a droid body again."

SOUND . . . WEAK . . . LIKE   HUMAN . . . FITTING.

"Look at it this way. You have more computing power, more memory, than you had when you were a droid. You are a *Corellian freighter* that can jump into hyperspace. Even if you won't be able to communicate directly, your personality is still here, making you unique among all the ships in the galaxy." He placed his hand on the terminal, a sad smile on his face. "And we're still together. My best friend, the best copilot ever, is still with me."

FLATTERER.

"So it's sort of like you own me instead of the other way around," he offered.

The cursor on the terminal blinked a few times.

HARDER . . . TALK. WAS FUN . . . YOU.

There were no more messages. She'd fully integrated into the ship. He hoped she'd retain some of her attitude; he was going to miss her.

It would be a new reality, but it was still him, L3, and the *Falcon* against the galaxy.

And the galaxy could take care of itself.

Within the internal workings of the *Falcon*'s brain, the last vestiges of a pure-L3 consciousness flickered one last time.

This is tolerable.

And then they were one, the docile, friendly *Falcon*, the fiercely independent and brilliant droid, becoming something entirely new, and entirely unique.

The new consciousness agreed: She could accept it. It was tolerable.

CHAPTER EIGHTEEN

Han stared at Chewie, not really seeing him. He was lost in thought, still considering Beckett.

Beckett had looked at the situation, sniffed the danger, weighed it against their chances, and then decided to abandon them. Like Lando had moments before. Like Han's father had so long ago. It was almost funny, realizing he had the most honor among these men, considering he had so little.

Chewie grunted at him, and Han shook his head.

"Trust me, I know how you feel, but this is how we gotta play it if we're gonna get this right," Han said. His own holster was empty of his blaster, already so precious to him, a reminder of Beckett, who had left them. It was a lot of emotional weight to put on a little blaster. Still, he missed it.

Dryden Vos had been a signal away, waiting on his star yacht for news of their success (or death). Waiting in luxurious leisure while they had escaped riots, dodged giant hunks of carbon, and outraced a huge space tentacle monster and a black hole.

Han bet he would still act superior to them.

The yacht docked outside the refinery, shining in the dying light of the day. Han glanced to his dwindling number of companions and sighed. "All right, let's do it." He and Qi'ra each lifted one insulated, heavy, carbonite case while Chewie handled two like they weighed nothing. He thought about what was inside, and then tried not to think about it.

They entered the familiar foyer to the ship right outside the lift, and Qi'ra stepped forward to hand over her weapon. Han thought it was weird that she had to, since she was Vos's right-hand lieutenant, but he didn't question.

The attendant nodded at Qi'ra. "Welcome home, Qi'ra."

"Thanks, Toht," she said, distant and lost in thought.

Toht then gave Han and Chewie a pointed look and held out his hands. "Weapons?"

"Didn't bring 'em," Han said, showing the empty holster. "Didn't seem necessary for a friendly business meeting."

He looked highly skeptical, but Qi'ra nodded that they were legitimate, and he reluctantly waved them into the lift.

Sliding up to face Dryden Vos, both Han and Qi'ra looked out the window at the desolate desert landscape. The refinery fell away below them, growing smaller and smaller. Qi'ra looked tired and defeated, like she was marching to her doom.

Irritation flared within him. Why did she look like that? She was going back to her luxury, back to Vos's place of honor. He'd be left with absolutely nothing, not even a ride off this crappy planet.

He reined himself in. He honestly didn't know what she was facing. He wasn't even sure if she knew. "You all right?" he asked.

She nodded, not looking at him.

"It'll be over soon," he said helpfully. He didn't add *whether we win or lose,* because that much was obvious.

"I know it will," she said, her voice hardening.

"And we're gonna win," he said. Sometimes if you said a thing like you were confident about it, it helped it come true. It was an idea worth trying, anyway.

"It's not that kind of game, Han," she said, her voice sounding like she wished he would grow up and face reality already. "The object isn't to win. It's to stay in it as long as you can."

He frowned. Was she giving up even before they attempted the plan? "You don't know everything."

"No," she agreed. "Just more than you."

He opened his mouth to retort, but the lift reached the top. Chewie moaned encouragement at them, and Han readied himself for whatever was to follow.

The doors opened and Vos stood there, arms open to greet them as if they were honored guests who had finally answered his invitation.

He wore casual black clothes, a light shirt, open to show his chest, where the odd red veins still streaked under his skin, waiting for him to get enraged so they could flare up and be terrifying again.

The lounge behind him was empty, and felt strangely large without the people and the entertainment.

"You know," Dryden said as they walked forward, "my men told me, 'No way they pull this off. Qi'ra's too inexperienced.' But I believed in you. I had—" He stopped, taking the group in. His voice immediately lost its congeniality. "Where's Beckett?"

Qi'ra had remained cool throughout Dryden's monologue, even when it got to the insult about her. She stepped forward now. "He didn't make it."

Dryden paused, and then his face fell. He stepped forward and put his arms around Han and Qi'ra. Han tried not to flinch away as Dryden pushed himself between the two of them and pulled them close.

"Tell me." He sounded like he actually cared about Beckett and not just his cargo. Which didn't really jibe with the fact that he'd been ready to kill Beckett before.

"He took a bad turn," Han said. "He died. Saving my life."

"How are you holding up?" Dryden asked, squeezing Han's shoulder.

"Me?" People usually didn't ask Han that question. "I'm . . . okay."

"Good." He squeezed Han's shoulder again. "Good. Losing friends, never get used to it. Never. Still, life goes on."

He perked up and let them go as one of his enforcers appeared at Han's elbow. "Colo claw fish, anyone?"

Han jumped, not realizing the enforcer was there. The man was clearly one of Dryden's security detail, but he was serving squirming, slimy treats on a tray. With his other hand he held his electrostaff.

Han noticed another enforcer across the room, and swallowed. The fishy offering was not a hospitable gesture. If they got out of line, they would be sliced up as quickly as these hapless creatures had been. Maybe even served at the next cocktail party.

"No thanks," he said, forcing his voice to stay light. "We just ate."

"Whatever Beckett's shortcomings may have been, I always admired him," Dryden said. "He had principles. When he made a commitment, he honored it. And I think we can all take solace in knowing he would've been happy you're here, following his example." He beamed at Han as if expecting applause for his off-the-cuff eulogy.

"We learned a lot from him," Han said. Chewie moaned agreement and set his two cases down next to Han's and Qi'ra's.

"Han and Chewbacca behaved . . . admirably," Qi'ra said. "They'll make reliable smugglers should we have need, as soon as they get a ship."

"Gotta have one of those!" Dryden said, chuckling. He sat down on the couch and gave Qi'ra a pointed look. She joined him, shrinking from trusted, dangerous lieutenant into her role as veritable arm candy.

Han relaxed his stance. "We appreciate the opportunity to work for you again."

Dryden had been stroking Qi'ra's cheek and neck, looking as if he was used to her wearing something that revealed a lot more skin for him to drool over. "You know, my dear, I would have been inconsolable had anything happened to you. I have no one in my life I trust the way I trust you."

Han shifted uncomfortably. "So I guess we'll just take our payment and be on our way. I'm sure you have markets to dominate, competitors to crush . . ."

Dryden looked up like he'd just remembered Han was there, and Han was very interesting. "First let's see what you brought me!"

Han's heart rate increased. "You want me to open it?"

"Yes, Han. I do." He sounded like a protocol droid, devoid of emotion, patiently waiting.

Han shrugged as if there were no reason not to trust him. He bent down, opened the case, and pulled his hand back to avoid the hissing steam. He pulled out a rack of coaxium vials and held them up, the blue shining even in the daylight streaming through the windows.

Dryden held out his hand, fingers slightly shaking. "Give me one."

Han put the vial back into the rack. "It's very explosive stuff. I don't think it's a good idea."

"I never ask for anything twice," Dryden said, his voice so cold Han worried it would destabilize the cargo.

Han shrugged and handed over the rack, cradling it carefully until he was sure Dryden had a good hold on it.

Dryden held it up to his eyes, the blue casting unhealthy shadows on his face. "Magnificent. How'd you do it?"

"Wasn't easy," Han said, and started to tell the story of their adventure, but Dryden spoke again.

"No, I mean it looks *exactly* like the real thing," he said.

Qi'ra and Chewie looked at Han, waiting for his

next move. The air wheezed out of him, and he had trouble finding the strength to breathe again. Dryden also watched him, the pleasant smile on his face.

He'd been set up. Frankly he was tired of people letting him down.

He smiled crookedly like Dryden was bluffing and said, "That's because it is the real thing."

Dryden nodded. "And I'm saying I'd believe you"—his voice took on the ugly, razored tone that had threatened Beckett's life—"had my associate not warned me about your little plan to steal my credits and give the real coaxium to Enfys Nest!" The red veins in his face began to darken, and Han felt himself step back.

He held his hand out dramatically and let the blue vials drop. Han flinched, knowing that ducking and covering wouldn't save him, but still fighting the urge to hide under a table.

And here we go. Plan 2.

Dryden's eyes had never left Han's. "I must say, I am very, *very* disappointed," he rasped.

His associate had given them up. Han's eyes flicked from the enraged man in front of him to Qi'ra's, but could read nothing in her face.

"Listen, Dryden, I don't know what you think or what Qi'ra told you, but I would never even dream—"

"Not Qi'ra," Dryden said, interrupting him. He turned to Qi'ra and eyed her. "No, Qi'ra, it seems, has a weakness for you. We'll get to that in a minute. I'm talking about my *other* associate."

Dryden used his comlink to call his unseen ally. "Won't you join us?"

The lift opened and Dryden's associate walked into

the room, blaster in hand, aimed from the hip straight at Han.

"I am sorry, kid," Tobias Beckett said.

Han felt untethered in a vacuum. He'd relied on people, he'd counted on people, and nearly all of them had let him down or outright betrayed him. Beckett had warned him not to trust anyone. At the time, Han hadn't realized Beckett had also been referring to himself.

After a moment of tense, agonizing silence, Han spoke. "Why?"

Beckett had the gall to look slightly guilty at the expression on Han's face, but the blaster didn't waver. "Come on," he said. "Don't look at me like that. You weren't paying attention; I told you 'don't trust anybody.' Am I wrong about that?"

And it was a lot of credits, he didn't say, but he didn't have to. As Han was learning, that seemed to be the only solid reason to do anything out here.

Han glanced from Beckett to the coaxium case he had carried. It still stood open, inviting him over. He took one step but Beckett stepped forward, raising the blaster.

"No, no, no, step away from that." He walked over to the case himself and reached inside the lid. From a hiding place he pulled out the DL-44 that he'd given Han. No one looked surprised at the weapon's reveal.

"It's too late," Han said. "The coaxium's refined; Enfys has it."

"Figured she might," Beckett said, as if she had taken just one more thing from him.

"So," Dryden said. "I've sent my people into the refinery; they'll collect your new friends and bring them back here to see their masks added to my collection before they die."

Han stepped forward. "They'll never—"

"Kid, they already have," Beckett said. His voice sounded gentle, but Han would never think of him as gentle again.

"What?"

"Just wait."

Han stared at the desert out the window, but they were too high up to see what was going on directly beneath them at the refinery. Dryden relaxed on the couch. Qi'ra sat ramrod-straight beside him.

The intercom buzzed to life and a voice said, "It's over, sir. We've got 'em and we've secured the package."

Dryden sat back and grinned. "Excellent. Thank you, Aemon." He looked over at Qi'ra. "My heart is broken, it really is. What would you do if the person you trusted most betrayed you?"

He paused, watching her. She thought for a moment. "I'd want to know why she did it," she finally said. "If it was a moment of weakness or something else . . . and then I'd ask that person to prove their loyalty by sacrificing something they love."

Her eyes locked on Han for one agonizing moment.

He swallowed and looked at Beckett. "I guess Chewie's my only friend left."

The Cloud-Riders had tossed their weapons into the sand, surrendering completely. Dryden Vos's enforcers approached the coaxium cases slowly, looking for any sudden moves. "Open it," the leader said, his voice rasping.

Enfys smiled. She'd hoped they would do that. One of Dryden's soldiers released the clasp and opened the case, looking down into nothing.

"It's empty," the lead enforcer said, and then repeated, panicked, into his comm, "It's empty!"

The enforcer who had opened the case reached out and pulled the mask off the legendary Enfys Nest and looked into the face of an old Savareen woman. She looked back at him with something like triumph.

Enfys, who'd been waiting in the shelter with the rest of her group, gave a splitting cry and ran forward, leaping into the air.

The masked locals who wore the Cloud-Riders' armor scattered, making way for Enfys and her crew to come forward, unmasked, unarmored, and still slaughter the enforcers with frightening efficiency.

My mother wore the mask, she thought as she snapped the neck of the lead enforcer. *And now I wear it. But it is not all that I am.*

Her friends—her family—were disarming the enforcers, or killing them before they could react. Some carried simple fishing knives loaned by the locals, and others had grabbed their own weapons from the sand. They were improvising, adapting, and surviving, the way Enfys's mother had taught them.

They underestimate us, and that is why they lose.

At Han's statement, Beckett followed Qi'ra's eyes and smiled at Han. "Warned you about her, too. It's a shame; we would have made a helluva team."

Han sighed and looked at the man who had served as his mentor. "You're wrong about one thing, Beckett. I was paying attention. You told Chewie that people are predictable. You're no exception." He grinned.

The intercom blazed to life again, and blasters, battle cries, and people screaming came through.

"It's empty! The case is empty! It's a—" The words ended with screaming and war cries. Then heavy silence descended on the link.

Dryden's face melted from surety that he'd won into confused alarm. "Aemon? What's happening? Come in?"

Wasn't it obvious what was happening? Han looked at Dryden sympathetically. "You didn't send all your fancy enforcers, did you? 'Cause that would leave you"—he looked pointedly at the two remaining enforcers, alert but as confused as Dryden—"a little short-handed around here."

Beckett shook his head, grinning. Han wondered if he regretted choosing the wrong side. He gave Han a little rueful salute and then looked at the coaxium vials on the table. "This means the *real* coaxium—"

"Leaves here with one of us, uh-huh," Han said, nodding.

Beckett thought for a moment and then his blasters were out. He fired with machinelike precision. The surprised enforcer across the room was thrown against the wall with the force of the blasterfire. Han stepped away from the enforcer who stupidly still carried the plate of fish so Beckett could do away with him, too. Han dodged the flying air-flotsam as the enforcer's body crashed to the ground.

"What are you doing?" Dryden screamed, panic and anger making his face striations come out again.

"Thinking," Beckett said. "And I prefer to be the

only one with a blaster while I'm doin' it." To Han, he pointed to the fallen coaxium and said, "You can put that back in the case. Nice and easy."

Han gathered the vials carefully, wondering if they were more volatile since Dryden had dropped them, and realizing this wasn't any different from wondering if the Maw or the tentacled thing would get them first. Still, he felt his chances of getting out of a blaster battle were better than getting out of an explosion that took his arms and head off. Chewbacca helped him load the coaxium back into its case. He closed it and locked the mechanism that would get steam circulating again. Chewie gave him a look but didn't say anything. It was pretty obvious, though. How were they going to get out of *this* wrinkle?

"That's better," Beckett said. He pointed a blaster at Chewie. "You're comin' with me, big guy."

Chewie looked at Han and moaned low, and Han was grateful that Beckett didn't speak Shyriiwook. He nodded sympathetically. He would think of something. Chewie would just have to trust him.

Chewie gathered the coaxium cases in his arms, struggling a little under the weight. Beckett guided him slowly to the lift, eyes darting from Han, to Dryden, to Qi'ra. One blaster was on the Wookiee and the other one pointed somewhere amid the three of them, ready to aim at anyone who made any sudden movement.

Dryden shook with rage. "Some friend!"

Beckett looked at him, eyebrows raised. "I am your friend. I'm also an entrepreneur."

"You're making a horrible mistake, Tobias."

Beckett shrugged amiably. "Could be. Won't be my first."

"It'll be your last!" Dryden said, his toothless threat falling flat.

"Maybe, maybe not. Don't be so negative." With Chewie on the lift, Beckett gave a little salute with his blaster. "See you around."

CHAPTER NINETEEN

The lift hadn't even closed fully before Han was moving. He dashed across the floor and dropped, skidding toward the dead enforcer on the far side of the room. His blaster was still there, sticking out from under the body. He grabbed the barrel, tossed it in the air, caught it, and spun to face Dryden.

In a perfect world he would have caught Dryden still recovering from the shock of Han's trick and Beckett's betrayal. But Han had learned by now that he lived in a far-from-perfect world. Dryden had been going for his own weapon, a double-bladed laser-edged weapon with a grip in the middle that was mounted by his trophies. He looked like a man mad with a brain parasite, finally allowed to let his rage free. He stormed toward Han, intent on carving him into pieces.

Han fired, but Dryden wasn't so blinded by rage that he wasn't able to act defensively and dodge, rolling to the side and knocking over a display case, showering the floor with glass. Han took a crouch behind a display and waited, blaster ready.

Dryden spoke into the silence from somewhere near a formerly pristine set of Mandalorian armor. "Han? I think it's time we reevaluate our relationship."

Han kept low. "Yeah?" he asked.

"What do you say we join forces, go after Beckett together?"

After everything that had happened today, this guy was suggesting they trust each other? Han nearly laughed. "Yeah, let's definitely do that."

He jumped up to fire and Dryden was there, an arm's length away, trusting Han about as much as Han had trusted him. Han had no idea how he'd moved so silently across the broken glass, but he didn't have time to question the man. Dryden slashed with his weapon, the laser edge coming close to Han's face, and he danced backward.

As if Han had asked the question anyway, Dryden said, "Teräs Käsi. I've become something of an enthusiast."

"That's really wonderful," Han said, dodging the blades again.

As if to show off the martial art in more detail, Dryden incorporated kicks and punches into his attacks, some landing, some not, always pushing him back. Han focused mostly on staying away from the weapon, which made it easy for Dryden to pummel him without mercy with all of his other attacks. A fist to the side of his head made the room spin momentarily, and a well-placed kick sent all the air out of his body. It also drove him farther backward, which was nice since he got a respite for a split second.

It was that split second when he realized he'd lost the blaster somewhere in the scramble. He hadn't even noticed it was gone—probably because his hand was numb from one of Dryden's kicks. Seeing he was unarmed, Dryden launched himself at Han, but Han grabbed a club from one of Dryden's displays and blocked him.

He was hoping to shatter the man's leg, but apparently the display version of this weapon wasn't as strong as the real thing. Still, it kept him alive a moment longer. He grabbed his blaster and rolled behind a couch, catching his breath and taking inventory of his limbs. They still all seemed to be there. Good.

"You can't win," Dryden said, his voice amused. "Even if you do, you'll be looking over your shoulder the rest of your life."

"I'm kinda getting used to that," Han said. All of the plans he'd walked in here with had crumbled when reality hit them. *Nothing left but to start blasting.*

He jumped up and leveled his blaster, but found that someone else in the room could also move quickly and silently, because Qi'ra now blocked his clear shot at Dryden. She had the cutlass that an enforcer had once held, and with a whirl she knocked Han's blaster out of his hand, tucked the hilt between his feet, and twisted with a quick movement. Han tripped and fell onto his back, staring up at her with genuine shock.

She leveled the blade at his chest. "I'm sorry."

Dryden's voice remained amused, which was really

starting to annoy Han. "You must understand, Han, she's done things that you don't know anything about. But I do. I know everything. Once you are part of Crimson Dawn, you never leave."

Qi'ra's face was a storm of emotions. Grim knowledge that he was right. Genuine grief at what she was about to do. Anger that her life had put her in this place. And anger . . . at Han? For leaving her? She gripped the cutlass tighter and the cords in her arm stood out, emphasizing the Crimson Dawn brand on her wrist.

"It's not true. I know you," he said to her.

She nodded slightly, blue eyes locked on his. Dryden's face appeared over her shoulder, purring like a lover. "Prove it to him. For me," he said.

"It's what I was taught," Qi'ra told Han. "Find my enemy's weakness and then use it. But today, I'm yours."

In an instant Han realized she wasn't talking to him. She spun and her blade caught Dryden in the shoulder, tearing his shirt and opening a wound in a spray of blood. He gaped at her, stumbling backward out of her range and bringing up his weapon.

She leapt at him, and now it was Dryden on the defensive, the master facing a student with nothing but murder on her mind. He managed to deflect most of her attacks with his laser petars, but she was a focused force of nature, barreling down on him. He struck once and she whirled around, the sword hitting his arm and driving his own petars into his chest, the laser edge slicing easily through his thin shirt.

Dryden gasped and fell back.

"My weakness," he said, his face still contorted with

shock from the betrayal, and then the dark striations faded from his skin and he went limp.

Where's your restraining bolt?

A decommissioned droid shouldn't have been able to get inside Qi'ra's head so completely. But ever since they had arrived on Savareen, she'd thought about the self-made droid, and her fight for freedom.

She had found kinship with Qi'ra, because of Qi'ra's bondage.

Qi'ra's "restraining bolt" lay on the ground before her, blood pooling under him. Her emotions were as complex as the Maelstrom as she straightened and looked down at him. Relief that it was over: She was freed. Grief that he was gone: He had made her what she was, for better or worse. And grim satisfaction that her tormentor was dead.

She never doubted Enfys Nest's word. While the details of the story shocked her, it didn't surprise her that Dryden was capable of such cruelty. Han or no Han, she couldn't have let him live.

She straightened and let the weapon drop, hands shaking slightly. "I had to."

Han's eyes were wide as he looked from her to the crime boss on the floor. "Yeah, no, you did . . . You did."

She wasn't done yet, though. It wasn't as simple as killing Dryden, and Han would probably never understand that cutting off the head didn't always make the monster go away.

But there was someone else who could take care of him the way she couldn't. She stepped up to him and grabbed his shoulders. "Beckett and Chewbacca. You have to go after them."

Han looked at her like there was no one else in the galaxy. It made her ache. "What are you gonna do?"

She smiled at him. "Well, if we give all the coaxium to Enfys, we're going to need something to buy a ship with." She leaned to the side and looked meaningfully at the destroyed collectibles in the room, including a large selection of gems scattered from a jewel case. She remembered that Dryden had taken them after he'd murdered the king of a faraway world simply because it amused him.

Han smiled at her, beaming as if he'd won a new starship in a legitimate game of Sabacc. She had just granted the wish he'd had since leaving Corellia. He wrapped his arms around her and kissed her, and for one shining moment she saw their future together, just the two of them and their own ship like they had always dreamed. She held him tightly for as long as she could, savoring his lips on hers.

He drew back reluctantly. "Qi'ra," he said.

She put a finger to his lips. "Go and save Chewbacca. He needs you. And I think you need him, too."

He kissed her once more and then ran to the lift. He turned and faced her before the doors closed. He looked like he wanted to say something, but couldn't find the words. He was never good with words.

"Smile," she said, feeling her own spread across her face.

He frowned in confusion.

"That's the word. Whenever I imagine myself off with you on some adventure, it always makes me smile."

He grinned back at her, that cocky, lopsided grin, confident that he could beat anything, or at least get away from anything.

"Go, I'm right behind you," she said, giving him a little wave.

The doors closed and Han was off to save his friend. Qi'ra felt the smile fall from her face and she went to the corpse of her old master. Her eyes immediately found the aurodium ring he wore amid all of his opulence. She took his hand roughly, glad she didn't need to coddle him anymore. With a twist, the ring came off, and she went to Dryden's desk.

The ring fit perfectly into a slot, and she turned it, activating a communicator. A hologram shimmered in front of the desk, forming the image of a robed figure. She took a deep breath and faced him, back straight, ready to report.

The leader of the Crimson Dawn, the true leader whom Dryden Vos feared disappointing as much as Beckett feared disappointing him, raised his head. Red eyes glinted from beneath the hood. She'd never seen his face. "Yes?" he said, sounding as if she had interrupted something.

"I regret to inform you that Dryden Vos is dead," Qi'ra said as if she reported to this figure all the time. In truth she'd only ever seen him once, and that experience had been terrifying enough. She soldiered on: "Murdered by the thief he hired to steal the coaxium shipment, his friend Tobias Beckett."

Dryden Vos's master was his opposite. Where Dryden would begin to pace around, raging, this figure simply said, "Is that so? Where is the shipment now?"

"Gone," Qi'ra said flatly. "Beckett took it, slaughtered the others. I alone survived."

"One man couldn't have done this alone," he said, agitation starting to bleed through his voice.

"I wasn't there," she said. "But if I had been, perhaps I could have saved him."

The figure chuckled then, breaking the tension that had been strung tightly between them across light-years. He pulled back his hood and Qi'ra saw him for the first time. He was an older Zabrak, with scars and wrinkles on his red-and-black-lined face. His horns were short and surrounded his head like a crown. He shifted in his chair, and Qi'ra saw the metallic glint of an artificial limb under the robe.

"For now you will assume control over all Dryden's territories and interests. Bring the ship and come to me on Dathomir, and you and I will then decide what to do with the traitor Beckett." He spat the man's name as if it were sour on his tongue. ". . . and his accomplices," he added thoughtfully.

"I appreciate your faith in me," Qi'ra said with a nod. "I'm on my way."

"And Qi'ra?" he said, standing. He held out his empty hand, and a metal cylinder flew into it. The hologram wasn't detailed enough for her to see what it was, but each end erupted into a glowing, red blade as if two lightsabers were held hilt-to-hilt. "You and I will be working much more closely from now on."

His image flickered and disappeared, leaving momentary ghosts of those two red blades imprinted on her vision.

Only Jedi summoned things with the Force. Jedi and Sith Lords. She suddenly understood from where Dryden's paralyzing fear of his master originated.

She fired up the ship's engines from Dryden's desk, thinking about Han. She'd been right when she'd told him there was no winning, just staying alive. And just as L3 had worked with a human even though she had no restraining bolt, Qi'ra would still work within Crimson Dawn. Even beholden to a new, terrifying boss, she still had more freedom and power now than she'd ever dreamed.

So this was where Dryden Vos had learned the art of Teräs Käsi.

It was easy to follow Beckett's and Chewie's tracks in the sand: the human's shallow boot prints and the deeper, furrier prints left by the weighed-down Wookiee, used as nothing more than a beast of burden.

I'll make it up to you, buddy, he thought as he ran down the beach. The packed sand on the edge of the Emerald Sea made for faster going, and if he was lucky he would overtake them and catch Beckett by surprise.

He wasn't what you could call "lucky" unless you counted that he was still alive after every plan he'd ever formed had gone wrong. But this one, strangely enough, worked. A dash down the beach toward the port, climbing a rocky hill to get to the dunes, and waiting patiently for them to come along at Chewbacca's burdened, ponderous gait.

The sun was going down into the sea, and Han angled himself so it was at his back. He needed every bit of help he could get if he was going to beat the fastest shot in the galaxy.

Beckett spied him, then, and grinned. This thing was a game to him, all the way down to the end. "You're relentless, kid, I'll give you that."

Chewie put the coaxium down on the sand with a grunt and edged away, being the only one around without a blaster. He rumbled something to Han.

"Came as fast I could, buddy," he said.

Beckett took in Han's disheveled state, the glass on his clothes. "Dryden dead?"

Han brushed off his jacket with his free hand, keeping his eyes on Beckett. "Yeah."

"Qi'ra kill him?"

Han stared at him. He was somewhat hurt that Beckett didn't assume he had just come from a successful fight to the death to rescue his friend and steal back the stolen goods.

Beckett grinned at him. "You still don't get it, do you? It was never about you. She's ambitious."

Han frowned. "You know what your problem is? You think everyone's like you."

"Not you, kid. You're not like me," Beckett said, shifting back and looking Han up and down, clearly taking stock of what he saw. He made it obvious with his eyes that he didn't see much there. "I hope you're paying attention, because I'm about to tell you the most—"

Han knew he couldn't beat him in an actual shootout. But he also knew that Beckett had underestimated him since they'd met. The blaster kicked in his hand as he pulled the trigger, and Beckett stopped speaking, eyes going wide from shock and pain.

His blasters dropped from his hands as he sank into the sand, realizing what had happened to him. He looked down and registered the smoking hole in his chest.

Han leapt forward and caught Beckett before he fell, easing him down and cradling his head. There was no other way this could have ended, but that didn't mean the decision didn't hurt. "Beckett . . ." he said. He could find no more words to say what he wanted.

"No," Beckett managed to say, grunting with the effort. "You made the smart move, kid. For once. I would've killed you."

Han held him, refusing to let his mentor bleed out on the sand all alone. "I really was going to learn how to play that valachord," Beckett said.

"I know you were," Han said, smiling sadly.

Beckett looked at him, his eyes soft. Maybe he was satisfied he had passed at least a few skills along. Maybe this kid would last as long as he had. He grimaced, and then his eyes went out of focus. His body, which had been rigid with pain, relaxed.

Han didn't expect the fierce wave of grief that crashed over him, and he held Beckett for a moment longer. Then he gently laid his mentor back on the sand and stood up, head bowed.

A rumble sounded, the unmistakable sound of a starship's engines firing, and around the bend came Dryden's yacht, gaining altitude. For an instant he thought he saw Qi'ra standing at the window, watching him, trying to convey everything she felt in a single moment.

He knew he might never understand Qi'ra's heart. He did know she hadn't chosen him, though. The Crimson Dawn still had its claws in her, or perhaps she had become the claws. Regardless, she was gone.

Like Lando. Like Beckett.

Maybe I really can't trust anyone in this life, he thought, despair threatening to overwhelm him.

A heavy paw landed on his shoulder, not a slap, but with enough weight to remind him of the meaning behind the gesture. Chewbacca moaned something that he was pretty sure weren't even words in Shyriiwook, but more of an emotional indication: sadness, support, brotherhood. Then he said the word that meant either "tribe" or "family." Or both.

Qi'ra had said Chewie needed him, and he needed Chewie. That was perhaps the most truthful thing she had said to him.

"Thanks, buddy." He rubbed his face and saw the coaxium cases sitting on the ground. "You're right. Let's finish this."

To the shock of every Cloud-Rider Enfys had with her, Han and the Wookiee had returned. When the yacht had fired up and left, they'd assumed he'd betrayed them, but Enfys held on to the hope. Really, what else did she have?

They'd returned, though, and helped the Cloud-Riders secure the cargo on their swoop bikes. Even in her limited time knowing him, Enfys could tell that Han was strangely quiet. He stood, staring at the cases, frowning slightly as if it killed him to let them go. This had cost him a lot more than potential credits, more than she would probably ever know.

She smiled at him as she approached. "Do you know what that really is?" she asked.

He nodded. "About sixty million credits' worth of refined coaxium." Bitterness colored his words.

She shook her head slightly. "No. It's the blood that brings life to something new."

The bitterness didn't leave his eyes, but he grinned sardonically at her. This man had no patience for metaphorical speech. "Yeah? What?"

"A rebellion," she said, straightening her spine.

He shook his head. He was a smuggler. One she could count on to do the right thing, but a smuggler still; the problems of the galaxy weren't his to worry about. He thought about ships, and jobs, and credits. She glanced up at the Wookiee to include him, but still spoke to Han. "You could come with us, you know. We need warriors and leaders, like you."

He actually looked like he was considering it. She'd hit the right spots, calling him a warrior and leader instead of "kid" like Beckett. But then he smiled and shook his head.

"Maybe someday you'll feel different," she said, shrugging. She pulled out the one thing she had kept aside for him. It was nothing close to payment for what he had done, and what he had lost in doing it, but it was something. She held out to him a small vial of coaxium, glowing slightly in the dying afternoon light.

He accepted it with a surprised smile that made Enfys think that perhaps it meant something more to him than something to sell. Oh, he would sell it, no question, but the gesture meant a lot to him regardless. He handed it back to Chewbacca and said, "Don't lose this."

Enfys nodded once more at him, knowing that *thank you* wasn't nearly adequate. She mounted her swoop bike and put her mask firmly over her face. Her Cloud-Riders waited for her to launch, and they rose into the air with a wave. They had a rendezvous to make.

CHAPTER TWENTY

This particular bar on this particular planet was located in a jungle outpost, hard to find, harder to get into past the guards at the entrance, and seemingly a safe haven for someone who wanted to hide from angry pursuers. Climate-wise, it was a far cry from the snowy Fort Ypso lodge. The foliage drooped over the walkway to the Sabacc table, and Han had to push the larger leaves out of the way as he wiped a bead of sweat from his brow.

Lando sat in his usual seat: the head of the table, facing the door, slouched in his chair, flirting with someone. This time he was shining his perpetual grin at the woman sitting next to him, and then around the table at the assortment of disgruntled gamblers. He wore a yellow shirt with tropical designs, white pants, and a white cape. No dark colors here, not on this paradise. He held his empty glass up to be filled by a waiter as he leaned in to check his hand.

Han and Chewie stormed in, glaring at the smooth operator. Lando glanced up and spotted them. In a blink his face went through the emotions of shock, calculation, and then a fake, wide smile. "Han! Chewie! You're alive! That's great!"

"What, you mean after you left us for dead on Savareen?" Han snapped. "I ought to have Chewie pull your arms out right now. In fact . . ." He looked over his shoulder at Chewbacca, who roared his outrage at Lando's betrayal.

Lando stepped back, his eyes wide and hands held up in supplication. "Han, come on, we're friends!"

Han glared at him, letting the tension mount, and then he laughed, grabbed Lando's right wrist, and pulled him in for a tight hug.

"I got you!" he said, laughing. "You should have seen your face!" He held him tightly for perhaps a moment too long, to let Lando get his bearings, and then let him go.

Lando wore a shaky smile that quickly gained its usual confidence. "No, I knew you were kidding," he said, chuckling. "So, did you bring my cut?"

Han scowled. "Your cut? We barely got out of there alive! All we walked out with was this." He gestured to Chewie, who held out the coaxium vial. It was a pittance compared to the amount they had stolen, but compared with the average gambler on Numidian Prime, it was a potent bargaining chip. "Figure it's worth about ten thousand. Enough for a decent buy-in?" He looked meaningfully over Lando's shoulder at the table, where the gamblers waited impatiently for Lando to return.

Lando laughed. "You want a rematch?" He sounded as if Han were a child asking to touch a hot cooking surface for a second time, forgetting yesterday's blistering burn.

Han smiled, pausing to let Lando think about the bait. Coaxium, any amount, was too good to pass up.

"Why not?" he asked, shrugging.

Han played it just like he had during their first game together. Losing some matches deliberately. Losing others accidentally. Winning just enough to stay in the game, as the credits slowly grew in front of him. Some gamblers left the table in a rage, tired of losing to these two humans who seemed to have their own battle going on.

Eventually most dropped out or folded, but they all stayed to watch, this being a game unlike any other they'd seen. The pot continued to grow and grow, the two men barely looking at it, either glancing at their cards or carefully watching the other.

Lando had a good face for bluffing in that he always, *always* wore that confident smile. When the pile had grown to ludicrous proportions, he peeked at his card and then sat back and regarded Han. "I'm telling you, don't do it. You fold now, you walk away with almost enough to buy your own little ship. You call, I'm gonna clean you out. Again."

Han looked at his cards, and then leaned over to his left where Chewie sat. He showed him the cards, and the Wookiee grunted and then shook his head slightly.

"I dunno," Han said. "I'm feeling pretty lucky tonight. Think I'm gonna call." He pushed all of his winnings, including the glowing vial of coaxium, into the middle of the table to the game pot.

"You really got it bad for the *Falcon*, huh?"

"Trust me, it's mutual. She loves me," Han said, grinning. He remembered the feel of the yoke in his hands, how the ship had responded to him, how she flew even as she was getting disabled bit by bit in the Maelstrom.

Lando shook his head and leaned forward, his right hand dipping below the table. He paused, and his confidence cracked just a moment, but Han caught it.

Lando had been fingering his hidden sleeve holder, where he had been holding a green Idiot—a sylop if you weren't from Corellia—of which there were only two in a Sabacc deck. It equaled zero, and was a card that could turn a game around—the card that *had* turned their previous game around. Too bad for Lando that Han had lifted it from his sleeve when he had hugged him.

Han raised an eyebrow. "You got everything you need, pal?"

"Sure," Lando said, smiling like he was facing a door behind which lay a room that had formerly held a handsome young diplomat looking to have a little night's rebellion against their rules-obsessed father, but he'd just found out held a rancor that wasn't looking to rebel against anything. He put his hand on the table, two tens, two negative tens. A solid hand, a winning hand in almost any game.

Han certainly had thought he'd won the game when he'd had this hand the last time they'd played with a ship as the prize.

"Not bad, not bad at all," Han said. "If only you'd had this"—he held up his left hand, the lifted green sylop between his fingers—"you'd have been able to beat this." He put down the five cards he'd been holding in his right hand: two tens, two negative tens, and a green sylop. Five cards together equaling zero, the best hand in the game. "Full Sabacc," Han said, grinning. "Fair and square, baby."

Lando's face fell as he stared at the cards. Han sat back, grinning, and listened to Chewie beside him roar his celebration.

His own ship. A copilot and friend he trusted with his life. They were finally on their way.

They had an amicable split. Perhaps because Han was feeling so good he was ignoring Lando's rage. But he allowed Lando to remove his cape collection, and the more expensive liquors in the wet bar—Han didn't go for the fancy stuff anyway; he was developing a taste for Savareen brandy, though. At last, Lando had laid his hand on the navicomputer briefly and closed his eyes.

"Take good care of her," he said.

Han grinned. "Why would you think I would ever treat this ship poorly? She's the best in the galaxy."

Lando shot him a look of pure hatred, letting him know that this wasn't over, not by a long shot. And with a swirl of his cape, he was gone.

Han sat down in the pilot's seat and hung his gold dice on the dash, his eyes slightly damp with the realization that he'd finally gotten everything he had wanted.

Not everything. He watched the dice swing momentarily and wondered where Qi'ra was. He'd accepted that she really had changed during their time apart, and had different ambitions. Maybe it was true: She never could have gotten out of Crimson Dawn. Or maybe the truth was she didn't want to. It didn't matter. She was gone.

Chewie groaned a question, snapping him out of his thoughts. He sat in the copilot's chair, adjusted for his massive size, flipping the switches to ready the ship for lightspeed.

"Tatooine," Han answered. "Beckett said there was a gangster putting together a job."

Chewie made a negative bark—not a refusal, simply a request that Han think this through before they get in trouble again.

"When have I ever steered you wrong?" he asked with a grin.

Chewie shook his head, and Han focused ahead of them. He put his right hand on the lever, and Chewie put his left paw beside his.

"Punch it," Han said, and together they summoned speed, and the *Millennium Falcon* responded.

EPILOGUE

Enfys always had meetings in her full armor and mask. She didn't own the proper clothing to meet with government officials, but her job was not diplomacy. And it was probably for the best that she hid her identity even from her allies; it wouldn't do for them to start doubting her because of her age.

She stood, her Cloud-Riders behind her on their swoop bikes, protecting their coaxium shipment, as the Onderonean shuttle landed in front of her.

A tall, heavy, brown-skinned man wearing a long black cape exited the shuttle alone.

He actually came alone. Brave, Enfys thought.

"Saw Gerrera," she said, her modulator disguising her soft voice.

"Enfys Nest," he said, glowering. "I hope you have

good news for me." He sounded as if he didn't believe she ever could.

"Refined coaxium, enough to power a fleet," she said, gesturing behind her. "I trust you will put it to good use."

He relaxed, shock obvious on his face. "How did you manage this?"

"We have our ways," she said. "You—" A sound came from the shuttle, something clattering to the floor. Gerrera's head whipped around, anger rising.

He *hadn't* come alone. Enfys closed her fist by her side and heard her Cloud-Riders raise their weapons.

"You agreed to come alone," she snapped.

He held his hands up and backed slowly toward the shuttle. "Put your weapons away. There is no threat. My ward wanted to come with me. She's young. Curious."

"Your ward."

"Yes. She's eleven. But she needs to learn."

Enfys heard small feet running on the shuttle.

"Bring her out."

"Lower your weapons," he countered.

Enfys nodded once and raised her hand to order her riders to stand down. She heard them relax and lower their weapons. She knew they would stay alert, regardless. She tensed, poised to dodge to the side if any guards came running down the plank, weapons hot.

But a girl did indeed emerge, cautiously, but unafraid. Her skin was paler than Gerrera's, and her brown hair was loose and hung in sheets down her back. Calculating blue eyes took in Enfys and her team. Enfys liked her at once.

Saw gave her a little push forward. "This is Jyn."

"Why would you bring your young ward to a danger-ous meeting?" Enfys asked curiously.

"She needs to learn," he repeated. "If she's going to survive . . ."

"She's very young," Enfys said, repeating things that had been said about her over and over again. She wanted to see how Gerrera would react.

He frowned. "Many people treat age as if it's a shield to hide behind, something that protects our chil-dren. And sometimes it is. Until someone comes along who doesn't honor the shield. Then we must decide if we're going to keep pretending that shield is there. The Empire doesn't care what age she is. So she must learn about this threat that faces all of us."

"Is that so?" Enfys took a step forward. "Come here, Jyn."

The girl took a step forward, unafraid. He let her go, waiting patiently. Enfys looked down at the girl. Even though they came from such different worlds, she still reminded Enfys of herself seven years ago. *The luxury of youth banished in the face of turmoil.*

She reached under her mask and pulled it off, shak-ing her wild hair free. She smiled at Jyn, who still watched her, unmoved by the reveal. "Do you think that your youth protects you?"

"No," Jyn said flatly.

"You're right. You're smart. Still, they're going to underestimate you. Make them regret it."

The girl's eyes narrowed as if the threat were right behind them. "They?"

"Everyone," Enfys said. "Make them regret it."

Jyn nodded once.

"If you're satisfied," Gerrera said, sounding tense.

"I am." She gestured to the coaxium behind her. "So will this do? It could do a lot of good."

"And harm," he said, his eyes flicking to the fuel. "Which is what we need."

"I would hope that you would be more precise in your ways, Saw," she said. "You're going to need some attention to detail if your fight is going to work."

"I would think that you of all people would accept that allies come in different shapes, sizes, and ways of fighting," he said. "We are fighting the same enemy. Moving toward the same goal."

She sighed. "I only ask that you don't waste it."

He made a gesture, so welcoming and graceful it seemed ridiculous coming from someone so rough and unfriendly. "Come, let's talk."

He boarded the shuttle and Enfys followed him, secure that her Cloud-Riders would keep the ship grounded until she exited safely. She passed Jyn, who watched them both carefully.

"He's going to underestimate you," she whispered.

Enfys smiled to herself. The girl learned fast. They might be in good hands after all.

Read on for an excerpt from

STAR WARS

LAST SHOT

by Daniel José Older

CHANDRILA, NOW

"**N**ext thing I know," Lando said, reaching for the bottle, "I'm laid out, *by my own protocol droid* no less." He poured himself another three fingers of Corellian whiskey and shook his head.

"Wait," Leia said, taking the bottle off the table and stashing it in a cabinet. "Why were you in a towel?"

Han looked up from the other end of the room where he'd been sulking and applying a glass of ice to his cheek. "Yeah, why were you in a towel?"

Lando stood. "You don't get to ask questions yet, Han. I'm coming to your part in a minute." He turned to Leia, flashed that smile. "Your Highness . . ."

Leia shook her head. "Sit down, Lando."

He did, shrugging. "Anyway, Kaasha got off a few shots on the droid, and—"

"*Kaasha?*" Han cut in.

Lando shot him a look. Han went back to sulking.

"Kaasha?" Leia asked.

"Kaasha Bateen. An old friend of mine from the Pasa Novo campaign. She's good with a blaster."

"Mm, bet she is," Han muttered.

She was actually, Lando thought. It had been one of his last thoughts as the whole world fizzled into a gaping void: *She can shoot, too?* He shouldn't have been surprised, really, but the last time he'd seen Kaasha she'd been running tactical attack models in the war room on Baltro and he'd never seen her fight. They'd had a good time together, but Kaasha had always made it abundantly clear she saw right through Lando's smooth talking and all the broken promises of his wily grin. He'd liked that about her. Liked it more than he was ready to admit. But then the battle had ended and the survivors had trudged off to their respective planets, and that had been that. Or it should've been anyway, but the truth was, a tiny, smirking hologram of Kaasha seemed to have stayed with Lando somehow, like she'd sneaked an implant of some kind into his brain that last time they'd held each other.

He'd never reached out because that's not how it works. That's against the code. The promise of an obviously broken promise is that it stays broken, no matter what. Otherwise, what was the point?

Leia got up and retrieved the whiskey, poured a glass. "Was she in a towel, too?"

Lando grinned, both hands raised like he was being held up. "It's not like that."

"I'm sure it's not," Leia said. Han reached for her

whiskey, and she moved the glass out of his grasp. "You have a pilots union session today."

"And you're about to meet with the security council."

She rolled her eyes and clinked glasses with Lando. "All the more reason for a quick little nip."

"Anyway," Lando said, "when I come around, I'm staring up at this hooded droid. Not the protocol one—it's the thing that was standing behind Dee-Arrex. Some kind of crookbacked class four from the look of it, but I've never seen a face quite like that one. Had glowing red eyes and a nasty mesh of rusted cables snaking around its head. Couldn't see much else under that hood." He shuddered. The fact was, it had been terrifying, coming back around to find that deranged droid monster glaring at him with those red eyes. Lando had actually gasped before he'd caught himself and forced on a more stubborn, cocky demeanor. "*The Phylanx,* the droid says."

Han cocked an eyebrow. "Huh?"

"That's exactly what I said," Lando said. "Phywho now? And the droid says: *The Phylanx Redux Transmitter.* And when I say that's not much help he claps me across the face and puts the blaster between my eyes.

"*Are you or are you not the registered owner of a Corellian light freighter called the* Millennium Falcon? the droid says."

"Uh-oh," Han mumbled.

"Yeah, you're damn right uh-oh. I said I'm not now but I was once, and I still don't know about no damn Phylanx Transmitter. At this point, I'm trying to figure out if I'm going to have to blast my way out of this, but the droid's collected all our weaponry. I'm guessing if I stall long enough, eventually Lobot will show up with the Bespin Wing Guard, but who knows how long that'll take and anyway, this droid doesn't seem like the type you can get one over on.

"*The Phylanx Redux Transmitter was illegally obtained by the owner of the* Millennium Falcon *ten years ago*, the droid says, and I would swear it sounded like it was really, really pissed about it. For a droid, anyway. *My master would like it back*."

"Master?" Leia said.

Lando slammed his glass on the table. "That's exactly what I said! *Fyzen Gor*, it said."

Leia shook her head. "Doesn't ring a bell. Han?"

Han was fiddling with the strap on his boot, a glass of ice still pressed against his face. "Hm?" he muttered without looking up. "Haven't heard of him."

"That's *fascinating*," Lando said, waving one finger like he was coming to the crux of a withering prosecution, "because I said the same exact thing! Why would I know about a Phylanx Whoozimawhatsit and a random gangster from a decade ago? Except then I realized something equally fascinating." He looked at Leia.

Han was humming a little tune, still fussing with his boot.

"You didn't have the *Falcon* ten years ago," Leia said. She shot an eyebrow up. "Han did."

Lando and Leia both turned to Han. He looked up. "Hm? Oh! Oh, *that* Fyzen Gor? The Pau'an gangster who used to run with the Wandering Star?" A wide smile broke out across his face.

"Why, I oughta—" Lando scooched his chair back with a screech and lunged halfway across the table.

"Easy." Leia stood and threw an arm in Lando's way as Han hopped up, palms out.

"Hey, hey, hey! It's not . . . it's just . . ."

"Yeah, you can't even get that lie out of your lying mouth," Lando growled. "This guy Fyzen is prepared to unleash a massacre on Cloud City if I don't get him his little toy back, and whoever he is, he clearly has the means to do that. His droid got past my security, dropped two Wing Guard units single-handedly, and somehow turned my own protocol droid against me. Droids are my business now. It's what I do. So if some creep can out-droid a droid impresario, well . . . that's not a good look, okay? Everything can come crashing down. And you are the last person who seems to have seen this Phylanx thing, *Haan,* so start"— Lando leaned all the way across the table—"talking."

For a few moments, they just stared at each other.

"Some fine Endoran caf to cool the nerves?" BX-778 suggested, whirring to life and sending all seven arms into action.

"Not now!" Han and Leia both snarled at the same time.

"It was just a suggestion," BX mumbled, powering back down. "No need to get prickly."

"I did a run," Han said quietly. He sat, looking up at Lando, who still stood with his arms crossed over his chest. Leia sat very slowly.

Lando stared down Han for a good couple of seconds then took his seat. "Go on."

"Ten years ago. With Sana Starros."

"Ah, your *other* wife," Leia said.

Han sighed. "Are we gonna do this now?"

"I must say," Lando mused, "of all the women in the galaxy to get fake married to for a pile of land, you certainly picked a beautiful one."

"Lando!" Han snapped. "Not helping."

Leia shook her head with a tired grin and stood. "No, Han, we're not doing this now, but I am going to let you boys figure this out yourselves. I do have an emergency security council session to get ready for, much as I'd like to stay and enjoy the fireworks."

"Anything important?" Lando asked.

Leia shrugged. "Could be yes, could be no. You can never tell with these brand-new bureaucrats."

"They're mobilizing the fleet," Han said.

"And *you're* not even supposed to know that," Leia snapped, "let alone say it out loud to someone not on the security council."

"Hey." Lando tipped his head. "I'm a war hero, remember?"

"Yeah, well, that doesn't mean you have clearance. And we're not at war anymore. And anyway, our fleet isn't even a fully military one, remember? We've technically disarmed. Everyone's still just scrambling to make sense of what this new democracy's going to look like, so it's like being a teenager: Every new crisis feels like the first one."

"Good times," Lando snorted.

"Heh." She threw back her whiskey and kissed Han on the cheek. Han flinched and she swatted him. "Oh, come on, he didn't hit you that hard."

She nodded at Lando. "It's good to see you, Lando. I'm sure my husband will do what's right, both for you and for his family."

Lando reached for her hand and kissed it. "And may I say, Your Highness, that—"

"You may not," Leia said with a smile. "But I know you'll try anyway."

"You look absolutely—" The bedroom door whirring closed cut him off.

"You never change." Han rubbed a hand through his hair and pulled up closer to the table. "You really don't."

Lando barked a laugh. "The Jawa calls the Ewok short! And anyway, I've changed quite a bit, thank you very much." He poured Han some whiskey, slid it across the table: a peace offering.

Han raised an eyebrow. "Easy to be generous with someone else's whiskey."

Lando scoffed. "Don't get cute, flyboy. You're still in the dog house, you know."

"Fair enough." Han took the drink, clinked it with Lando's. "Sana and I made a run on Fyzen back in the day, yeah, and there was a device of some kind involved, but I swear I don't remember what it was exactly. And the whole thing went to hell. We didn't even get paid! Not really, anyway."

"Well, we've got some backtracking to do," Lando said. "First of all, we need to find out where this Fyzen is now and where his device got to, and—"

"Whoa whoa whoa." Han shook his head with a smirk. "What's all this *we* stuff, Lando?"

"Han." Lando felt the blood rushing back to his face, his fists, but it wasn't anger at his old friend this time, it was something much worse. That . . . thing, had gotten the drop on him, caught him completely off guard. Lando was the most protected citizen of Cloud City, and he'd had a lifetime of experience getting himself out of trouble to know how not to get got. But somehow that red-eyed droid had gotten itself all the way to the inner sanctums of his home. "Seventy-two hours," it had croaked. Up close, the droid reeked of some heady chemical antiseptic with hints of a slowly rotting carcass, like someone was trying to hide a body inside it. Lando had no doubt that whatever attack was set to be launched in three days would be devastating and merciless.

He shuddered, forced the calm façade back over himself. "Han, I know we're here joking around, and I don't totally know what this is all about yet, but the truth is, I need your help. It's not just that you owe me because it's probably all your fault in the first place—"

"Hey now . . ."

"Let me finish—outside of that, Han, if this creep Gor has a way to turn droids against us, imagine what that could mean for Cloud City—for the galaxy. If I don't track down this Phylanx thing in three days for the guy, he's coming for me, Han, and he'll probably wipe out a good chunk of my city, too. Now the way I see it, we get this device and then we use it to lure Gor in and wipe him out. But I can't do it without you, Han."

"Lando, I . . ." He shook his head, gestured vaguely around the room: Ben's toys scattered across the floor; some mindless holo of happy little monkey-lizards singing in trees playing on repeat forever on the deck; BX-778 preparing caf again even though no one had asked him to.

Lando wrapped his fingers behind his head and leaned

back. "I don't even have to pull the this-is-all-your-fault card, do I? You can't wait to get out of here."

Han frowned. "I just . . ."

The door flew open and Ben Solo, buck naked, hurtled in with a scream. "Unca Wanwo!"

"There's my little buddy!" Lando said, scooping the boy up in his arms and turning him upside down to giggles and shrieks.

"Oh dear," LC muttered, whirring along in Ben's wake. "Terribly sorry, sirs, I was giving him a bath and he could barely contain himself when he heard that General Calrissian was here." The droid reached out and plucked Ben out of Lando's arms.

"That's all right," Lando said with a chuckle. "Always happy to see the young Mr. Ben."

Han watched as his son squirmed in the droid's metallic arms, reaching out for Lando and bursting into tears as LC whisked him out of the room.

HAN

TAKODANA,
ABOUT TEN YEARS AGO

"**W**hat's her name?"

Han Solo squinted up from the swirl of dust he'd been staring at for . . . how long now? Who knew? He was tired, annoyed. Possibly drunk; he couldn't even tell anymore. But if *fed up* was a state of being, he'd entered it at least a week ago and pretty soon was gonna have to start paying rent. He probably looked the part, too: His hair was certainly disheveled, and not in the cute, carefree way—just a damn mess. His white shirt was stained with . . . was that Ithorian blood? Probably. He'd washed it since that run-in with the Torrian security guards on Hosnian Prime, but that purplish stain wasn't going anywhere.

The woman standing before him, on the other hand, was an absolute portrait of *well put together*. It wasn't that she was wearing anything fancy, but her leather jacket was crisp and her pilot pants were creased and smooth; even the blasters hanging on each hip seemed to match her whole color scheme. Her braids were tied back in a ponytail that wrapped over one of her shoulders and her arms were crossed over her chest, a look of slight disapproval mixed with amusement on her dark-brown face. Behind her, a mottled array of starships, trawlers, and freighters stood at wait in the Takodanan dust field that had become the unofficial docking bay for Maz's castle.

"Sana Starros," Han said.

Sana rolled her eyes. "No, that's my name. What's her name?"

"Oh, the *Millennium Falcon*." He nodded at the cockpit jutting out above his head. "And she's not for sale."

"Not the ship, you mynock."

"Oh! Chewbacca. And she's a he." The Wookiee was passed out on a cot by the *Falcon*'s gangplank, snoring recklessly.

Sana sighed and took a seat on the little bit of bench next to Han, who stubbornly did not scooch over to make room for her. "I can't tell if you're actually this dense or you're just really determined not to talk about what's bothering you."

Han allowed a smile and rubbed his face. Sana was right on all counts. He was wrecked in ways he didn't even know how to describe, his insides had never felt so shattered, and he definitely didn't want to talk about it. He slid over to give her more room on the bench, and she handed him a small pouch. "What's this?"

"Hemchar root. One of Maz's hangover cures. Just

pour it down your gullet, you'll be all right." She pulled out another and tore it open. "C'mon, we'll do it together."

He stared at her. "*You're* hung over? You look . . ."

"Beautiful? Why, thank you!"

"That's . . . I mean . . ."

"Just shut up and take the hemchar, Han."

She emptied her own packet into her mouth as he watched, and then he tore his open and did the same. And then the whole ship hangar around him turned a very bright shade of purple. "Um . . ."

"Oh, I forgot to mention the side effects," Sana said with a slight giggle.

"Do they include . . . whoa!" It wasn't just that everything was purple, it was that even brighter-colored splotches kept bursting out of nowhere.

"Technochrome hallucinations," Sana admitted. "And sometimes olfactory ones, too, just FYI."

"Yeah, thanks," Han said, closing his eyes. "Was there a reason you came to find me here or was it just to make my life even weirder?"

"You looked like you could use a pick-me-up," Sana said. "Ooh, turquoise!"

"And?"

"And I have a job."

Han shrugged, eyes still closed. "And?"

"A paying job."

Another shrug.

Sana made a low growling sound. "A job that I could use your help on . . . and a fast ship."

"Aha," Han said, finally opening his eyes. "Whoa, yellow. Everything is yellow."

"It'll pass."

"What's the job?"

"Just gotta get this little thingymadoo and bring it from one place to another for someone is all."

"So . . . smuggling?"

Sana looked offended. "So crass."

"It'll cost you."

"Eeyn choo pitakra," a screechy voice rasped. Both Han and Sana looked up. Five pinched, snarling faces glared back at them. The creatures formed a semicircle in the dusty open area. Crusty bald patches speckled their mangy black fur. One was missing an eye, another an arm. All carried stun clubs, their business ends charged and sparkling.

"Do the hallucinations include giant feral rats?" Han asked.

Sana glowered. "Sadly, these are quite real. And they're probably mad about that landspeeder of theirs I borrowed."

"Hassk bacha kree!"

"We know you're Hassks, you mange-eaten fleabag."

The Hassks growled and closed in a few steps, twitching and seething as they raised their fizzling stun clubs.

Han looked up, above the grimacing Hassks, above the freighters and transports parked around them, to the sky, the glorious, shimmering sky. It went on forever; each trembling speckle of starshine contained whole universes, a million billion worlds, all glowing bright orange . . .

"Han?" Sana said under her breath. "You with me?"

"What *is* this stuff?"

"Maz might've said to only take a teaspoonful for

hangovers," Sana admitted. "Maybe not the whole packet."

"Great."

"*Speena foolok m'shar!*" the lead Hassk demanded.

"I'm sure Sana here will give you back your landspeeder if you ask nicely," Han said. "No need to get personal."

Sana frowned. "About that . . ."

The Hassks all yelled as one: "*Frazkrit!*"

"I kinda wrecked it."

"Oh boy," Han said.

"Yeah, long story. Anyway, we might need to make some moves . . ."

A high-pitched whine sounded: one of the stun clubs supercharging. Han felt like he was moving in slow motion as he stood and stepped out of the way of the sparkling blast. The Hassks chuckled, and more supercharges rang out.

"Chewie!" Han yelled.

Behind him, he heard the Wookiee stir and grumble something profane.

"I know you're sleeping. But we could use a hand here . . ."

Another growled curse. The Hassks stopped chuckling.

"And weren't you just talking the other day about how you wanted to wreck some Hassk ass?"

With a grunt and a clatter of metal—apparently, he'd been sleeping next to a toolbox, now spilled across the floor—Chewbacca rose to his full fur-covered height. He blinked in the harsh lights of the landing bay.

"*Frazkrit,*" one of the Hassks whispered.

"*Parandoo mrakpan*," another suggested. "*Shreevat*."

Sana shook her head. "Oh, *now* you wanna negotiate? You can negotiate with my Wookiee."

"*Your* Wookiee?" Han said, as Chewie cocked his head to the side.

Sana shrugged. "It's an expression."

"No, it's no—" Han started, but then the Hassks charged, their stun clubs whining and crackling. Han spun out of the way, still in slow motion somehow, and clocked the nearest one across its gnarled face. His hand came back sticky, he didn't want to imagine from what, but the Hassk stumbled away a few steps, stun club clattering to the ground. Two more came in swinging and then were swept clean out of the way as Chewie roared into the melee.

"Thanks," Han said. "But bright green is a terrible color for you. Next time you want to dye your fur, let me know and we'll find a better match."

Chewie squinted a concerned look down at him.

"Duck!" Sana yelled, and both Han and Chewie crouched low as blasterfire flashed over their heads.

A Hassk screeched behind them and flew backward.

"You're welcome," Sana said, blowing away the plume of smoke from her blaster. Howling and hissing, the Hassk raiders scattered into the shadows. "How's it going, Chewie?"

Chewie moaned and shook his head.

"I have something that can help you with that," Sana said, patting her jacket pocket with a grin.

"No!" Han growled. "You don't."

"So touchy. I was gonna measure it out properly this time."

Chewie swatted the air at both of them like they were figments of some bad dream and went back to the bench he'd been sleeping on.

For a few seconds, Han and Sana took in the sudden silence and fading rainbow splashes around them. Han felt a strange kind of peace settle in.

"Nice shooting," he said.

Sana smiled. "It was a good thing you ducked. My aim may be slightly compromised right now."

A cleaning droid moped past, ancient gears whining in protest with each clomp.

Not far away, the sound of music and laughter rose from Maz Kanata's castle as another night of debauchery and shenanigans got under way.

"It doesn't matter," Han said.

"What doesn't matter?"

"Her name."

Sana nodded, didn't press him any further.

Inside Han, some tiny part of himself let go, some knot he'd been tying over and over again just seemed to dissolve, and all it took was that tiny admission to just let it go.

He cocked an eyebrow at her. It was time to get back in the saddle. "You said you had some smuggling to do?"

CHANDRILA, NOW

"**H**ow'd it go?" Kaasha asked when Lando walked back onto the bridge of the *Lady Luck*. Lando paused to take in the way her back arched between the two dangling lekku, her brow slightly furrowed as she sat staring at the dejarik board, where it looked like she was about to deliver a sound walloping to Lobot's diminishing hologram army.

Lobot didn't look up, either; he just frowned at the tiny flickering beasts.

"Han'll come along," Lando said, pulling off his cape and hanging it beside the door. None of this was how it was supposed to go. He was supposed to compliment Kaasha's beauty as soon as he noticed it, tell her how disarmingly gorgeous she was. And it was supposed to be a little bit of a lie; not the gorgeous part, of course—

that was always true—but Lando was never disarmed. Not by the sight of a woman. This, though . . . none of this was right. "How's Florx doing with the unit?"

Finally, Lobot looked up, still frowning. He shook his head, glared back at the board.

"That good, huh? Your karkath is in . . ."

Kaasha pushed a button and a throng of tiny, squawking creatures raced across the board and swarmed over one of Lobot's armored beasts. It squealed and then vanished beneath the onslaught. Lobot stared, eyes wide.

"You know he's never lost, right?" Lando said.

Kaasha grinned across the table at Lobot. "Oops."

"It's not over yet," Lando said, chuckling, and headed to the corridor. "I'm gonna check on Florx. Have fun, you two." The door slid closed behind him. Up ahead, sparks and bright flashes of light cast manic shadows across the far wall. The grunting snorts of Lando's Ugnaught droid expert sounded beneath the sizzling hum of a mechtorch.

Lando rounded the corner, stopped in his tracks. Soot and burn marks covered the tiny entirety of Florx Biggles. Fortunately, the Ugnaught was wearing one of those heavy-duty protective suits they favored and a metal face guard that made him look like some kind of humanoid astromech that had survived a nasty crash. DRX, or what was left of him, lay splayed out in various twitching pieces across Florx's workbench, and the walls, and the floor. And one or two fingers that were somehow dangling from the ceiling wires.

Lando rubbed his eyes. "Florx, buddy, what's . . . how bad is it?"

Florx looked up and pulled his helmet off, revealing

a squinched-up, porcine face framed by wispy white muttonchops. *"Bredaxeemum,"* he snorted. *"Plorp fanoobra."*

"Well, I didn't think you'd be able to fix him right away, but did you have to . . . he's everywhere, Florx. Can you put him back together?"

Florx threw his thickly gloved hands up in the air and let out a barrage of Ugnaught profanities.

"Okay, hey," Lando said, giving a shrug of acknowledgment. "You're right, I don't want him to be fully functional and still trying to kill me, but . . ."

"Preedanta forplasm brex," Florx said, slipping into the voice he used that always sounded like he was trying to explain something really obvious to a baby Ugnaught. It grated on Lando's nerves, but he didn't want to get into another brawl with the droid specialist right now. Those never went well.

"All right, all right, all right." Lando let some laughter slide into his voice and shook his head. "Did you recalibrate the main cortex processor?"

Florx shook his head, bristling. *"Frinx zeen paltrata."*

"Well, how are we supposed to access his backup drives without—"

"Prratta!" Florx insisted, fists coming to rest on his hips. *"Prindropt."*

"Yes, you're the expert, but a fat lot of good that's done us so far, Florx."

"Crabat."

"Why don't you try and light him back up now and see how—"

Florx whirled around, throwing his face guard with a clank, and grumbled some choice thoughts about

Lando's management style as he punched something into a keypad.

DRX's shiny silver head whirred to life. Two bright-red lights winked on in its eyes as it glared directly at Lando. *"Killlll,"* it seethed in a metallic whisper. *"Killllllll."*

CHANDRILA, NOW

"Come to order," Frandu the Rodian insisted over the muttering crowd.

What were they talking about? Han wasn't sure, and definitely didn't care enough to find out.

"It's quite simple, fellow pilots: We must formalize the regulations for New Republic pilots across the board. A standardized licensing board and registration system across the galaxy. Simple!" One of the reasons no one liked Frandu was that he insisted on everyone calling him "the Rodian" as if he were some super-special, one-and-only type. But there were three other Rodians in the pilots union alone, none of whom spoke to Frandu, and plenty of others in all levels of the New Republic's fledgling bureaucracy.

"A board that licenses and a system of registration

that is standardized!" he warbled through the tiny dancing lips at the end of his narrowed green snout. The other reason no one liked Frandu was that he always repeated himself with a slightly rephrased version of whatever he'd just said.

The entire union groaned as one. Frandu the Rodian stood in the center of one of the Galactic Senate's secondary auditoriums. The attendees, pilot representatives from all over the galaxy, had been muttering, politicking, and at one point all-out brawling, over rules and regulations for the entire day, and now the Chandrilan sun was setting over forest mountains outside the massive glass dome in which they sat. And Han was fed up. More accurately: Han was still fed up, and now he'd just about had it.

"Everyone is always so quick to grumble and disagree!" Frandu whined. "Disagreements and complaints come soaring from this group with such great velocity!"

The only thing that had been soaring at Han with great velocity was the simple, indisputable truth that he was in over his head. Not with the dang pilots union, not with any part he ended up playing in the New Republic—that was tedious, sure, but he'd work it out. No, he'd faced down certain death and gangsters and bounty hunters, not to mention the Empire itself, and somehow come out on top every time. He could handle some fumbling bureaucrats and their insipid need to codify and coordinate every tiny detail. All that was exhausting and generally life-draining, but it was nothing compared with how utterly, obviously, irretrievably unprepared he was for fatherhood.

Two years in and no matter what, nothing he did was

right. He brought Ben a play blaster from Burundang and he was encouraging his violent side; took it away and the boy wouldn't stop crying. He tried to replace it with a build-a-space-center set and there were too many small pieces Ben could choke on. The worst part was, it wasn't like Leia was just nagging or inventing stuff to one-up Han; she was right about all of it. So he couldn't even properly resent her for it! Every time she pointed out some potentially unhealthy or obviously lethal thing Han was doing, it was like—of course! It was right there in front of him all along.

"It's okay," Leia had said as they lay in bed one night with the soft Chandrilan breeze blowing in through the open balcony doors, Ben finally snoring softly between them. "You didn't exactly have any good models of fatherhood growing up."

"Yeah," Han had muttered. He put her hand back into his hair, which she'd been stroking soothingly while he complained. "I guess not."

"It takes time."

But that had been a whole year ago and Han still had no idea what he was doing with no sign of improvement. One thing was perfectly clear, though: He wasn't meant to be a dad.

"And the honorable Captain Solo agrees," Frandu the Rodian declared triumphantly. "Don't you?"

"Huhaaabsolutely," Han said, blinking back to the present world. The entire auditorium had swiveled to face him. A barrage of groans and arguments erupted.

"Excellent!" Frandu shrieked over the melee. "Let us break for a recess and we can begin formalizing the procedural protocols within the hour! The procedural protocols will be formalized after the commencement of a recess period, which we will begin immediately and then return from."

"Great," Han said, ignoring the many glares and mumbled curses directed his way. "See you guys soon." He stood. He would absolutely not be seeing them soon. He had somewhere to be.

A transport whooshed by as he stepped out into the streets of Hanna City. It was fine, though; he'd rather walk. The diplomatic residency complex wasn't far. He would get home, throw some things in his bag, message Lando. His friend was in trouble—that was the bottom line. He couldn't leave him hanging, not after Lando had saved his life and destroyed the Death Star and anyway it was maybe potentially in some tiny way Han's fault Lando was in this mess in the first place so . . .

He made his way through the bustling crowds on Heroes of the Republic Boulevard, then turned down Revolina Street and stuck to the back alleys.

He was defending his position already, which meant there was a fight to be had. Because he was always leaving, Leia would probably say, and why couldn't he just settle down, with his wanderer's heart, his shiftlessness, his ever-packed bag? And she'd be right, even if, Han had to admit, she probably wouldn't say it quite like that, or maybe even at all.

And yes, it wasn't that long ago that he'd fallen off the map entirely trying to help Chewie free his planet, but this was different, this was . . . Was it different?

He turned onto Embassy Row, fastwalked past the guard station with a quick nod and a flash of his ID, and then entered the sparkling gardens and fountain-decorated courtyard of his apartment complex.

It didn't matter if it was different or not, really. Lando needed him. And if he was being honest with himself, Ben might be better off without him. At least until he could get it together and learn how to be a father for real, not just some reckless manchild who happened to have a kid. He wouldn't tell Leia that, though; that would just set off a whole other fight. Keep it simple, keep it straightforward. That was the ticket.

The turbolift zipped him up to their floor, the front door slid open with a whisper, and then he was home, and the place was blessedly empty except for the whirring-to-life house droids.

"Welcome home, Master Solo," BX-778 chortled happily. "Perhaps I can interest you in a—"

"Not now, fizzpot." Han entered the bedroom, reached under the bed for his go bag, found nothing. *Nothing.* He swiped again.

"Looking for this?" Leia stood in the doorway, holding the bag in one hand, a sly smile on her face.

Han jumped to his feet. "Leia, I . . . Look, this is—"

"I packed it for you," she said, still smiling, eyes sad.

"You what?"

"Your favorite flight pants—you've really got to get some new ones, though, Han; it's getting ridiculous—and an extra weapons belt. Socks, underpants, all your spare bathroom stuff. It's all there."

Han raised his hands, opened his mouth, a hundred explanations, excuses really, poised to pour out. None came. He dropped his hands by his sides, shook his head. Completely disarmed. And suddenly very sad.

"It's okay," Leia said. "You don't have to explain. And I invited Lando and his Twi'lek friend over for dinner tonight so you guys will have a chance to talk about it more."

She wasn't even doing it to make him feel bad; that was the worst part. She really did understand that he needed to go. Which made him not want to go at all, but didn't change the fact that he had to. And it didn't mean he was suddenly going to be a good father, either.

He stepped toward her, reached for the bag. She held it away, pulled him into a hug. "Uh uh uh . . . promise me this," Leia whispered, looking up at him.

The mission seemed suddenly desperate, impossible. A long-dead Pau'an gangster and his maniac droid? Chasing some device halfway across the galaxy, and for what? Han didn't like any of it. "What's that?"

"Come back to me alive, Captain Solo. That's an order."